THE MILK WAGON

Also by Michael Hewes

Watermark

The Tempestuous Trial of Maybelline Meriweather

THE MILK WAGON

A Novel

MICHAEL HEWES

ISBN: 978-1-64704-110-6 (Print)

ISBN: 978-0-578-67237-3 (Ebook)

Samntoff Press

Gulfport, Mississippi

Cover Design by Berge Design

To my sons.
May the friendships forged in high school
be forever part of your story.

PROLOGUE

*If you could go back, knowing what you know now,
which would you choose – high school or college?*

The question appeared on my Facebook feed as a sponsored ad for a dating website attempting to match me up with someone who shared a like-minded yearning for those carefree days gone by. Even though I am now happily married and clearly not the person the poll was targeting, I suspected the pop-up wasn't totally random. I had spent the past few nights looking through high school class reunion websites searching for ideas for our thirtieth. Usually I don't give online questionnaires, chain mail posts, or other similar data traps a second look, but I lingered on this one.

Hop and I were the only two alumni from our class who still lived in Gulfport, and truth be told, ever since we'd been tasked with planning our reunion (by default), I'd been thinking a lot about our high school days. Still, I had never thought to compare them to my four years in college. At first glance, it was a no-brainer, and somewhat unfair to line up the beauty of a sprawling, oak-tree laden university against the institutionalized cinder block and linoleum domain that we called St. John's. Apples and oranges for sure, but not quite for the reasons I initially expected.

I was fortunate enough to spend the majority of my high school years with my best friends Hop and Mark. The three of us were thick as thieves back then, and when we were together, we were sure enough bulletproof. Or so we thought.

We stumbled, mostly unblemished, through junior high, and by the time tenth grade rolled around, we had started to come into our own. We tried drinking and did our best to talk to girls, but we weren't very good at either. We had classes we hated; we had classes we loved. There were days when the fog of boredom slowed time to a point where I could literally feel myself aging as I sat in my desk. Others passed like a flash of light, and there were some mornings where I truly felt most at home in homeroom. Still, I suspect our early high school experiences were much like those of other kids, and if my last two years had continued along the way of my first two, I think I may have picked college as my Back to the Future option. But one Friday the summer after our sophomore year, I came home to find a beat up 1980 Suburban parked in our driveway under the rusted out basketball goal with no net, and things were never quite the same again.

Even now, I don't know why my dad bought it. It was a rare event for him to give a gift of any type, as benevolence was not his strong point. My guess is he either had a good night gambling or had bartered it in some type of sketchy deal. I didn't care and I didn't ask. He threw me the keys from the front porch, said "now you can drive yourself to school," then went inside and slept the rest of the afternoon. We didn't discuss it again.

I took a long, slow walk around, and the more I inspected it, the more it took on the feel of a vehicular stray dog. It was big, it was ugly, and it was most definitely a rescue. It couldn't have been any more different from the pedigreed, decked out Suburbans currently wheeling through my neighborhood by latte moms on the way to spin class. But it did have something theirs lacked. It had character.

The remnants of a *Gulfport – Where Your Ship Comes In* logo shadowing the driver's side door was just one of the scars from its prior job as a workhorse for the city. The body had turned a dusty, powdery white – any luster from the paint had long since faded after spending a lifetime parked out in the elements. There were holes in the floorboard, the back smelled like wet clothes, and I found out later that the windshield wipers only worked if you leaned your arm out the window and gave them a pull start. When I slid onto the front bench and turned the key, all eight cylinders roared to life. At that moment, any angst I had felt from my dubious first impression disappeared behind the cloud of smoke coming out of the exhaust. I was so happy to have something to call my own, I drove it to Hop's second annual back to school party that very night. Within an hour after arriving, someone dared me to try and fit fifteen people inside it. We loaded up nineteen, plus one or two hanging off the bumpers before it started getting ugly – and we were just warming up. Later in the evening I pulled it in the backyard where it served quite handily as a makeshift bar, a stargazing perch, and, much to our surprise and good fortune, a righteous make out machine.

It didn't take long for the Milk Wagon to become the go-to vehicle for pep rallies, football games and afternoon food runs. It was a gathering point in the morning before school, and a rallying point at late night parties and parking lots. We double- and triple-dated in it, and even took it camping one weekend where we draped my cousin's Army-issue mosquito net over the open doors and slept in the back.

It was also a keeper of secrets. Unspoken ones steaming up the windows in the parking bays by the beach. Deep ones discussed cruising around town, free from parental intrusion and judgment. Lighter ones, too, like when a particular dickhead cop pulled us over on the way to a party and totally missed a twelve pack of Schaefer Light and a pint of Seagrams smuggled away and out of sight.

And then, of course, there's the big one.

I opened the bottom drawer of my desk, moved a two-decades-high stack of expired At-a-Glance yearly calendars to the side, and pulled out an old manila envelope that had been handled, bent, and wrinkled so many times that the paper had taken on the soft buttery texture of a fine fabric. I turned it over in my hands, surprised at how light it had become, and gave it a closer look. The bank's logo in the upper left corner – once a navy blue – had finally faded to the point where I could barely make out the edge of its signature magnolia blossom. The rest of the return address had been reduced to blurred smudges and an occasional semi-legible street number. Or was that the zip code? I couldn't tell anymore.

The four names handwritten on the front, however, had maintained their crispness, so much so that when I put it up to my face and inhaled, I swore I picked up a distant essence of black magic-marker. Just the smell put me back behind the wheel, white knuckling down that country road with a lead foot – too naive at seventeen to fully consider the implications of what was about to take place, and too emboldened to care. I remember it being especially cool that morning, and I had the driver's side window down, singing along to "Dancing with Myself" as loud as I could. It may very well have been the last pure moment of my childhood.

The laptop going blank caused me to lose my train of thought, and when I tapped the touchpad to wake it back up, the question that set me adrift in the first place was still waiting for an answer. Which one would I pick? I leaned back in my chair and crossed my hands behind my head. It was a no-brainer all right.

High school.

I would definitely go back to high school. And if I was truly going to get a do-over, as the ad suggested, I would start right where Hop's party left off: the first day of our junior year. After all, it was the year that changed everything, and the year that everything changed. It was the year I fell in love. It was the year Mark started a band. It was the year Hop actually almost, kind of, but not really got a girlfriend.

And it was the year Nate Mayes disappeared.

CHAPTER 1

I have always liked the first day of school, ever since I can remember. I even dug it in first grade, although based upon the pictures from that early September morn, it was obvious my parents were enamored with brown plaid. Everyone had shiny new metal lunchboxes filled with sandwiches, chips, and some sort of treat (the lucky kids had Twinkies), and we always had new shoes that would remain looking that way for only about three days. Our hair was slicked down in that back-to-school 'do favored by our folks, our shirts were tucked in, and we were ready to face the brave new world, unaware that our parents were more nervous than we were as we stepped off the curb and onto the big yellow bus.

In high school, the ritual may have been different, but the anticipation remained. My friends and I would get together the week before to compare schedules and notes, and to speculate as to whether there would be any new talent gracing the halls upon our arrival. It wasn't like we were tired of the ladies we had been seeing for the past ten years – they still looked good (and some were starting to look better) – rather, it boiled down to the spirit of competition. If you're the only retailer in town, you can relax a little and not worry so much about your advertising and selection, because people are going to buy what they can where they can. As soon as the ground is broken on that new Kmart, however, you'd better tighten your ass up or you'll be usurped by a clean, bright, modern store hocking goods that were impulse buys in the first place. Kind of how it was with the girls – they didn't like the competition a bit, but they reacted the same – new clothes, new bows and, for the most part, a well-tanned body. This attention to detail always impressed us, even though we were never the intended beneficiaries of their efforts.

The boys, on the other hand, never really gave much thought to the new guy or two who came in, and we certainly didn't undertake any extra efforts to polish the chrome. Usually, he fit right in anyway with one crowd or another.

Usually.

Our first day back as juniors started out not much different. We were all supposed to meet in the parking lot at seven-thirty, and since we were now officially upperclassmen, we got to park in the back next to the seniors, no longer relegated to the few crappy parking spaces by the drop-off line in the front. I left early and stopped by the Bayou View Grocery on the way in to get a Coke and drove up at a quarter after, wheeling in right behind Hop and Mark. We were the only ones there. I got out, grabbed a doughnut from Hop's Quality Bakery bag, and leaned against the Milk Wagon. I could smell the fresh cut grass down by the practice fields.

"Welcome to paradise, boys." I said, taking in another deep breath and wondering how long the dew would stick to the ground with all the humidity. Mark hadn't gotten out of the car yet. He considered himself a bit of a musician and was waiting for "Blister in the Sun" to end before he officially started his day. He was spitting powdered doughnut crumbs on the dash with every chorus between drumming. Hop was digging in his pockets for his schedule, seemingly oblivious to the fact that he had checked it twice already that morning, once before his shower and once while taking his morning growler.

"Who you got for first period?" he asked, uncrumpling the blue mimeograph that smelled like a chemical weapon. "I thought I had English, but it says here chemistry," he said through a grimace. "I don't know if I can handle a nun first thing in the morning." I couldn't blame him. No one wanted a perimenopausal celibate as their eight-fifteen a.m. warden.

"El Español," I replied. "I've got Ms. Mander."

"Lucky bastard." He took another glance at his sheet and began cleaning his glasses.

Jason "Hop" Hopkins and I met in the seventh grade playing on the basketball team. We were two goofy-looking, skinny white kids who played at about the same level – fair to middling. We didn't know each other well, and during a full-court-press exercise, I tripped him and he busted his ass. I helped him back up, we continued to play, and the rest, as they say, is history. Whether or not I did it on purpose is still the subject of much dispute, and he brings it up way more than he should. Truth be known, I barely even remember it, and I doubt I did it with intent to harm. Unless, of course, he was getting the edge on me. Then I might have.

The Femmes tape ended, and Mark got out, chewing on a straw and picking his nose. "Am I clear?" he asked, cocking his head up for us to verify. After we ignored him, he checked it in the side mirror and came around to join us. "You're taking Spanish? What the hell you going to use Spanish for?"

Mark was a relatively recent transfer, having just started at St. John in the ninth grade. He moved over to Gulfport from Biloxi and didn't make a peep his first couple of weeks. He and Hop knew each other from back in elementary school when they used to play each other in peewee baseball, and once Mark realized he was not alone, he followed us around like a puppy. Before we knew it, Mark was one of the guys, despite his clothing choices, which were questionable at best. Black Chucks and torn Levis were cool; red Chucks not as much, but still acceptable. Wearing a gold necklace with a St. Christopher medal so it showed – even on the outside of a button-down – was a bit much. Mark's roots were primarily Italian, but he had just enough redneck in him to make things interesting.

"I don't know," I said. "It had an opening."

"I'm taking French," he said, tucking his shirt in. "I think I'll get more out of French."

"French? Really? Pussy."

Mark smiled real big and took a draw on his chocolate milk. "Say what you want; I know what I'm doing. You ever see the makeup of one of them French classes?"

"You ever see any real French girls?"

"Yeah, on the Olympics. And I liked them." Now I can guarantee Mark hadn't seen a real French girl on TV, and I'm certain he'd never watched the Olympics, but to him it sounded cool. "Plus, Blondie sang some French on one of her B-sides – I think it was 'Sunday Girl.' And the backup singer in 'Eyes Without a Face' did too."

Billy Idol played in my head as he spoke. Mark wasn't wrong.

"So what classes *do* we have together?" Hop asked. We checked, and it looked like Hop and I would suffer through algebra; I would have biology with Mark, and the three of us would share the religion and English comp classrooms. Homeroom was a toss-up; we might have had the same times, but we would likely get split up into different groups. Mark believed it was part of a conspiracy, but he thought everything had some sort of furtive backstory.

More cars started creeping in, and before I knew it, our little corner of the parking lot was filling up with classmates. I didn't see any new vehicles, and from the looks of it, several folks carpooled.

The metal girls gathered around Shayna Haddock's pickup truck, smoking cigarettes and listening to Warrant. They wore a lot of paint, and the sheer size of their hair was always a source of amusement to me. I could not imagine how much ozone they burned to tease those helmets out that high. I wanted to comment, but I didn't because I thought some of the girls, especially the thicker ones, could whip me if it came down to it, and that was never a good thing. Also, I knew if they couldn't take me, their redneck, roach-killing boyfriends – several of whom finished high school early and now worked for the city – could do the job for them with ease. And by finishing "early," I don't mean they were part of the gifted program.

Trey Kratz pulled up in the Whale, an antique, beat-up baby blue Mercedes with a rusted-out hole in the back seat so big you could drop a tennis ball through it. Chad Harkins followed in the Firechicken, Travis Wilson in the Dustbuster, and Ben Sands, Antonio Adkins, Rush Atherton, and Sammy Mallette arrived in Ben's mom's Cadillac – affectionately named Freddy after the notorious pimp who ran the whores up in North Gulfport. Ben was embarrassed to be driving such a behemoth, but Sammy thought it was funny and was laughing about it when they got out of the car. Sammy laughed at everything. Rush was the redheaded kid of the class. He always wore a crew cut and dreamed about being a Navy SEAL. He was laid back, easy to talk to, and had a good-looking older sister with fantastic cans.

We eventually decided we had hung out in the parking lot long enough, and it was time to comb the halls to see what piqued our interest. I was hoping one particular white BMW would roll in, but seeing none, there was no need for me to stay outside any longer. I borrowed a pen from Hop, who grabbed his notebook and a sack lunch. Mark didn't bring anything. No paper, no books, nothing. He figured the first day was a pass. Actually, he considered the first week a pass.

As we started to make our way to the side door near our lockers, a shiny, red four-wheel-drive F150 pickup crunched through the oyster shells and pulled in next to where Mark had parked.

"Who is that?" I asked. Neither Mark nor Hop answered, and judging by the looks on the faces of the rest of the gang, no one had a clue. The door opened and out stepped a cat who looked like a cross between pre-Army Elvis and post-*Outsiders* Tom Cruise.

He was crisp, polished, and clean – much like his truck. His hair was Lego perfect, and when he closed the door and started walking towards the school, it was like a slow-motion scene from a movie, with the Kenwoods from Andy Tanner's Camaro over in the senior lot pumping out the soundtrack. He looked toward us and scanned the crowd, then nodded, glanced at me for a second, and headed for the door.

"Must be a new kid," Mark said.

"You think?" Sammy chimed in from behind us, still laughing. I put the pen in my mouth and checked out the truck again while everyone headed towards the door. It looked like it had just rolled off the lot.

New kid indeed.

CHAPTER 2

St. John Interparochial High School opened in Gulfport, Mississippi in 1956 as a place where Catholics, pseudo-Catholics, and the occasional Protestant could go for an education purportedly built on truth, honor, and the antiquated tenets of the Roman Catholic Church. Back in the day, hardline nuns patrolled the classrooms with the precision of drill sergeants, swapping out boots and fatigues for orthopedic shoes and habits. Banging erasers after class and writing lines were relatively light sentences; a hand smacking, a cheek pinch, or an ear grab were more the norm. Years and years of pent-up sexual frustration coupled with bunking in bleak, yellowed rooms with groups of other similarly situated women took its toll. Somewhere along the line, much like husbands and wives who have been married for a long time, the nuns started to look alike. Other than variations in weight, nearly every nun over the age of sixty favored the other. Dirty glasses, questionable teeth, and bad haircuts flourished. It was as if Velma from Scooby-Doo had several ripened aunts who suddenly retired and moved in together.

The St. John student body drew from three feeder sources – St. James Elementary and St. Alphonsus Elementary made up the majority of the Catholic contingent, while the remaining kids came from a scattering of public schools up and down the Coast. I was a bit of a hybrid. I attended St. James for first and second grade, but in third grade, my parents moved us out of Gulfport proper and relocated the family further north, deep in the county. Said they were tired of living in a cookie-cutter neighborhood, wanted more land, and something else about taxes and my dad's job. I found out later our move was tied more to our being strapped from my old man's binges at the greyhound track in Mobile than any desire to experience country living at its finest.

To say I wasn't happy with the transfer would have been an understatement. One year, I was surrounded by friends in a school I loved, and the next I found myself square in the middle of Lyman Elementary, a public school way out in the sticks where the dirtline mustaches and permed-in-the-back mullets were sported without a hint of shame. I made an observation early on about one particularly egregious haircut and almost got my size eight tail kicked by another third grader who looked like he drove himself to class. Over time, of course, things got better, and by the time I left three years later, we found common ground that led to some pretty tight alliances. What I didn't know then was those bonds formed on the red dirt of that worn-out kickball field would end up saving my ass – not once, but twice.

When I returned to St. John in 1981 after my involuntary secondment, I happily fell back into the fold within my first week as a seventh grader. There were still some nuns, but the majority of the classes were now led by teachers who had come over after a career in the public schools, checking out of the zoo as soon as they put in enough years to qualify for state retirement. The ratio continued to lean more towards the secular with every season after that, and as I began my junior year, there were no more than a handful of sisters left. The principal, on the other hand, had been a staple at St. John's for at least ten years, and he made it clear he intended to stay. Petty Officer Johnny "The Chief" Beattie was a fireplug of an Italian man with a short fuse and a Navy pension who transitioned from a 25-year career in the military into "hiya" education. The Chief's stubby arms made him genetically predisposed to swing a paddle, and the first time he lit me up when I was a freshman, it hurt so bad it made me cough. He had a history of trying to set the disciplinary tone the first day of school, and it was often not pretty for whoever ended up on the receiving end.

I saw him as soon as I stepped into the building and did my best to keep from crossing his path. I was able to avoid him by cutting through a classroom, and I eventually made it to my locker unscathed. Per tradition, I taped my tattered picture of the Blues Brothers on the inside door, then pulled out my Spanish book, Hop's semi-chewed pen, and the sixty-page Mead spiral notebook with the orange cover. I had been there less than an hour, and the metal coils were already bent and misshapen to the point of being nonfunctional. I started to make my way down to the cafeteria to see if the rumor about an improved lunch menu had any merit.

I barely made it three steps before a voice stopped me in my tracks.

Suddenly the dissonance of five hundred day-one conversations, the scraping of desks across freshly waxed linoleum, and the slamming of cold steel locker doors fell away like someone pressed a selective mute button silencing all sounds but one. The question hit me like a sucker punch.

"Where do you think you're going?"

I should have had more situational awareness. I should have picked up the scent of Lauren perfume, which even now slingshots keen memories to the forefront of my brain as sudden and as vivid as the Christmas I got a full Hot Wheels track, complete with garage and working elevator. My periphery should have noticed the parting of the crowds, the sudden change in pitch of some of the voices closer by. My radar should have been moving in overtime, because, at least for this year, the main reason *I* was looking so forward to the first day of school, was for this very moment.

I turned, and there, in front of me – crossed arms cradling books across her chest – stood Emily Miller.

CHAPTER 3

Emily and I had been classmates, kind of, since first grade at St. James. I would have been on track to go the entire distance with her, but my temporary relocation screwed that up. It didn't really matter, though, because I barely even noticed Emily back then – nor were her antennae pointed my way, but in eighth grade, after several months of pre-pubescent posturing, we became friends. During the next two years, we became close, and somewhere toward the end of our sophomore year, a spark lit. The glances across the hall became more frequent. The conversations got a little deeper, the physical space between us drew closer, and the end-of-class locker visits were becoming a daily event. She was all I thought about. Then summer happened.

Her parents had money. Real money, although you would never know it by the way she carried herself; in fact, she downplayed it as often as possible, even if the BMW was hard to ignore. It was the kind of money that allowed them to spend most of their summer traveling in Europe and taking three-day theatre weekend trips to New York City. My family, on the other hand, was not exactly knocking it out, which meant I spent the summer between my sophomore and junior year busting my ass at Murphy Electric as the default attic rat and the go-to mole cricket. Pulling wire under crawl spaces and digging ditches in the South Mississippi summer sun was not glamorous, but it kept me busy, and the forty-hour-plus weeks put a respectable amount of change in my teenage pocket. We promised to keep in touch, but neither of us did, and as soon as I laid eyes on her, I instantly regretted not writing.

She was wearing faded Guess jeans, a pullover Esprit shirt, and earrings that dangled and swung when she moved her head. She was a bit of a close-talker, and her sudden proximity caught me off guard, turning my mouth to cotton. If someone *had* to be a close-talker, however, I'd much rather it be Emily than any of my cretin friends.

"What?" I swallowed quickly and tried to recover while doing my best, quite poorly I might add, to avert my eyes. I didn't want to stare, but I hadn't seen her since we got out of school and I could not comprehend how it was possible for her to become exponentially better looking here, the first day back.

"Were you heading somewhere?" Underneath her perfume, I could smell vanilla and Faberge Organics shampoo, and when she spoke, I picked up a hint of Big Red.

"Yeah, I was just, you know, going down to the cafeteria."

"The cafeteria?" She looked over my shoulder and nodded in the direction behind me. "Really? You sure you're not following your boy Hop down there to check out the new junior high prospects?"

To her point, the only legitimate date Hop went out on during our sophomore year was at homecoming, and he weirded everyone out by taking an eighth grader. Some eighth graders looked like their mom still tied their shoes. I followed Emily's gaze. Sure enough, Hop was halfway down the hall and moving with a purpose.

"You know, maybe I should go rescue him. Or maybe not. His efforts last year did yield results. Granted, she had to be back by nine-thirty, but technically, it was a date."

"Y'all are sick."

"What other options did he have? After all, he could never get anyone from our class to go out with him." I grinned. "I couldn't either."

"From what I hear, you didn't have any problems over the summer."

"What?"

"I heard Hop had some killer parties while I was away." She looped her index finger in between the first and second buttons of my shirt and bunched the fabric from the placket into a fist, pulling me closer. Then she stood on her tiptoes and put her lips to my ear. "And I heard you were quite friendly with some of his guests," she whispered, teasing out the words. Then she smiled without showing her teeth, slapped her palm on my chest and pushed me away.

While Hop's back to school soiree indeed proved to be fertile ground for snagging, I hadn't expected reports of my dalliances to reach Emily's ears. At least not yet. Not that it would have mattered much to her anyway. Or would it have?

I wanted to say something snappy in reply, but after she lobbed that grenade, she moved on, oblivious to the cut eyes from the girls and turnaround checks by the dudes. I couldn't blame them, and as I moved down the hall in the other direction, I found myself wanting to restart the conversation. I wondered what she was thinking at that very moment. I doubted she was dissecting the dialogue like I was, and the unpleasant revelation occurred to me I might not be in her thoughts at all. But I could have been, right? She searched *me* out, not the other way around, right? In fact, I was pretty sure I saw the same flash of happy-to-see-you-recognition in her eyes that I had. Didn't I?

I felt another tap on my shoulder. My instincts had been on point all along. I knew she'd come back, and I spun around, ready to re-engage. But the person standing in front of me was most certainly not Emily Miller.

It was the new kid. And he looked as if he might throw up.

"Uh, excuse me, I, uh, hate to bother you, but I saw you this morning in the parking lot and I was wondering if you could help me with something?"

"Yeah?" I held my tongue.

"I - I can't figure out where to go."

Even though this dude was probably six-foot-two, he looked smaller up close, standing there hunched over, schedule in hand. I really didn't want to be rude, but I also really wanted to catch back up with Emily. I glanced down past the lockers, but by this point she was long gone, and probably already in class. I narrowed my eyes and looked back at him. I remembered what it felt like starting up at a new school where everyone's a stranger, so I couldn't leave him hanging. I had been there not too long ago myself, and it could be tough no matter your age.

"I saw you as well," I said, "Matt Frazier. Nice to meet you –?"

"Nate."

"Nate?" I shook his hand and it felt like a chicken breast two hours into a thaw.

"Nate Mayes."

I nodded my head. "Where you from, Nate?"

"Sacred Heart. Hattiesburg."

"Oh yeah?" Hattiesburg was about an hour north of Gulfport.

"Yep."

"What brings you to Gulfport – and what landed you here in this fine institution?"

"Ah, my, uh, my old man got an opportunity to open up shop down here." To look so good, the kid could barely talk.

"Well, lucky you." We had a lot of military kids move in and out due to our proximity to the Seabee base. At first I thought he could be one of those, but changed my mind once I gave him a look over. Diction issues notwithstanding, the boy looked put together. He had all new clothes, and they were expensive. Girbauds, Polo shirt, and leather Stan Smiths. Maybe trying a bit too hard, like someone dressed him or something. I hoped he wasn't going to be one of those asshole preppies. We had enough of them already.

"Let me see what you got." I took a look, and the brain trust in the office had him doubled-booked. "Here's the problem. Looks like they got you in Spanish and chemistry first period. That's crazy."

"Yeah," he said, oblivious to my comments. Actually, I don't think he was even listening. "Should I go back up, up front to the, uh, desk, and check –"

"Look, I'm heading to Spanish right now. Why don't you just follow me? Arguably, you'll be half right. Plus, our chemistry teacher, Sister Joanne, can be incredibly shrill. You do not want her first period."

"Thanks." He shifted his weight, threw his book bag over his shoulder and looked at me for direction. I jerked my head back toward the senior end.

"This way. Room seven. Can't miss it. Miss Mander may look like a linebacker, but she's a real softie once you get to know her." I took a few steps and then turned back. "How'd you end up way down here, anyway?"

"Weird," he said, looking relaxed for the first time. "Some old dude just a few lockers back was yelling and screaming at everyone and got me all – got me turned around."

So Nate met the Chief. "Greasy, short bastard?"

Nate laughed. "Yeah, looked like he combed his hair with a pork chop. Had a perpetual grimace on his face like he just crapped his pants."

No stuttering there. I smiled and gave him a second look. We continued to class, and the more we talked, the more I got the feeling Nate wouldn't be an outsider for long.

Who knows? We might even be friends one day.

CHAPTER 4

Kathryn Cooper's father, a career Air Force Colonel, had a way with words and neither enlisted nor officer could escape his aphorisms. They became so prevalent during his command days at Keesler that they regularly appeared on the announcement board near the front gate. *Be careful what you wish for* was one of his favorites, and he often paired it with the other principles he swore by: *always tell the truth* and *be accountable for your actions*. He once told Kathryn during her feisty teenage days that the former was not nearly as important as the latter, but it was still a good piece of advice to heed, especially when your head – *your* head, Katy Bug, he pointed out – stayed perpetually turned toward the horizon looking for greener pastures.

She sure wished she could have his counsel now. It had been five years to the day since he dropped dead of a heart attack in the commissary parking lot, holding a brown paper sack containing a gallon of milk and a box of Ginger Snaps he had picked up for her mom. His passing absolutely devastated Kathryn and she wore her grief like a veil: she could still see out, but it clouded her view of everything.

Her year in the ditch ate away at nearly every meaningful aspect of her life. She walked away from her friends, isolated her work colleagues, and to her surprise, even found herself blaming her mother. Sex became nothing more than a distant memory, and romance was altogether off the table. It took her hitting rock bottom one Saturday morning – hunched over, cross-legged, tears dripping on the ceramic tiles in her crappy apartment kitchen before she realized there were two paths ahead. One led to an early grave; the other, she wasn't quite sure, but it was somewhere *else*, and at that moment it was enough. The epiphany may have been unpleasant, but it was necessary, and over the next four years, she scratched, clawed and climbed her way back to those verdant fields where everything was right again. Except it wasn't. Not yet, at least.

Yes, she became one of the most buzzed about FBI agents from her class, having been promoted from Agent Trainee to Senior Special Agent in record time. Yes, she had flown to DC twice to meet with the Deputy Director in person. And yes, she was in line to make her next rank – Supervisory Special Agent – faster than any female field agent in FBI history. But she still hadn't been able to close out one of the highest profile homegrown FBI cases since the days of the Capones and Gambinos. Not yet, at least.

Kathryn slid a Hall & Oates CD into her stereo and turned on the shower. As she butchered the lyrics to "Out of Touch," she let the hot water rinse the shampoo out of her hair. She liked the way it felt running down her face and between her breasts, and as the steam collected to the point that the walls started dropping out, her mind turned to Tom Chrestman – the witness who would, that very morning, give a statement that would finally blow the case wide open.

Lord knows she needed it. A few missteps in every investigation are allowed, but some of Kathryn's choices of late had brought her dangerously close to what some would consider unacceptable, if not incompetent. She was painfully aware of her predicament, and had taken extra efforts to avoid another derailment, to include arranging the meeting so it would just be her and Tom – plus his lawyer, of course. She also purposefully selected the time – early in the day, outside the scope and purview of the press and other prying eyes. She wanted to make it as easy on Mr. Chrestman as possible, and the more secure and private he felt about it all, the better the odds were of Kathryn getting what she wanted.

Of course, that was the plan *prior* to him giving up the goods. After she had his sworn affidavit in the can, it would be a different scene, and she had made special arrangements for that as well. She gave a local reporter the heads up that she would be providing her own statement on behalf of the Agency that afternoon, and to prepare for the inevitable cameras, interviews and upcoming *atta girl* meetings with the higher-ups, she spent the weekend getting a makeover. Kathryn got her hair cut and colored, treated herself to a manicure, and even bought a new outfit. It was more than she could afford, but it would be offset after two months at her new pay grade, and as she slid into it, she confirmed once again how good it made her thighs and butt look if she turned just the right way. She leaned into the mirror and put on her lipstick, touched up her mascara, and stepped back to inspect her work.

"Wow." She couldn't recall a time when she looked this put together. Confident even. She grabbed her purse and the file folders and locked the door behind her. As she walked to the car, a feeling she hadn't experienced in some time came over her. She didn't know if it was her new look, her new clothes, or the heady thoughts about what would happen if she did close the case, but there was a confidence in her stride that hadn't been there before. In just a matter of hours, the world would finally see Kathryn the way *she* wanted to be seen.

It was something she had wished for all of her life.

CHAPTER 5

Project Pestle was the code name given to the prolific money-laundering scheme that had been growing by leaps and bounds from the day Kathryn was assigned to the case. She was fortunate to get on board early, and through a combination of luck, skill, and immersive working of the files, she eventually became the lead agent over the Southeast region, where the bulk of the operation had been taking place.

The primary perpetrators were a collusive network of compounding pharmacies and doctors working together to defraud Uncle Sam out of millions of dollars. Through a combination of bogus prescriptions from the doctor end, and false reimbursement requests from the pharmacists, a pseudo-cartel had been formed, and it remained reasonably under the radar until the players started getting careless. When the FBI got involved, Kathryn picked out the project's code name herself and thought it quite clever considering the subject matter. But lately, she felt like she had been on the receiving end of the grinding, and was looking forward to some relief.

She spent the first two years behind the scenes, going through boxes and boxes of records, cross-referencing bank deposits and withdrawals with receipts and checks. It was mind-numbing and labor intensive, but she was a detail person, and the meticulous spreadsheets she generated led to multiple rounds of arrests, convictions and confessions. With each doctor or pharmacist she put away, a layer of the onion peeled off, and Kathryn could feel herself closing in on the main target. The problem was, she hadn't quite been able to get there.

Her first real chance came after she collared Joe Birdsall, a manager of several pharmacies near Jackson. Kathryn had hard evidence proving that he was the primary launderer on the compounding side *and* that he played a leadership role on the recruiting front. When Kathryn approached him trying to cut a deal prior to sentencing, he made it clear he wasn't interested in talking. Kathryn wasn't deterred. She had seen his type before. Through his façade of arrogance and faux-bravado, she could tell he was scared, and instead of spinning her wheels trying to broker an early plea in exchange for information, she made the call to wait him out. She was sure a more comprehensive confession would be forthcoming once his inevitable date with the warden grew closer, and was willing to wait.

That was her first big blunder. She misread him, and he put a bullet through his head within days after her walkout, spinning her into a spiral of depression and self-doubt reminiscent of those months after her father died. She soon realized, however, that no one blamed her directly for the failed outcome, even though she was the one who set the chain of events in motion by her own arrogance and need to show everyone how tough she was. After all, a suicide is a suicide, she was told, and there was not a lot she could do about it. When people discussed it on those terms, Kathryn took no effort to dissuade them – partly because she didn't know how she would handle the criticism, and partly because she had a backup plan of sorts.

Enter Tom Chrestman.

He was a minor fish, she was led to believe; friendly and more than willing to talk the first time she interviewed him. It wasn't until later that she found out he had been playing her all along. That's when she contacted Tom's lawyer and told him, quite curtly, that they now had evidence to put Tom away for years, if not decades, and if he had aspirations of cutting any type of deal, then it was his last chance to come clean. Of course, she was bluffing and didn't have *all* the evidence, but she baited the hook anyway to see if she would get a bite. She was surprised to learn not only that Tom was willing to meet, but that he insisted the sooner the better. Kathryn wasn't quite sure what triggered his change of heart, but she had a hunch, and if she was right, Tom would come busting through the doors with bells on, ready to sing.

That is, if he showed up at all.

CHAPTER 6

Tom Chrestman wasn't sure why, but the Mercedes was the one new purchase they let him keep. The feds took his 911, his Range Rover, and even the old Bronco he was going to have restored. He was hoping they would take the 560SL, too. At one time he considered the car – a convertible with a low profile built for speed – his prized possession, but now it seemed like yet one more display of excess, and it stood out as a sore reminder of who he once was.

He had suffered through having to air his dirty laundry publicly, humiliating his wife, Jessica, in the process. He felt the sting of friends peeling off one by one as he faded from principal to pariah over a period of time measured by headlines documenting the drama as it unfolded. Now, according to his lawyer, Tom was a few days away from an indictment, and the severity of charges to be levied against him – along with potential prison time – would be dictated largely by how cooperative he was with the special agent waiting to interview him at the FBI office downtown. He had been released on bond a few days after his initial arrest because he was not considered a threat to flee, and every day of freedom since then had felt like a breath of fresh air.

But now the noose had begun to tighten. A plea agreement had been put on the table, and as Tom adjusted the knot on his tie, he weighed just how much he should – or could – say. He didn't want to go back to jail, but at the same time, he shuddered at the thought of what might happen if word got around that he snitched his way to a deal. On the way out the door he kissed his wife on the cheek and pulled the covers up on Julia, his three-year-old, careful not to wake either. Jessica had no idea he was going in for a second round. The less she knew, the better.

He took the long way to the federal building. He was in no hurry to get to the confessional, and he figured more time would clear his head and better prepare him for the inevitable. As he drove, he cursed the day he left his job at K&B Drugs to open his own compounding pharmacy business. Yes, working at K&B had been mind-numbingly boring. Counting pills day after day, week after week, answering the same questions time and time again – often from the same customers – wore thin quickly, but it was stable, paid well, and was only a few minutes from his home. Hindsight was 20/20, and suddenly, a repetitive and mundane life sounded good. Comforting, even. Much better than convicted felon, that's for sure.

The back roads led him to Archibald Park, a stretch of land donated by the descendants of a prominent turn-of-the-century sailing captain who made his fortune exporting timber. It stretched over several hundred acres, split primarily between a nature preserve on one end and a sportsplex on the other. Tom pulled into the parking lot where the two public spaces converged at a large playground. He parked on the side closest to the woods and smiled as he thought of Julia tiptoeing down the nature walk to try to see a bluebird or a redheaded woodpecker. He loved that she showed little interest in the slide or the swings and always made a beeline for the trees. He looked around; there were no cars, but he saw a red, white, and blue Schwinn Sting-Ray with a silver banana seat leaning against the wood sign at the trailhead.

"Dang, Marty, you're here early," Tom muttered, killing the ignition.

Marty Deen was the son of Grant Deen, the long-serving city councilman of Tom's district. Growing up, Marty – just a few years younger than Tom – was referred to as retarded. Of course, you couldn't say that anymore, so now Marty was either "mentally challenged" or "slow," depending on who was doing the speaking. Neither sounded good to Tom.

Marty was well known among the Gulfport locals. He worked part time for the city's department of leisure services, mowing grass around the park and striping the ball fields. When he got off work in the afternoons, Marty would ride his bike over to the park, loaded up with the remains of his lunch, a sketchpad, and a pair of binoculars. Even though he suffered from some developmental and cognitive deficiencies, Marty was not without talent. God had given him the ability to draw, and his obsession was birds, which he would sketch from memory using colored pencils or pastels. He was enough of a prodigy that the Holden Gallery in downtown Gulfport slated a New Year's Eve exhibit for Marty that was already starting to get some buzz. At one time in a prior life, Tom had hoped to go and pick up an original to hang in Julia's bedroom. Fat chance of that happening now.

Tom got out and stretched his legs to see if he could see Marty across the way. Anything to burn a few more minutes. He strained his eyes and even waved but got no response. The scent of the pines hung heavily in the air, and he thought about how the ground would soon turn slippery with straw once the cooler weather kicked in. He had spent many a fall raking it into piles and wondered if this year he would be relegated to watching the seasons change through a prison window. Off in the distance he thought he heard the hum of a mower cranking up near the soccer fields. He leaned on the hood of his car and checked his watch. Tom was scheduled to meet with his lawyer at eight before his appointment with the feds at nine. He started running the facts through his head again and again, and no matter how the different scenarios played out, he always ended up hitting a wall. He knew he bought some time with the first interview a few months ago, but he hadn't been exactly forthcoming with everything. The agent who interviewed him had apparently come to the same realization, and when Tom thought of facing her again –

Tom nearly ripped his shirt collar trying to loosen the button and forced himself to breathe through his nose. He fumbled in his pocket for a Xanax and washed four tablets down with a Mountain Dew. He wiped his face with the cuff of his sleeve, then stooped over, hands on his knees, to collect himself. After a few seconds, he took a deep breath, then picked up a rock and zinged it toward a garbage can where it banged off the side. Yes, Tom thought, this time would be different for sure.

This time would be a reckoning.

CHAPTER 7

It had been a bit of a crapshoot lately as to exactly how the Xanax would impact Tom's mood, and the outcome was not always as expected. Sometimes it was euphoria, infrequently it was paranoia, and on most days the medicine just took the edge off, which was usually enough for him. A lot of it had to do with how he felt when he swallowed the pills, his mood impacting the pharmacologic effects of the chemicals as they metabolized and flooded his central nervous system. This time he was hoping for a pleasant escape or at least a tamping down of the anxiety raging inside of him, but instead, he was greeted with a melancholic introspection that caused his thoughts to turn, yet again, to the events that led him to his sorry state of affairs.

It all began with a too-good-to-be-true offer just a few years back from his pharmacy school running buddy Joe Birdsall. Tom ran into "Birdy" at the annual Southeastern Pharmacists convention in Birmingham. It was Birdy who told Tom over drinks that he had opened a compounding pharmacy just north of Jackson, and it was Birdy who suggested Tom join him and open one in Gulfport.

According to Birdy, the world was changing. Big box pharmacies had grown too corporate, and patients and physicians were seeking a more personalized approached for their prescription needs. Compounding – the old-time practice of preparing custom medications – was enjoying a revival, and the benefits on both sides of the coin were numerous. Customers weren't forced to take a stock medication that might or might not be exactly right for whatever afflicted them, and pharmacists could actually exercise some creativity and utilize their learned skillset for a change. This second fact alone had great appeal to Tom. He would no longer have to bide his time counting out capsules and filling bottles, and he could finally feel like he was making a difference. Plus, it had the potential for profit. Real profit. Six figures and more per year with the sky being the limit if you worked hard enough.

Tom didn't need to be told twice. He worked out an arrangement with Birdy, quit his job at K&B, and after a short stint shadowing Birdy up in Jackson, opened Cat Island Compounding – not too far from Gulfport Memorial Hospital, and just a short drive down Highway 90 from the Seabee base. Birdy told him the location was ideal because it allowed Tom to serve the most profitable subset of patients – retirees serviced by Medicare and servicemen covered by Tricare.

Tom enjoyed the work and was proud to finally be in control of his life. He did his best to drum up business; he read everything he could get his hands on and tried to make himself available to patients and providers 24/7. But as the first quarter stretched into a year, his receivables could not keep up with his overhead, and he was soon deep in the red. He had poured all his money into the store and could not get any more loans. He even moved his family into a small apartment to save money, but it didn't help. He woke up each morning with his stomach in his throat and a throbbing headache from grinding his teeth at night. He quit eating from worry and lost twenty pounds. When he couldn't take it anymore, he called his old boss at K&B to set up a meeting, but when Jessica found out, she encouraged him to reach out to Birdy one more time. Jessica didn't exactly trust Birdy, but at this point she didn't care. Birdy was doing something right, and she quietly wondered if Tom could use some additional guidance on the management front. Plus, she had lived through the K&B years and did not want to do it again.

Birdy showed up the next day in a convertible Porsche with a big-breasted blonde named Charlotte riding shotgun. He introduced her as his "number one sales rep." Tom remembered them both coming into his office, their eyes excited with the prospect of – something. Tom sat them down and started to walk through his story. He was a bit taken aback and embarrassed when Birdy asked to see his financials, but Tom showed them to him anyway. Birdy read over them for less than five minutes before nodding to Charlotte. When she got the signal, she put her purse on the table and pulled out five stacks of $100 bills – $10,000 total – and lined them up across the front of his desk, right next to his framed picture of Jessica and Julia.

"What is this?" Tom asked, standing up. "Look, I didn't ask you to come down here for a loan."

"Not a loan," Birdy said, "far from it." He looked over at Charlotte and she smiled. "That's one week of sales. Net."

Tom's mouth opened slightly. "One week?" He tried to do the math in his head but could not figure out any reasonable sales activity that would generate this kind of income.

"I've been waiting for you to call," Birdy said, leaning back and cracking his knuckles. "I told you there was money to be made in this business."

Tom whistled slowly. "And you made this compounding?"

"Indeed I did."

He looked at him and then over at Charlotte, wondering what she did for Tom, other than the obvious.

"Legally?"

Now Birdy leaned forward. "Paid straight to me from the United States government."

Tom shut the door, sat down, and listened as Birdy laid it all out for him.

* * *

Nearly two years to the date of Birdy's and Charlotte's visit, Tom watched a breaking news report showing Birdy being cuffed and stuffed into a police cruiser after his pharmacy got raided by the FBI. For a brief time, Birdy took the position – quite publicly – that he intended to prove his innocence in a court of law. He hired a big, toothy lawyer out of Jackson with a penchant for expensive suits and press conferences. On the day his indictment was unsealed, Birdy didn't appear at the federal courthouse for a mandatory hearing, leading the magistrate to issue a warrant for his arrest. When the police arrived at his house, they found Joe Birdsall dead from a self-inflicted gunshot wound. Tom's personal situation was as bad, if not worse, than

Birdy's, but he couldn't imagine what it would take for a man to even think about doing such a thing.

After Birdy died, things started happening to Tom that at first seemed innocuous. A few phone calls where the person calling remained silent after Tom picked up. Missing mail. A broken window at the pharmacy. It was not until Tom came home to find his door unlocked and opened that he started to get uncomfortable, and he became downright nervous when he realized someone had been tailing him on the way home from work. Rehashing it all made Tom even more anxious, and he fumbled in his pocket for another Xanax. He knew he had taken too many already, but he had to calm his nerves. He popped two just for good measure, and as he waited for another layer of fog to set in, a movement in the woods distracted him. He sat up and waved one more time for Marty, but still got no response. He thought he might have seen a lens flare and stared for another second or two, but when no one came out, he climbed in his car, slid in his Tears for Fears CD, and backed out. A sudden lurch of his vehicle snapped him out of his daydreaming.

"What the hell?" Tom said, looking in his rearview mirror. "Today of all days, some son of a bitch rear-ends me," he said under his breath as he threw his car in park, unlatched his seatbelt and stepped out. As he walked to the back to inspect the damage, he noticed the driver of the truck start to get out. He hadn't even realized anyone had been behind him.

"I hope you have insurance," Tom said, fuming and glancing at his bumper, "because –" he froze, and the burn he felt just a second before morphed into something darker as the man now walking his way came into focus. Tom put a shaky hand out in front as the man raised his arm. "Wait, let me explain. You don't understand, I wasn't going to talk. I –"

A Sig Sauer P-250 fitted with a screw-on absorption silencer fired, putting three bullets in a tight triangular pattern through Tom's forehead. He dropped into a heap on the shoulder, and the shooter holstered his weapon. He stepped over the body and performed a cursory search of the vehicle. Finding no documents, tapes, or things of interest, he picked up the spent shells and left the scene, being careful to avoid any patches of dirt on the pavement that could be used to match up his tire tracks.

The entire encounter had taken less than a minute. After a slow loop around the premises to make sure no one else was around, the shooter made his way to the Triplett-Day cafe, where he ordered a plate of beignets and a small chocolate milk.

At eight a.m. sharp he walked outside to the pay phone by the Coke machine and dropped in a coin. When the prompt from the beeper on the receiving end chimed, he entered a code, hung up the phone, and walked out to his truck.

The message had been delivered.

There would be no further statements from Tom Chrestman.

CHAPTER 8

Kathryn watched through her office window and let herself breathe when a car finally drove through the gate and parked two spaces down from hers. The make and model of the brown sedan that pulled in told her it was probably the lawyer's, and based upon its condition, it also told her he worked full time as a criminal defense attorney – and not a very good one at that. She craned her neck to see if she could get a look at Tom, and was especially interested in how he was carrying himself, but when the lawyer got out, lit a cigarette, and locked the door, a revelation hit Kathryn as swift and powerful as a slap across the face.

Tom Chrestman was not with him.

Out of habit, Kathryn smoothed her blouse with her hands, which were starting to sweat. A hangnail she had been biting snagged on a pleat in the silk, but she didn't notice. What if she had been fooled again? What if it had all been a ruse? What if he had never intended to come back all along?

She looked back outside. The lawyer was leaning against the car, his elbows resting on the hood, overseeing the parking lot. *He* wasn't nervous, but he didn't look very happy either. That was no surprise, though. Most defense lawyers didn't look very happy. He looked at his watch, snubbed his butt out and walked toward the building.

Nine o'clock came and went. Thirty more minutes of Kathryn making awkward small talk with him clicked by. Nothing. Tom's lawyer looked even worse in person, and the acrid smell of smoke on his clothes and breath were too much – even from across the room, so Kathryn pretended to turn back to her work. Thankfully, he got the hint and left just before ten. He left a card, and told Kathryn to call him if Tom showed up. He also promised to let her know as soon as he found out anything, but Kathryn could tell by the look on his face that he wasn't exactly hopeful. On the way out, he turned at the door and said that in his entire career, he only had a few of his clients skip town, and was certainly disappointed to now count Tom as one of them.

By the time he pulled off, she had cycled through everything from pissed off to panicked, and now found herself reluctantly having to face the music. It was time to inform the troops, and she wasn't quite sure how to spin this one. She pulled the file and started a pot of Maxwell House, but the phone rang in her office before she could pour her first cup.

"Hello."

"Gulfport Police Department calling for Agent Kathryn Cooper."

"Speaking."

"Please hold while I connect you to Chief Papania."

Kathryn stood up a little straighter and cleared her throat. The last time she spoke to Rick Papania was at a first responders' breakfast hosted by the Kiwanis Club a few weeks prior. He was divorced, she had never been married, and she swore she picked up a flirt or two while making small talk in the buffet line. She had given that encounter more thought than it deserved, but she couldn't help herself. This call was a pleasant diversion, and for no apparent reason, she fixed her hair while she waited.

"Morning Chief," she said when she heard the line click, wondering if she was being too formal.

"Morning Agent – uh, Kathryn."

"It's not every day I get a call from the man in charge, and I know it's not just so you can hear my beautiful voice." She put her hand to her forehead and closed her eyes. She could not have said anything more cheesy, but before she could recover, he responded.

"Well, it's not every day I have to deal with a homicide first thing in the morning."

"A homicide?" Murders happened in Gulfport, but they were few and far between, and usually involved a drug deal gone bad or a domestic dispute – almost none of them involving her department. She certainly never received a heads up from the locals while the body was still warm.

"Yeah, so, I called you because I wanted to speak to you personally – before the word gets out and your phone starts ringing off the hook."

"The word?"

"Do you remember a fellow named Tom Chrestman? If memory serves me, at one time he was one of the suspects in the big money laundering case you've been working on."

Kathryn's stomach dropped. "Yes."

"One of my officers radioed in to me a few minutes ago that they found his body this morning."

"His body?" She took a seat. "Where?"

"Archie Park."

"You said homicide, and not suicide, right?" Kathryn grabbed her pad and started scribbling notes. "You sure?"

"Hard to commit suicide by shooting yourself three times."

After making another entry, she spun her pen in her fingers and tapped the paper. "This morning?"

"Yep."

"You been to the scene yet?"

"Heading that way shortly."

"I'll meet you there. Make sure no one touches anything until I have taken a look."

"If you say so. I'll let my boys know. And uh, Kathryn –"

"Yeah?"

"There's going to be a lot of press about this. If it gets to be too much or if I can help you out with anything don't be a stranger okay?"

"You got it. See you in a few minutes."

Anything? At least the day didn't turn out to be a total shit show. Kathryn grabbed her keys, her weapon and her lipstick and headed out the door.

CHAPTER 9

Her Crown Victoria couldn't get her there quick enough. She even used the siren, a rarity for her, and when she arrived, Rick was waiting next to a taped off area.

"Here you go," he said, pointing. "A jogger came up on the body just after eight during her morning run."

"I imagine she had quite a shock," Kathryn said, taking her first look at the victim. She walked near his head and leaned over to try to get a visual on the exit wound. She had to step over his legs, which had buckled under him when he fell. His right arm was extended above his head, Saturday Night Fever-style, and his face was locked in that ghastly open-mouthed death mask she had seen so many times before – like he was trying to get one more word in before he crossed over. It was sure enough a homicide.

She always felt bad when she showed up in the time frame between the murder and the notification of next of kin. Right now, someone out there – spouse, parent, child, whoever – was carrying on with their day, blissfully unaware that their lives had been forever altered in the most horrifying way imaginable. It was unusual for Kathryn to have known one of the corpses she was called to investigate, and it was especially hard to see Tom, lying there with the back half of his skull blown off. His was definitely not a "good killing" – the term those in law enforcement privately gave to those individuals whose demise could only be considered a positive. Tom was no saint, but from what she gathered, this man could have contributed something to the world.

"Shells?"

"Nope."

"Prints?"

"Nothing. Not even tire marks," he said, squatting down and surveying the parking area.

"What about the jogger – the lady? Anything from her?"

"Nothing. Had a Walkman on. Didn't hear a thing. She lives just a few blocks from here and I have a team at her house right now." He stood up and pulled his pen out of his front pocket. "You talked to this fellow once before already, right?"

"Several months ago."

"Anything stand out to you? Demeanor-wise, I mean?"

"Um, it was pretty standard. Background stuff, you know."

"Did you ever get the impression he was in danger?"

Kathryn thought about just how much she should let on. The feeling she got the first time was that Tom had not come forward with all of the pertinent information, which she had intended to address when they met again. Since he was dead now, Kathryn really had no reason to keep what she knew under wraps. Plus, it was Rick Papania who was doing the asking, after all, so, of course, she would tell him.

"Actually," she said, standing, "I think he believed he was."

"Really?"

"Yeah. He was on his way in this morning for a second round. His lawyer said he was acting real squirrely. Talking big about working out a deal – and fast. He thought he needed protection."

Papania rubbed his mustache. "I would say he was right."

"You think?" Kathryn knew he was right but she wanted a concurring opinion before she said anything – and she hoped Rick would be the one to provide it.

"I do." He squinted his eyes and looked back down at the body as the coroner pulled the sheet over it. "This was no ordinary murder, Kat." Rick Papania had never called her 'Kat' before. She tried to remain focused.

"No?"

"No," he said, and ran his fingers through his hair – another move Kat could not ignore. "This was a hit."

CHAPTER 10

His daddy had told him time and time again not to go by himself early in the morning or late at night. He said bad people sometimes sleep there. But Archie Park served as a resting place for migrating birds, and the day before when he was riding the John Deere with the yellow seat, Marty Deen had seen warblers flying in and out. He didn't have any drawings of a warbler, and he wanted one for his show. Since they would be heading further south soon, he thought – just this once – it would be okay, so he took off at the crack of dawn, happy to have the morning ahead of him. He didn't have to be at work until ten.

Marty had just settled down at his favorite spot just inside the woods, when he saw his friend Tommy pull into the parking lot and wave to him when he got out. Marty wondered how Tommy even knew he was there. He wanted to wave back, but if anyone told his daddy he was out there this early, he would surely take his binoculars away – and maybe his bike.

His bike.

That's how Tommy knew Marty was there in the woods. Marty left it out front by the trail post like he always did. He thought about getting it and craned his neck to look out. Then he saw something he hadn't seen before – a blue pickup truck parked behind the dugout near the girls' softball field.

Marty also knew not to talk to strangers, so he surely wasn't going to come out now. He looked back at Tommy, who had quit waving by then, and watched as Tommy threw rocks at one of the garbage cans. Marty wished he wouldn't do that because some of those rocks get into the grass and when they do, the lawnmower sometimes slings them out super-fast. It was dangerous. Could break a window or even hit someone on the swings. Eventually, Tommy quit, and when he did, Marty eased back down and tried to relax.

He heard a ruffle overhead and turned his binoculars high up towards one of the pin oaks. He spotted a big male with a puffed-out golden chest, and it was even more beautiful once he got it into focus. Marty hoped the bird would preen or spread his wings so he could get a good look at the feathers, but as soon as Marty propped his elbow on his knee to steady his arms, a thump coming from near the play area got his attention. Marty looked towards the noise and saw the pickup truck had run smack into Tommy's car, and boy was Tommy mad.

Then Marty saw the man get out. He was holding a gun.

Marty had never seen a real gun before, so he flopped down on his belly and put the binoculars to his eyes. His hands and face were sweaty, but he was able to focus on Tommy and that man. As soon as he did, the gun jerked and made a weird noise. It wasn't loud, but it wasn't totally silent, either.

Then just like that, his friend Tommy fell over on the ground.

That man must have been one of those bad people his daddy told him about, and Marty wondered if the man heard the binoculars bounce off the root in front of him when Marty dropped them after the shot was fired. Now Marty really wished he had pulled his bike in. If Tommy saw the bike, the bad man surely had seen it, too, and would be coming for Marty next. Marty put his fingers in his mouth and started rocking back and forth. If that man shot Tommy, he would surely shoot Marty. He squeezed his eyes closed and waited. He could feel tears running down his cheeks and dripping on his legs.

But the man didn't come. Marty jumped when he heard a door close, and when he looked up, he saw the truck drive off. Marty waited and counted to be sure the man was gone. Once Marty hit fifteen Mississippis, he snatched his bike, threw his binoculars and sack over his shoulders, and pedaled as fast as he could down the backwoods trail that led home.

He didn't stop or check behind him until he wheeled up to the garage his dad had turned into his apartment. He kept his Millennium Falcon key ring under the mat out front, and once he opened the door, he yanked his bike inside, locked it back, and then threw himself on his bed, burying his face in his pillow so no one could hear him cry.

No matter how hard he tried, Marty couldn't erase what he had seen. Over and over in his head, he kept replaying that man walking to Tommy and shooting him. Every time he closed his eyes, the gun went off. It scared him, but he didn't know what to do. He couldn't let his daddy know where he had been. He couldn't even go outside. What if that man had seen Marty and followed him?

The thought that the man might be tracking him made him nervous all over again. He sneaked up to the window and peeked out but didn't see anything unusual. He checked the lock on the handle and unhitched and rehitched the chain to make sure it was secure. He paced for a bit, looked back out the window one more time, and drank some water.

He climbed in bed, pulled his New Orleans Saints bedspread up high just below his chin, and watched the door. He wished he could turn back time like Superman. He wished he had never left his room. He wished he would've listened to his daddy, because his daddy was right.

There were bad people out at Archie Park early in the morning.

Really, really, bad people.

CHAPTER 11

"This truck needs a name," Hop said from the back seat, slurping his drink before throwing his head back and letting out an epic, multi-pitched burp. It was Friday night, a month and change into the semester, and Nate was taking me, Hop, and Mark to his house to play pool. We were ready to chill out after having just suffered through the first round of exams, and we were finally feeling a bit better now that our bellies were full after tearing up some Burger King. The back-to-school fifty-nine cent special was still in play, and collectively, we destroyed nine cheeseburgers, two large orders of onion rings, two orders of fries, and four Dr. Peppers. For good measure, Mark topped it off with one of their cardboard apple pies, and soon we were all paying for our gluttony.

It was a shame Nate had finally volunteered to drive because the secondary effects of our meal were fouling up a truly pristine vehicle. Leather interior. Pioneer stereo with cassette player and equalizer. Eight speakers with a subwoofer, electric windows, and to top it off, a sunroof. If he put a fridge in the back and hotwired a TV, I think I could have lived there.

"A name?" Nate asked, and looked over at me. I shrugged my shoulders, and he looked up in the rearview mirror. "Never crossed my mind. What do you think, Mark?"

"I agree," Mark said. "A truck without a name is just a truck." The first three weeks had been a bit of an adjustment for Nate, but nothing out of the ordinary for a new student. He followed me around pretty close at the outset and soon bonded with Mark, due in part to their somewhat similar new-guy histories. Eventually he started to feel comfortable enough around us to chill out a bit and act like a normal person, even if, more often than not, he had a look on his face like he was perpetually lost in a room he had been in many times before.

"I could go for a name," Nate said.

"Like the Milk Wagon.'"

"Exactly. Like the Milk Wagon. How'd y'all come up with that anyway?"

"It was actually pretty easy," Mark said, "happened at Hop's back to school party. Rush Atherton named it."

"Rush?"

"Red-headed kid. Quiet; wears flannel all the time. Likes Van Halen."

"Oh yeah. I know who he is."

"So the party was pretty wild before Matt drove up in that beast. I mean one of the best ever. Full of chicks, lots to drink, and everyone dancing and absolutely just throwing down. Some folks had come outside to take a look, but it didn't get too much attention up to that point, even though Matt parked it in the front yard."

"It was the perfect spot, if you ask me."

"Nobody asked. Anyway, Matt and I step out on the front porch to shotgun a few beers after Hop caught us drinking in the living room."

"Y'all were getting it on everything."

"You should have made that room off limits. The door was wide open. Can I finish the story?"

"If you hurry up."

"We get through round one and are catching our breath when Rush walks up, longneck in hand, to take a leak. He leans up against a tree to do his business, and lays his eyes on that big hunk of junk for the first time."

"Careful now," I said, "you're talking about a classic."

"A classic?" Hop said, turning his cup upside down and banging it on the corners of his mouth to get at the ice. "A lot of words came to mind that night, but classic was not one of them."

"Bite me."

"So, we're watching Rush, and the whole time he's doing his business, he just stares at it. Like he couldn't figure out what it was."

"The majesty of it put him in a trance."

"Shut up, Matt. Seriously. Then, he zips up, slams his beer, says 'nice Milk Wagon,' and goes back in and cranks up 'Dance the Night Away.' I looked at Matt, he looked at me, and we knew right then it was golden."

"And that's how the legend began," Hop said. "If memory serves me, we got nineteen people in it that night."

"Was that the time Sammy surfed it?"

"Yeah. Guess he technically makes twenty."

"That was earlier in the night. We had a, uh, more intimate group of eight pile in it later."

"Eight?"

"Four couples, Nate," Mark said. "I'll explain the details to you later. Geez."

"Oh, I get it now. Awesome."

"Yes. Awesome would be one way to describe it."

"You see?" Nate said. "Matt's right. It *is* a classic."

"Thank you, sir." I looked over at Nate and nodded, and Mark and Hop groaned. Then Nate upped the ante.

"I wish I had one."

I blinked. Mark stared at him. Hop shook his head like a seven-year old refusing to go to bed. "No, no, no. Bullshit, no. Are you serious?"

"Serious as a ghost." Nate let out a goofy, staccato laugh that sounded like he was clearing his throat. It was the kind of noise people make when they are trying to fill a void after they've told a joke and suddenly realize it's terrible.

"As a *what*?" Mark asked. "Just how old are you? Five?"

"Nate, *you* are a classic," Hop said. "A classic dumb ass. That's what we should call you. Nate the dumbass." Hop made finger quotes when he said it. "Even better."

"An enigma," Mark said, nodding – more to himself. He was proud to have worked such a word into the conversation and more proud that he knew that I knew it was spot on.

"I guess what I'm trying to say is – anybody can have a *new* vehicle."

"Really?" Mark said, rolling his eyes. "Wrong."

"Y'all know what I mean,"

"No, Nate, we don't. I have never seen a new car in my driveway."

Neither had I, for that matter, and I didn't expect to see one anytime soon, either. In fact, considering my family's shaky financial situation, there was a real question as to whether I would even get to finish out at St. John. Tuition was a luxury, not a necessity, and things were tight around the Frazier house. Hop and Mark knew this was a real possibility for me, and Mark told me the finances weren't exactly in the black for him either, but I didn't want Nate to know. I was too embarrassed, so I moved off the topic, as usual, with an attempt at levity.

"It hasn't been too bad, actually. In fact, as Mark noted, the extra space has already served us well."

"Well, at least two of us," Mark said, and leaned up to give me some skin.

"My man."

"Not cool," Hop said, "not cool at all."

"Sounds ideal to me," Nate said. "Hey, speaking of extra space, does it really have a secret compartment? What do y'all call it? 'The Trapper Keeper' or 'Trapper' or something like that, right?"

I whipped my head back around and glared at the second row. Knowledge of the Milk Wagon's most distinctive feature was shared by a chosen few, and its existence was rarely discussed in public. Hop and Mark shook their heads. They didn't tell.

"How'd you hear about the Trapper?" I asked, probably with too much edge.

"Em- Emily Miller mentioned it to me the other day."

"Emily?" My mind snapped back like a rubber band. Of course Emily did.

Emily was the only other person in our class who actually had money − real money, and when Nate mentioned her name, I had a revelation that was not entirely comforting. Nate's family, like Emily's, appeared to be flush with cash. He was the only other person I knew who had been to Europe − he did a whole semester of ninth grade in Austria as part of an exchange program. It all made me wonder if their not-inconsistent histories would cause them to cross paths in a way that ended up in a coupling. She had already shared one of our cardinal secrets with him − even though she swore to me she would keep it between us. Who knows what else they discussed? I felt the ugly tinge of jealousy rear up, but I ignored it. I really wanted to like this cat. But I couldn't quit thinking about Em.

Hop took the sting out of the air.

"Ferris,"

"What?"

"Ferris. I think we should name it Ferris."

"What the hell kind of name is that?" I asked, still a bit ticked off.

"This truck reminds me of that Ferrari from *Ferris Bueller's Day Off*," Hop said, rubbing the finish on the seat. "Red. Sleek. Awesome."

"But Ferris didn't even own that car," Mark said. "It was Cameron's."

"It was actually Cameron's dad's," I said, "and if you recall, the Ferrari was destroyed after Cameron had a breakdown because his old man was such a dick."

"Then let's call it Ferris," Nate said. We all got quiet for a second and thought about it.

"But -"

"That works," Hop said.

"It's perfect," Nate said, and continued north. We drove past my old stomping grounds in Lyman, and crept dangerously close to Saucier where the population started to resemble what most people think most of the people from Mississippi look like. We slowed down on Highway 53 and turned down an unmarked road not too far from a stable, then drove another mile through the woods to what looked to me like a dead end. It was not. The overgrown jumble of underbrush – woods, pine, pecan, and oak trees so dense the tree line transitioned from green to gray to black just a few feet off the shoulder – hid a road that led us to a well-manicured alcove flanked by two dwarf magnolias bordering a wrought iron gate with brick posts that must have been ten feet tall. Behind it, a cobblestone driveway twisted through a thicket until it disappeared. Looked like Sleepy Hollow to me – and this was during the day. I couldn't imagine what it must look like at night.

"Sweeeeet," Hop said, leaning into the front seat and ducking his head down below the visors to get a better look. Mark rolled down his window and let out a slow whistle.

"Daaaaamn."

Nate keyed in a code on the pad, and the gate started to open.

"Perfect," Nate said again, and put the truck in gear.

CHAPTER 12

I have been to all my friends' houses at one time or another. Depending on the day, the season, and what was going on at that particular moment, we could spend a few minutes, an overnight, or even a weekend hanging out – and it was not altogether unusual to drop in uninvited.

There were those houses where everyone gathered because they were comfortable, and the parents were conspicuously permissive – like Hop's. His folks didn't provide a lot of oversight, so their house was the default for spending the night when we didn't want to go home because we were going to be out later than our respective curfews would allow.

There were houses where everyone gathered for an entirely different reason: food. Mark's Italian mom always had large pots on the stove or trays in the oven – lasagna, spaghetti and meatballs, ham – a buffet of samples from what Mark deemed "the motherland." I had some of my finest meals at Mark's house. Plus, they had one of those toilets with a cushioned seat.

A few of our friends – Trey Kratz for example – had nice parents and sweet houses, but they were like museums on the inside. The furniture consisted mostly of antiques, and there were certain chairs we couldn't sit in and certain towels we couldn't use. When I was there, I felt like I was trapped at a perpetual dinner party and kept expecting old ladies to walk in carrying plates of shrimp cocktail and deviled eggs talking about their azaleas.

Some houses were memorable because of the way they were decorated, and some houses I barely remember at all. A few were close to the beach, and some were within walking distance to Archie Park where we would play pick up games of basketball or football. Some came with siblings, which might not seem very important on its face, but to this day, I have not forgotten how Sammy's older brother taught us how to undo the elusive front bra clasp with three fingers. I never quite understood why he kept a bra under his bed, but I never questioned it either. That skill ended up serving me all my life. Like typing.

To a great extent, each house was different, and each house had its own personality – good and bad, and I thought we had seen it all.

Until we went to Nate's.

When the gates swung open, Nate crept into the thicket, and we emerged on the other side into what must have been fifty acres of rolling hills. The truck snaked its way down the cobblestones, and we took it all in – Hop and I with our faces stuck to the windows, and Mark hanging halfway out the sunroof. We passed over a small bridge and drove through a pecan orchard that was being tended to by a lanky old yardman driving a golf cart. He had a big straw hat and stopped and watched us as we passed.

We eventually turned onto the final stretch that led to an estate flanked by a tennis/basketball court; a small, prehistoric looking shed; and a freestanding garage. We parked in a circular brick drive with a fountain in the middle that had bronze birds perched around a little naked kid shooting water out at all directions into the bowls below it. It was like we had been dropped out of the suburbs of Gulfport into some alternate living area where they take photos for magazine covers.

"How come I've never seen this place before?" I asked.

"Probably because you weren't supposed to." Nate said. "Used to belong to an old money family from New Orleans. They liked to escape over here from the Big Easy to disappear for a day or two. They ended up dumping it after the wife found out there was some sneaking around going on that didn't include her. When the house came up for sale, my dad jumped on it. He said he liked that it was out of the way and that it didn't need a whole lot of work."

"How many of you Mayeses live here?" Mark asked.

"Just me, my old man and my stepmom."

"Just three of you? You need a boarder?" Hop asked.

"Stepmom?" Mark asked. "How's that working out?"

"About like you'd expect," Nate said, "for a rebounder. Typical trophy wife." He looked at Mark. "You'd probably like her."

"I might," Mark said, raising an eyebrow. "And she might like me. I do have a reputation as quite the stallion, you know."

"Stallion, my ass," Nate said. "When she sees you, Mark, she'll wonder how the lawn man got inside."

It was actually a pretty good line for Nate.

"Well, I look forward to meeting her, and, after I do, she may indeed want me to mow the lawn." He smacked his lips and made a motorboat sound.

"You are not right," Nate said, "and you're out of luck – at least for tonight. She works with my dad at the clinic managing the books, and they are heading out to dinner straight from the office."

"Cool," Hop said as we started to walk in. "Hey, you going to pull Ferris around to that barn of a garage over there or leave it here? If we're going to shoot hoops later, I should probably go ahead and get my glasses."

Nate checked his watch and then glanced at his truck. "We should be okay. Since I have to take y'all back tonight, I'll just keep it parked here. They shouldn't come back for some time, anyway." He pushed open the door and looked over his shoulder at the gate.

"Yeah," he said, mostly to himself, still staring out towards the road. "I think we'll be fine."

CHAPTER 13

"Rack 'em," Nate said, blowing the blue chalk off the top of his stick, "my break."

In the back of Nate's house, overlooking the swimming pool was the ultimate game room. On one end was a sectional sofa and big screen, and on the other end, a pool table and a *Black Knight* pinball machine that looked like it came straight out of Aladdin's Castle, the Edgewater Mall arcade that ate our quarters as fast as we could feed them into the slots. Nate had already whipped me and Hop in two games of cutthroat. Mark didn't play, because once he found out Nate had a satellite, his one and only focus was trying to dial in the Playboy channel.

The game room was a microcosm of the rest of the house; everything looked new, expensive, and to some degree, clinical. The place was spotless and uniform – even the towels in the bathroom were lined up and spaced out just right. I used one to dry my hands and did my best to put it back just how I found it, but it still looked like a homeless person had hung it up. I wondered if Nate kept his bedroom the same way as they kept the house – clean and orderly. I guess we would see soon enough. He just got Donkey Kong for his Nintendo, and we were going play a few games before a pizza run, which I hoped was not too far off because I was already starting to get hungry again.

"Hop, you in?" I asked.

"I'm going to take a break. Mark's looking kind of lonely over there."

"Okay, just don't sit too close to each other. Y'all are making me nervous." I grabbed the chalk. "Looks like it's just you and me, Nate. Eight ball?"

"Sure."

"I hope I get stripes. I'm always better with stripes."

I arranged the balls, making sure I put a few extra solids on the outside, and waited for him to break. He leaned over, pulled back his cue and took a couple of practice strokes. He reared back his elbow and tagged the ball as hard as I've ever seen one get hit. It made a beeline for the other side of the table, and I waited for the rewarding crack, hoping his shot would scatter the rack and set me up for a good run, but I never heard it.

Before the cue ball could get there, the front door slammed open and crashed into the wall, whipping all of our heads around in unison. It scared us for sure, but it was just a teaser, because the screaming that followed it made my stomach hurt the way it did when my parents fought in front of me and my brothers.

"DAMMIT, NATE."

It was an angry bellow, the kind spewed out with a pointed frown and clenched fists. The kind someone works up to over a period of seconds, if not minutes. The kind fueled by longstanding, deep-seated resentment. Perhaps most telling, it was the kind reserved for a soft target – upper hand vs. lower hand – where the one dropping the bomb does not expect any flack in return.

The commotion caused Nate to jam his stick into the felt, leaving a powdery blue divot. It scared Hop and Mark straight off the couch, with Mark a second or two behind as he scrambled to change the channel. It jolted me too, and I looked over at Nate for context. He was white as a sheet.

"I DIDN'T BUY YOU THAT DAMN TRUCK SO YOU COULD LEAVE IT OUTSIDE IN THE FRONT OF THE HOUSE LIKE WHITE TRASH." It sounded like he would go hoarse if he kept going at that volume. "YOU MIGHT AS WELL PARK THAT PIECE OF SHIT IN THE YARD. ARE YOU IN HERE, SON? CAN YOU HEAR ME?"

Nate set his stick down and turned his body toward the hall. His eyes had gone from vibrant and alive to flat and lifeless within a matter of seconds. Me, Hop, and Mark just stood there, and when the shrieking commenced, I suddenly wasn't so hungry anymore.

"ARE YOU RETARDED OR SOMETHING? ANSWER ME, BOY. I WANT TO KNOW WHY YOUR DAMN TRUCK IS NOT WHERE IT IS SUPPOSED TO BE."

A man who appeared to be in his mid-40s turned the corner into the game room, shadowed by a woman at least ten years his junior. Both were moving fast, clearly intent on engaging their prey – both hostile, their expressions deformed with anger, and looking for a beat down. That is, until they saw us.

They were expecting Nate – gunning for him even – but our presence threw them for a loop. I couldn't tell who was more surprised, although if I had to put odds on it, probably the man.

Either way, it was a terribly uncomfortable scene.

CHAPTER 14

"Why, I didn't know you were having friends over tonight, son." The bottom half of his face started to show friendly, but his eyes were still rimmed with fury, and he reminded me of the Heat Miser. He managed to work up a fake smile, and was trying so hard to keep it, his lips barely moved when he talked. "Nate, why don't you introduce us to these – these gentlemen?" I could tell he had put this mask on before; it came too easy and too fast. On the other hand, the bitch standing next to him did not seem too worried about first impressions. She held the same look of contempt the whole time – like *we* had ruined *her* evening somehow.

"Y-yes, yes sir." Nate became a robot, suddenly stiff-armed and barely able to move his head as he did his best to make our acquaintance. "This is Hop – J-Jason Hopkins."

"Jason, you say?"

"Yes, sir. Uh, nice to meet you." Hop was nervous.

"An- and this is M-Mark Ragone."

"Mark, how are you?"

"Good, I guess." Mark was looking down at the floor. He was getting angry but didn't know where to channel it.

I watched his father size us up as Nate made the introductions. He wasn't paying his son a lick of attention – he just parroted our names as Nate did his dead-level best to disperse the heat. His dad was assessing what we were wearing, our haircuts, what kind of shoes we had on – basically trying to figure out whether we fit his preconceived idea of what one of his son's friends should look like. I am sure we failed on every level, but I didn't give a damn. He didn't measure up to my preconceived notion of what a parent should look like, either, so I guess we were even. Since I was behind the pool table, I had some ground to cover, and I made my way to the center of the room before Nate had to stammer through another introduction. I spoke as I walked, and I was soon standing front and center.

"I'm Matt Frazier," I said, and held out my hand.

He gripped and bent my fingers so hard it felt like two of them might break. I tried not to flinch but fluttered for a second, and when I looked him in the eye, I picked up a gloat.

"I'm Ford Mayes. Nate's father. But you can call me 'Doc'."

Governor. Captain. Mayor. Esquire. Principal. *Doc.* I have heard them all, and as a rule, I don't like anyone who asks to be referred to by their title. Apparently, some feel their lot in life bestows on them an expectation of what amounts to a modern-day kissing of the ring, and this man was no exception. I, however, am neither a kisser of rings nor a kisser of asses. I get that some might enjoy having their ego stroked every time they're addressed, but they won't get that satisfaction from me. Not now. Not ever.

"Nice to meet you, *Mr. Mayes.*" Then he blinked. Back on even ground.

Now that I saw him up close, he didn't seem as intimidating as he did at first. He was a guy who was used to getting what he wanted, sure, and I suspected there were more than a handful of terrified people left bruised and battered in his wake. But he also looked like he was halfway through his second midlife crisis, and the effects of years of trying to remain relevant were starting to show. His pants were a little too tight and his Chiclet teeth a little too bright. He had wavy hair that he probably teased out back in his college days, and whatever goop he applied made his curls look wet and crunchy at the same time. He had on too much cologne and wore pointy-toed shoes I am sure his wife purchased. I turned my back to him and looked her way.

"And you are?"

"Vicky."

She looked like a Vicky. My guess was that she, too, probably turned some heads back in the day, but years of too much time in the sun coupled with an affinity for the bottle were starting to take their toll. Crow's feet around the eyes, sallow cheeks, and a chin that made me wonder how she changed pillowcases.

"Nice to meet you as well, Vicky." She didn't say it was nice to meet me. But she did snort and put her hand in the crook of her husband's arm. I was about to say something else, but Nate misjudged the temperature of the room and jumped back in.

"Dad, I thought y'all were going out to eat, which is why —"

"Well you thought wrong, son. We had to come by here so Vic could change out of her work clothes."

"Yeah —"

"Don't interrupt me. You should try to think more about others and not so much about yourself."

I appreciated Nate trying to let off some of the steam; I get it. But there was no way this asshole was going to stop humiliating him. Not at that moment. I certainly wasn't going to let it continue.

"It was time for us to go anyway, Mr. Mayes, so please forgive us if we have delayed your evening." His fake smile had withered to where it looked as if he smelled something bad. "You have a beautiful house – and a beautiful wife." I gave her a wink and I thought she might explode. "Hop, Mark, y'all ready?" They were dang near through the door before the words spilled out of my mouth. I turned to Nate. "You okay giving us a ride?"

Nate cut his eyes at his dad, then back at me, not quite sure what to do. There must have been some unspoken direction I missed, because without a word, he walked over to the bar and grabbed his keys.

"Yeah, I'll take you. Let's go."

The drive back was completely silent, so I turned the radio on. The Cars were playing. How Rick Ocasek scored Paulina Porizkova remains a mystery to me even today. I tried to engage them on this very topic but got nothing but crickets. Hop and Mark were glad to be out of the line of fire, and they sat in the back not making a peep. Nate just looked ahead and drove.

It felt like one of those nights during basketball season when our team came up short at a grueling away game, and we had to suffer the silence of a two-hour bus ride home in the dark. We were frustrated, exhausted, and confused, and for what might have been the first time ever, no one – not even Mark – had anything to say.

CHAPTER 15

The old saying in the Bureau was if you don't close a case within the first week, then you don't close a case. It was well over a month since Tom Chrestman was murdered, and despite Kathryn's initial burst of optimism, neither the FBI nor the Gulfport PD were any closer to identifying a suspect than they were on the day he was shot. Kathryn was at her desk, going through her morning routine of perusing through the day's paper. She still had not given a statement, and as Rick had predicted, a stack of messages and requests from reporters – local and national – were starting to pile up. She swore she would not talk to the press until she had a valid lead or some progress to report, and she was starting to feel the heat of inactivity, so she turned to her partner, Agent Ethan Davis, as she was prone to do when brainstorming.

"Someone knew he was coming."

"Who?" Ethan was stirring artificial creamer into his coffee. He liked it flavored a certain way and he prided himself on being able to pour in just the right amount based solely upon the tint.

"What do you mean, who? Tom Chrestman, that's who. Do you think someone knew he was coming here?"

Ethan closed one eye like he tended to do when he was working an idea through his head. "Of course someone knew he was coming." He took a sip and swished it around. "Dammit."

Ethan was a recent hire at the agency, having worked as both a compliance officer for the Department of Justice and as a cop before joining the FBI. He was in on some of the early pharmacy busts in and around Hattiesburg, and when he showed some promise, Kathryn had him transferred to the Coast after her raid on Tom Chrestman produced more documents than she could handle. Ethan was a few years her junior and a bit green – having come from compliance – but he did well at Quantico; his supervisors gave him good reviews, and she was glad to have a helping hand. She could have pulled worse, for sure.

"But how?" Kathryn asked. "Tom was highly motivated to keep our meeting private."

"In theory, yes," Ethan said, adding another splash of creamer and taking a follow-up sip. "There we go. What was I saying? Oh yeah, he may have been motivated to keep it quiet, but I bet he told a friend, his wife – maybe someone else – and the word got around. It's hard to sit on a secret. Especially one this big."

Ethan was right. Tom Chrestman had been running quite the racket, and his role in the scam was as simple as it was profitable. The more prescriptions written, the more Tom could bill, and the more bills he submitted, the more money he made. There was no overhead, no loss of inventory, and no out of pocket on Tom's front because the prescriptions were never filled. At one point Cat Island Compounding was turning over hundreds of claims per month – to the tune of up to $8,000 per claim – and the government was paying them without any audits or background checks.

When the checks came in, Tom took 60% off the top and shuttled the remaining 40% to his doctor friends in return for repeat business. He ran the cash through Cat Island, and Kathryn calculated Chrestman laundered anywhere from $1 million to $4 million in cycles every six months. She was able to link most of the kickbacks to a physician's group out of the Hattiesburg area, and due to Ethan's snooping and Kat's bulldogging, those physicians were now either doing time or seeking a new line of business, as their licenses to practice medicine had been revoked.

When one of the doctors she had busted asked her why she was chasing just the small players Kathryn realized that, she, too, had been sloppy. He told her that Tom, as part of his recruitment pitch, often referenced one particular doctor who had made millions and millions working the system. Although Tom never mentioned the doctor by name, word on the street was that he practiced in Hattiesburg.

So Kat brought Agent Davis in to dig. He went through the mountains of documents, one by one. He coordinated with the comptrollers at the departments of Medicare and Tricare and detailed every transaction that could have possibly been related to Tom's business. He looked through haystack after haystack and came up empty handed time and time again – and while he was not able to identify the doctor by name, he did find a needle.

Turned out Tom kept a separate, offshore private account, under a shell company – Cape Island Compounding – that shared a remarkably similar name to his brick and mortar store, Cat Island Compounding. When Kathryn looked through the Cape Island records, she learned nearly $20 million had been paid directly to the company. While this number was significant, the discovery that $6 million of the $20 million in payments never made it to the bank was what turned her head.

"Six million dollars. How did I miss that?"

Ethan didn't want to say anything. Kathryn's *modus operandi* when she ran out of ideas was to start from the beginning. He had already personally swept the file twice and was not excited about the prospect of one more round.

"Look, Kathryn, Tom snowed you that first time. You can't blame yourself." She didn't say anything. "Maybe it's best we set this aside for a bit before you kill yourself trying to check every box. Let our minds rest and regroup. We've been going a hundred miles an hour since the murder. Sometimes those pieces come together better when you let them breathe."

"You could be right," she said, pushing her glasses back on top of her head and squeezing the bridge of her nose. "But before we table the whole thing, there may be one more lead we should check out."

Ethan walked his chair to the edge of the rug pad. "Another lead?"

"Yeah." Kathryn thumped her pen on the desk and then clicked it closed. She tossed him a folder. "I'm not sure it will bear much fruit, but I think it's worth a shot. See if you can find Charlotte Gutherz."

Ethan opened it and looked at the picture paper-clipped to the inside flap. "The sales rep? I thought we didn't have anything to pin on her."

"We don't."

"Plus, didn't she say she would never speak to you?"

"She did."

"So?"

Kathryn picked up the Sun-Herald. The press had been a thorn in her side since the investigation began. The reporters had been relentless, and every single mistake she or the agency had made since day one had been magnified, editorialized, and exploited for the public's consumption. For once the paper may have run with a headline that could actually play in her favor. "You think she's been following this?" It read: *Pharmacist Murder Suspect Still at Large.*

"Probably."

"They're not letting this story go."

"I still don't see what this has to do with Charlotte Gutherz."

"Don't you think if she even got an inkling that her name may be publicly associated with this it would scare the crap out of her?"

Ethan shook his head. "I would agree – if she was a suspect – but she's not."

"Says who?" Kathryn leaned forward in her chair.

Ethan set his coffee down. "Special Agent Kathryn Cooper, you are not thinking about doing what I think you are thinking about doing, are you?"

"Special Agent Davis, that's exactly what I am thinking about doing. A little misdirection never hurt anyone." She pointed at Ethan and then past him. "Phone."

He blinked, and a smile crept across his face. Then he scooted back to his desk and started dialing.

CHAPTER 16

"Do you know what a smurf is?" Kathryn asked the witness.

"Excuse me? A *smurf?*"

"A smurf."

As suspected, it did not take much arm-wringing to get Charlotte Gutherz back in for another interview. She was a bit huffy on the phone, but when Kathryn reminded her that two of her former employers were now dead, it got her attention. She showed up dressed to the nines, wearing a blouse that left little to the imagination. She didn't even bring a lawyer. Cocky one, Kathryn thought, and sure enough, now a half hour into the interview, the only thing she and Ethan had gotten out of Charlotte was attitude.

"Are you serious? Do you mean those blue guys?"

"There was a girl smurf, too," Ethan said. He grabbed a chair across from her and straddled it, crossing his arms over the back "But no, we're talking about something else."

Charlotte put her chin on her hand and leaned forward, undeterred. "Do tell."

"A 'smurf'," he said, "in the parlance of our current investigation, is best described as a money runner. Ring a bell?"

"No."

"Okay, because banks have regulations, and because large transactions are flagged, the bad guys like to break their big hauls into smaller deposits and spread them over multiple banks or accounts to avoid scrutiny. But the man behind the money can't – and wouldn't – do this himself. So he hires someone to do the running for him. A smurf."

"Fascinating. Really."

"The smurf takes the cash, makes the rounds to all the banks and makes deposits, one small piece at a time."

"He – or she – gets his cut after the deposits are confirmed," Kathryn said, "and the boss stays happy, rich – and anonymous."

"I bet you're wondering why they're called smurfs." Ethan said.

"Nope. Not even a little bit."

"The bag men back in the heyday of the Colombian cartels weren't men at all. They were Grandmothers. Old blue-haired ladies." Ethan slapped the desk, and Charlotte jumped. "Smurfs. Get it?"

Charlotte looked from Ethan to Kathryn then back to Ethan and clicked her fingernails on the desk. "Thank you for the history lesson, Agent . . ." She squinted at the nameplate on his desk across the room. "Davis, is it? Now are you going to tell me why you called me in?"

"Because," Kathryn said, "I have looked through every single document produced in this investigation, and having done so, I have developed a pretty solid appreciation for the amount of money your former employer, Tom Chrestman – God rest his soul – generated over the years. And try though I might, I can't shake the fact that your name is all over the place here."

Charlotte rolled her eyes. "Of course it is. I was a contract sales representative. Compounding medications, even now, is still a bit of a novelty to some in the medical field. My job was to generate business, and I was paid for my services, fair and square."

"That you were," Kathryn said, "but I think your services were more than just sales and marketing."

"Oh yeah?" Charlotte said.

"Yeah. I think you were receiving kickbacks in addition to your salary."

"Really?"

"He made millions."

"Good for him."

"I think you were one of his smurfs."

Kathryn saw a smile creep on to Charlotte's face and her defensive posture disappear. Kathryn had seen it before with other witnesses – Charlotte took the bait and believed she was off the hook. Kathryn knew Charlotte wasn't a smurf when she asked the question, but she wanted to test the waters anyway. The response was predictable.

"A smurf? You brought me in here because you thought I was a – a smurf?" Charlotte threw back her head and laughed. "Oh, my dear, you have wasted your time and my time."

"Have I?" Kathryn asked, acting confused and disappointed. "Do you think so?"

"I do."

Kathryn leaned in close, just a few inches from Charlotte's nose. "Now, listen here, Ms. Gutherz. Here's what I think."

"Ew." Charlotte recoiled a bit and turned her head to the side, leaving Kathryn staring at her earring.

"I think you were taking payments on the side. I think you were taking dirty money and sticking it in your pocket or down your shirt, or wherever you think you could without anyone noticing. And you know what else? I think you know more than you have been letting on."

Charlotte grinned that same grin but said nothing. Kathryn pulled out a legal pad and pen and sat it next to Charlotte on the desk. "Here's your chance to clear the air. It is a rare gift – one that could work out well for you if you cooperate. All I need you to do is write down every single doctor, every office, clinic or healthcare provider Tom Chrestman paid in exchange for prescriptions."

Charlotte leaned down in her seat and picked up her purse to leave.

"Sit down," Kathryn said, "and write."

"You have nothing on me," Charlotte said. "If you think I have committed a crime, then you should arrest me. Otherwise, I'm out of here."

"Not so fast," Ethan smiled and handed her a manila folder. "You may want to take a look at what's inside, Ms. – is it Mrs. or Ms. Gutherz?"

"I don't see how that is any of your concern." She opened it and eased back into the chair.

"What you have there is a set of documents we retrieved from Tom Chrestman's files, showing numerous payments to you totaling tens of thousands of dollars. Now what you told us earlier is that those payments represent your salaries and bonuses you earned, to use your words, *fair and square.*"

Charlotte flipped through the pages and stopped about halfway through. Then her expression changed.

"Ahh, I see you've found the tax documents," Ethan said.

Kat stood up and started pacing the floor.

"You see, after your story didn't totally check out, I did some further investigation on my own. Started with my friends at the IRS. Contrary to popular belief, they have some lovely people over there and were quite willing to provide me with your income tax filings for the last ten years." The arrogance faded from Charlotte's face. "It appears, through my cursory review of your documents that you have been, let's say, less than forthcoming with your earnings." Truth be told, Charlotte had indeed fudged a bit on her taxes, but according to the IRS folks, it could be rectified fairly easily with not much more than a negligible fine and a slap on the wrist. Charlotte didn't realize it was nothing, however, and Kathryn kept on. "I can rectify this with a phone call, but whether or not I do is in your hands now. You help us; we help you."

"Ooh, can I jump in?" Ethan asked. "When you are considering whether or not you want to deal with us, keep in mind we will have to let the press know that yet another person may go to jail because of this compounding mess. Do you really want that out there?" Charlotte didn't say anything. She kept flipping the pages in the manila folder, looking but no longer reading. "I mean, once the reporters get a hold of this, your name will be plastered all over the state. If history is any indication, that kind of exposure may not be good for you. Agree?"

Charlotte closed her eyes and took a deep breath. When she opened them, Kat nudged the pad her way. "Write."

She took the pen and twenty minutes later, she filled out a page and a half of names. She passed the pad back to Kathryn.

"That's it," Charlotte said. "All of them. Can I please leave now?"

Kat picked up the pad and read the list of names one by one. She flipped to page two and stopped eight lines down and circled one she hadn't seen before.

"Cool your jets, Ms. Gutherz. I'm going to let you go, but not yet."

Kathryn showed the name to Ethan and he nodded back. Then she sat right next to Charlotte and turned the two chairs so Charlotte had no choice but to face her.

"Tell us what you know about Dr. Bradford Mayes."

CHAPTER 17

The four of us had shared a very difficult – and very humiliating – moment at the Mayes house, and while I was a little worried when Nate didn't show up for school on Monday, I was glad to be able to put off the inevitable – and hoped the extra day would put enough space behind us so that we wouldn't have to talk about it all. But when he strolled up to my locker Tuesday morning, he had other plans.

"What's up, Matt?"

"Same old, same old. Didn't do my homework, as usual, so I hope Ms. Mander doesn't call on me. Could be ugly."

"Yeah, me neither." He stood there, waiting for an opening, and stared down toward his books. It looked like he had dressed on the way in. His shirttail hung out the back of his pants, and one of his shoelaces was coming undone. His face was pinched and squinty like he had been napping, and he rubbed his neck when he talked.

"Look, man," he said, "about Friday." He stopped and let a group of kids pass before continuing. "I'm sorry y'all had to see that."

"No problem, Nate. No need to explain. You should see what goes down at my house sometimes."

His eyes, which hadn't been focused on anything in particular, finally found mine, and I hoped he didn't ask me to provide any personal details. Then his gaze drifted off again.

"This isn't the first time I've had to deal with something like this with my dad," he said. "In fact, crap like this happens all the time."

"Well –"

"He's a control freak. Do you know he makes me run two miles every morning before school? If I don't run, I can't drive. He takes the keys. But that's not it. If I don't do my homework by nine o'clock every night, I lose all privileges. Oh yeah, if I somehow forget to brush my teeth, I don't eat the next meal. And God forbid, I don't clean up my room."

Damn. "I'm sorry, man." He wasn't finished.

"I used to think he would change, you know? Once I got older, I hoped we could find a connection or something. But he's not interested. Not interested in talking, not interested in changing, and not interested in me. It's actually gotten worse now that I'm in high school. It's beyond embarrassing. I just wish he could be just a dad. Just once. Like everyone else's."

I looked at Nate and thought about what to say next. I really didn't want to air any of my family's dirty laundry – and there was a lot of it – but he was carrying a lot on his shoulders, and this was not about me anymore. I had to set that free.

"You're not the only one who has problems with their parents, Nate. And while my dad has not put his thumb on me like yours has, I've got my own issues at home."

"Yeah?"

"Yeah. My dad is a compulsive gambler. He has blown paycheck after paycheck – not to mention whatever piddling savings we had – at the dog track over in Mobile. When he goes, he may not come home for days, and when he does, he and my mom get in a knock-down, drag-out fight that cannot be silenced by pressing two pillows over my head. Trust me on that point – I have tried. In the last year alone, he has changed jobs twice, and now he's humping it for minimum wage at an auto parts shop, but that won't last either. Unless something changes on the financial front, I doubt I'll graduate from St. John's. This year has been a pretty rough one, and if it wasn't for my mother, our family would have long since been done."

I hadn't meant to let that much spill out, but once I got on a roll, I couldn't stop.

"But – but you never act like anything is bothering you."

"You're right. I don't. Sometimes I have to force myself to act like I don't care, but most of the time it's because I made the decision when things started blowing up a few years ago to not let someone's actions – even my dad's – dictate how I live my life."

"Easier said than done."

"True, but I don't go it alone. I lean on my friends a lot – and I mean *a lot*. There is no value that can be put on what Mark and Hop mean to me. Of course, I have more history with them than with you, but you're part of our group now, too, Nate. You know that, right?"

I was glad I threw that second comment in there, because it was well-received. It was also true. In a relatively short period of time, Nate made it into the inner circle, and all indications were he would stay. The run-in with his dad might have actually made us tighter – a point I still needed to address.

"The second thing, Nate, is you have to stay focused on what's around the corner. In less than two years, we will be in college. *College*. Out of the house – for good, if we choose to be – and neither you nor I will have to deal with any more of this bullshit. That fact alone can be a lifeline. And if you can't make it until then, there may come a day when you have to stand up to him. Let him know you're a man. I did last year, and while it was ugly, my old man has backed off. You may be surprised at how things change if it comes to that."

"Sometimes I guess you do have to take a stand," he said.

"Indeed."

"No matter the implications."

"Well –"

He pushed out his jaw until his bottom teeth caught his upper lip. "You certainly stood your ground at my house."

"Umm." I believe Nate was off on this point. If memory served me, I hauled ass once the heat started to come down.

"No, seriously. Did you see my dad's face when you walked up to him? Don't know that anyone's ever done that before. He actually backed off."

"Well, Nate, maybe you saw it different from me, because –"

"Dude, you had more balls than any of us." He blinked away the thought and closed the book on the subject. "Now we're almost late for Spanish. We don't need to give Ms. Mander another excuse to jump you. Let's go." He slapped me on the shoulder and walked into the classroom.

And that was it. He never mentioned it again, and neither did I. We acknowledged it; we recognized it impacted each of us in some way, and we moved on. Of course, it continued to nag at my brain. What if my advice had been wrong? Sure, taking a stand worked for me, but my dad was kind of weak when it came down to nutcutting – I knew he wouldn't resort to violence, no matter how hot it got.

With Nate's dad, I wasn't so sure.

CHAPTER 18

At lunch our crew sat together at our spot at the round table under the magnolia tree just on the other side of the library. It was unseasonably hot that October – even for Mississippi – and I was thankful for the shade the green leathery leaves was throwing off. A few days had passed since Nate and I had talked, and other than Nate still showing up to school looking like he was on a week long bender, things seemed back to normal – or as normal as they could be. Of course, during lunch, it was always hard to have a lull in the conversation with Mark and Hop present, and they were wound up way more than they should be – especially for a Thursday. During morning announcements, the Chief informed the school that this year's homecoming theme was "Hooray for Hollywood," and the two of them wouldn't shut up about it. Truth is, no one cared much about the theme. We were more concerned about getting dates.

Because St. John was smallish by most standards, and because the Chief and his stormtroopers did what they could to tamp down any school-sanctioned activities that could potentially become hotbeds for hand-holding, grazing, touching, grinding, or slow dancing – there was no prom. The school did allow a dance or two each semester, but those were monitored with a heavy hand by faculty members who, by default due to their nonexistent social life, had nothing else to do on a Friday night than watch a mix of hormones, sweat, and Halston Z14 jerk across the dance floor to "Freak-A-Zoid."

But we did have homecoming, and over time, it evolved from an after-the-game party, to a dance, to a dressy event, and eventually worked itself up to a tuxedo-and-shiny-gown occasion that loomed large on everyone's social calendar. It took its current form so slowly the school never really saw it coming, and once it reached the point of an ersatz prom, no one took any efforts to dial it back down. Probably because homecoming often brought graduates back, which allowed the Diocese another unabashed opportunity to ask for more money from those chasing the cheese.

Homecoming also seemed to loosen the chains on the domestic front, and for that one night, most parents seemed to pull back on the usual archaic curfews. Some of us got to stay out past midnight. Most seniors were even allowed to book hotel rooms with the understanding they may be subject to pop-ins by chaperones (although the adults usually were long gone before the clock rang twelve). Even my parents seemed to fall into line as I had been dropping hints since day one about my plans. I tested the water by suggesting that me, Mark and Hop would hang out at Jeff Haase's room after the dance – and mom didn't even blink. Of course, that was just a decoy because Haase was a super nerd and perennial parent favorite because he aced the ACT and played the French horn. Nice enough dude, but I did not intend to spend my one true night out playing Dungeons & Dragons and sipping on wine coolers served by a sweaty, if not buxom, fifteen-year-old girl wearing a Renaissance Fair outfit and a daisy chain.

Even more important than scoring a late night out was finding the right date. I'm not much for most of the school-sanctioned functions, but homecoming was the exception. We could still personalize it a bit – get a velvet tux, put on some Vans, or have our dates wear dresses bordering on the obscene – so participation wasn't a total sellout. And if attending this soiree made us Neanderthals even remotely interested, you can imagine the effect it had on the girls. They went all out, planning like it was a warm-up for a wedding. People started pairing up mentally the first day of school, trying to figure out first, second, and third options. No one wanted to go NDA – No Date Available – so the net for prospects was cast much wider than would be expected for a typical weekend. This entire homecoming discussion caught Nate off guard. He thought it was just another dance.

"So, you don't have a prom?"

"Right," I said.

"What school doesn't have prom?"

"Ours." Mark said. "Yours now."

"It's formal? Like really formal?"

"Yep," I said. "Sucks. Picking gets slim the longer you wait." I hesitated to offer him too much advice, or to prod him to act too quickly. The dance was in early November – just over a month away – and while I fully intended to ask Emily, the right opportunity had not presented itself. I felt some electricity every time we talked, but I couldn't step out of the box long enough to objectively see if she felt the same way, and I was just insecure enough to run all of the what-could-go-wrong scenarios on a loop. I gave it some more consideration as I watched the eighth graders play a pickup game of soccer down on the football practice field.

"You asked anybody yet?" Nate asked. He was running the metrics in his head as well.

"Not yet." I leaned back on the rail and turned back towards our group. "Keeping my eyes open, though. Had a productive encounter with Chrissy Pisarich last week, and I think she'd say yes, but I don't think I want to go with her."

"Why not?"

"I don't know. She's good-looking, but she's kind of out there." An understatement.

"Bad breath," Hop said, not even looking over at us.

"Snakes in her head." Mark chimed in. "Rattlers."

"You should know, considering that prize you showed up with," I said.

"Hey, don't knock her, man," Mark said. "The weird ones are open to suggestion, if you know what I mean. And *her* name is Wendy, by the way."

"Wendy? Like the restaurant?" Hop said.

"No, not like the restaurant."

"Hmm. I wouldn't peg her as a Wendy."

"I don't know what that even means, but as of this weekend, you can peg her as my date. I'm locked in."

We all looked his way, and Hop piped up. "Seriously? You are the man."

"I had to move," Mark said. "It was time. She's pretty cool, actually. Not only does she play the guitar, but I think I'm on the cusp of having unfettered access to all things above the waist. Hard to argue with that." I couldn't agree more. "What about you, Hop? Who are you going to trick into coming?"

Hop started cleaning his glasses, and a slow grin spread from ear to ear.

"Don't tell me you have a date already, too." I said.

Hop nodded his head. "Tell the wenches to take a rain check. The Hopster is off the market." For once, Hop led with the high fives.

"With who?" Mark asked. "You never told us this."

"I never kiss and tell."

"Because you never kiss. Who is it?"

"Let's just say Kristin Bennett could no longer deny my charms."

To say Hop was not exactly a ladies' man would be putting it lightly. Sure, Hop was able to get girls to talk to him, but he rarely leveraged his exchanges into anything more than a conversation. On the exceptional occasion when he did have a chance to snag on someone, it usually didn't take because he was all hands and one-sided overgrinding, so this was a big deal for him. Not so much because he *got* a date (which should never be discounted); but instead because of *who* his date was. Hop developed an unrequited – and somewhat unhealthy – crush on Kristin Bennett sometime around second grade, and it never truly faded. We picked on him about it some, but we had to be careful because the scab could get raw pretty quick.

"Really? Good for you, Hop. I really mean it. Restraining order finally expire?"

"Says the man who has no date."

Dang. He had me there. Nate didn't either, though.

"What about you, Nate?" Mark asked. "Who are you thinking about asking?"

"Emily Miller. For sure." Mark quit chewing his ice, and Hop leaned in ever so slightly. Nate realized there was a tonal shift and sat up. "Whoa. She doesn't have a boyfriend, does she?"

"No," I said, feeling eyes on me, and trying to look cool and unfazed. One half of my mind was raging, but the other took a little comfort in the fact that a date with Emily could help bring Nate back around to the living. Still, if I was being honest with myself, I wasn't happy about it and pretended like I was still watching the soccer game. "No, she doesn't."

"Good," he said.

Now Hop smelled blood in the water. "What do you say to me, Matt, whenever I go on and on about Kristin? What is that phrase again?"

He got me and I glared at him to let him know we would discuss this later. "The phrase?"

He wasn't letting go. "Yeah, something about home . . ."

You couldn't be thin-skinned around these guy, and I knew I couldn't push back any more, so I said it. "If you can't keep her home, let her roam."

Nate started snickering, and Mark laughed as well.

Hop was smiling at me and then opened his notebook back up. "Yeah, that's it," Hop said, tapping his pencil eraser on his cheek. "Let her roam."

Dick.

CHAPTER 19

Yes, it drank gas like a camel. It's true there was no cassette player, and without a doubt, the cooling effects of the AC were marginal at best, but for a high-schooler, Nate was right. The Milk Wagon *was* ideal, and with three full-sized traveling couches it was better than a dark movie theatre when the opportunity for some one-on-one time arose. Me, Mark, and Sammy had put that to the test on more than one occasion with varying degrees of success. I had hoped one day to familiarize Emily with its finer points, but what I hadn't foreseen was that she would be sharing the backseat with someone other than me.

Things had been a little strained between the two of us since our respective homecoming dates were finalized. Of course she agreed to go with Nate, and I, of course, defaulted to Chrissy, not having any other legitimate options. I really wished I had asked Emily first and kicked myself for not getting ahead of it. Emily's and Nate's nose-to-nose chat fests in the hall gave me the uneasy impression that my procrastination might have unwillingly lit a fire that had the potential to burn long past November, and I certainly didn't want the Milk Wagon fanning any romantic embers.

Mark, Hop, and I had originally planned to take Wendy, Kristin, and Chrissy on a triple date to the movies, but Hop was a bit skittish about exposing Kristin to all of us in the same vehicle, so he said they would just meet us at the theatre. When Hop bailed, Mark called up Nate without checking with me first and gave the extra Milk Wagon slot to Nate and Emily. Like Hop, I wanted to avoid being in the same car as Emily and Nate in the event we ended up parking. It would be difficult – but not impossible – to pay proper attention to Chrissy with Emily literally arm's length from me. I suggested we take another ride, but Nate would have none of it. He wanted to drive the Milk Wagon because he liked the way he could click the brights on with the toe switch on the floor.

We ended up seeing *Commando* at the Hardy Court Theatre, a local four-screen, famous for its good popcorn and lack of ushers. Even though the movie was crappy, the date ended up going better than expected because I was able to avoid the parking thing altogether. Nate had a strict curfew at ten o'clock due to an early morning obligation. He had to drive up to Hattiesburg to pick up a chair Vicky had ordered, and there was no way he could get out of it. We all shared some ice cream at Chillville then took the girls home.

The ladies graced us with some good night tongue, and Mark ended up scoring the longest make out session at Wendy's house. Her parents went to sleep early so he didn't have to worry about any front porch hawks. I couldn't even bring myself to watch Nate walk Emily up, so I played with the radio until he came back. I dropped Chrissy off last, and she didn't hesitate to show her appreciation for the date either. By the time our marathon snaking session was over, I had a crick in my neck, a bite mark on my left ear, and my jaw clicked whenever I opened my mouth all the way. As I slid back behind the steering wheel, Mark bounced his head up and down from the second row.

"Well, well. That certainly appeared to be productive."

I smiled and wiped my mouth with the back of my hand. "Yeah. She's nuts." I turned back down Washington Avenue and headed to the school to drop Nate off. I pulled into the front by the gate and parked next to Ferris.

"I know it's kind of early, Nate, but it's time for you to roll."

"Yep. Thanks for the ride. Appreciate you letting me drive the Milk Wagon earlier."

"No problem."

"Mark, you were right," Nate said. "The roomy interior does make for a sweet ride."

"If you got the right seatmate, for sure." Mark and Nate gave each other one of those half-high fives that morphs into a handshake. They tried to snap their fingers at the end like the black kids but failed.

"Terrible," I said as Nate stepped out and Mark climbed over the bench and into the front seat.

Nate closed his door and leaned through the passenger window. "Look Matt," he said, pinching his chin into a dimple, "You know she really likes you, right?"

"Yeah, Chrissy's not too bad. I guess I could do worse for sure, although –"

"Not Chrissy. Emily."

"Emily?" Mark's head whipped toward Nate and then back to me.

"Talks about you all the time."

"About me? Really?"

"Really. In fact, when I walked her to the door, she had a lot to say – about you. And Chrissy, of all people. Emily is *not* a fan, by the way. I barely even got a good night kiss in."

"Nate, listen, I –"

"Matt – I'm good with it, all right? Seriously, it's okay; it's not like this is a surprise or anything. Let's just get homecoming out of the way and see what happens." He leaned in and held out his hand for a real handshake. Mark pressed himself against the back of the seat, trying to avoid contact at all costs. I slapped Mark on the chest just to make him jerk, then shook Nate's hand. He was for real.

"Deal. We'll circle back on this in a few weeks, and if your theory still holds, we'll talk about it then."

"Right on." Nate rapped the side of the Milk Wagon twice and walked off. "See y'all Monday," he said, waving over the back of his head.

"Later, Nate," Mark yelled and watched him get into his truck. Mark leaned his elbow out the window and put one foot up on the dash. "Geez, what was that all about?"

"I have no idea. But it sounds promising."

"Yeah. For you."

"You hungry?"

"You know it. Let's go."

I put it in gear, still floored by Nate's comment, and not just because the door had potentially been opened with Emily. I was more stunned by the revelation that perhaps I had misjudged Nate from the outset. All this time, I thought he was goofy, aloof, confused, and somewhat disillusioned. Truth was, he had been watching, listening, and observing everything, and had been fully plugged in from the beginning to the undercurrent between Emily and me. It made me wonder what else he was keeping to himself.

Maybe Mark was right. Maybe Nate was an enigma.

CHAPTER 20

It had been several weeks, and Marty still had not returned to work – or to Archie Park, for that matter. It scared him too bad. When his daddy asked him why he didn't want to go back, Marty halfway told the truth and said he didn't want to in case the bad man was still there. Marty was very surprised his daddy didn't make him go. In fact, his daddy was nice about it and told Marty he could go back whenever he wanted to.

Marty looked out his window and saw that the fog had crept in, making the night even scarier that usual. He pulled the shade down all the way then closed the curtains on top of that. He rarely ventured out, even during the day, and when he did, he stayed close to his house. Close enough that he could make it back in under a minute if need be. He timed himself with his watch to make sure. His bike remained where he put it. Inside, kickstand down, parked at the foot of his bed.

The one thing Marty did have that calmed him down was his art. He had a big exhibit coming up soon, and even though most of the drawings had already been selected, they wanted some extras. He was going to meet with the lady soon and wanted to show her what else he had done. He had already sketched a heron, a least tern, and a mockingbird. He also drew some ducks that he had watched down near the marina in Bayou View earlier in the summer. He just had to add some color and more feathers, and they would be done. They all came pretty easy, but there was one bird he just couldn't get right.

No matter how hard he tried, he could not bring himself to draw a warbler. Even though he saw several of them in the woods that terrible day, every time he put pencil to paper, nothing took shape. The only details that came to him from that morning were Mr. Tommy getting shot. In fact, those visions surfaced almost every day and they terrified him, over and over again. They were bright and loud, and when he dreamed, they moved.

He wished he knew how to get them to go away. He tried praying, he tried playing video games, and he tried singing, but it didn't work. He wished they were just in a photograph so he could just put it away in a drawer and not have to look at it anymore.

Then it came to him. What if he could make them like a photograph? He didn't know if it would work, but he might as well give it a go. The thought excited him, so he grabbed his pad and box of pencils and sat Indian style next to his bed. He moved his hair out of his eyes and did the only thing that had ever come natural to him in his life.

Marty drew.

CHAPTER 21

D r. Nathan Bedford Mayes had just poured himself a Maker's Mark on ice and was settling in to watch the Tonight Show. When the phone in his home office rang right as Johnny Carson's first guest came on, however, he knew he had to take it. Only a handful of people had that number, and most of those were bankers who were only allowed to call during the day. When he picked it up, he was surprised to learn it was a man he had instructed long ago to break off all contact. But before he could protest, the reason for the call became clear. He swished the whiskey in his highball glass as he listened, no longer interested in his nightcap or in what Robin Williams was saying. In a matter of seconds, the message had been delivered, and the line went dead.

If the caller was right, his immediate interests were best served by taking care of things downtown, and he wondered what excuse he could give for leaving the house at that hour. He crept back in the den and called out to his wife, but she didn't budge, much less look up. The effects of the wine usually started to set in with her just after the evening news ended, so he had a pass there. His son had just come home from the movies, but he went straight up to his room without so much as a peep, and wouldn't be down until morning.

Dr. Mayes returned to the office and grabbed his wallet from the top drawer, then took the Emmitt Thames painting off the wall so he could get to the safe, where he pulled out a stack of documents. He eyeballed the rest of the contents and figured they could wait until he got back. He thought about taking his shredder with him, but the one at the office was a heavy duty, commercial grade machine and could handle more volume. He swiped the keys off his desk then sped off in his Porsche.

In his haste to leave, Dr. Mayes made three errors – an unusual slip-up for a man who demanded precision and perfection in everything and from everybody. First, he failed to close the safe all the way; it never latched, and the door kicked out just enough to not be flush with the wall. Second, he misjudged the actions of his family. Yes, his wife was on the couch, barely coherent, and long since disinterested in what he was doing. His son, on the other hand, was not. In fact, he had been in the kitchen making a sandwich the entire time.

Of course, the first two wouldn't have mattered if Dr. Mayes hadn't made his third – and most egregious – mistake: he failed to hang the painting back up properly. Instead of being aligned with the floor and ceiling, the frame leaned a bit to the left, causing the bucket of apples on the canvas – perfectly painted using egg tempera and watercolors – to give the appearance that they would spill out on the ground.

It was the first thing Nate noticed when he walked by.

CHAPTER 22

Mark and I met Hop at Sonic for a Coney and some chili cheese tots. We sat outside, dodging mosquitoes and solving the world's problems while we ate. Since Mark and I didn't have to be in until eleven-thirty, we all decided we would head to Hop's for some Nintendo, but when I opened up the driver's side door of the Milk Wagon, something fell out onto the ground that made us reassess our plans.

"Hey, guys, looks like Nate left his wallet."

Hop looked at his watch. "Too late to call his house."

"What do you think?" I asked. "Should we drop it off?"

"I don't know, man," Mark said. "You know what happened last time we showed up unannounced. Not sure it's a good idea to go busting up in there again."

"Yeah," Hop said, "but if he's driving to Hattiesburg tomorrow morning, he's going to need this. And if his old man is looking for an excuse to jump his ass, this would be it."

"Especially since his stepmom is involved. You know she won't cut him any slack."

They were both right. I didn't want to go to Nate's house, but I didn't want him to get reamed out again. I had an idea. "Didn't the gate have an intercom thing? I thought I saw a call button."

"I don't remember," Hop said, "what are you thinking?"

"Why don't we try that and see if Nate can meet us out front? That way we don't have to go in."

Everyone agreed and Hop jumped in. I cranked it up, and we headed north.

It was much harder to navigate the roads at night. There were no streetlights that deep in the country, and only one car passed us once we started moving. I felt like I was doing okay until I got to what I thought was the last turn before Nate's street. I should have paid more attention when Nate had been driving, and I wasn't entirely sure I was where we needed to be. The headlights on the Milk Wagon were cloudy due to the yellowed lens covers, and instead of illuminating the road, they cast more of a gauzy glow – even when I clicked on the brights. I couldn't find any break in the woods heralding a gate, a driveway or anything resembling a road, and I eventually came to a complete stop to try to reorient myself. Condensation had started to form on the windshield, so I rolled down my window to lean out and get a better view.

"Any of this look familiar?"

"Nope," Hop said from the back. Just woods all around."

"I feel like I'm in a horror movie," Mark said.

"Thanks. Thanks to you both. Very helpful." Mark rolled down his window as well.

"You think we ought to backtrack and see if we can figure out if we missed that turn?"

"Maybe," I said. "I wonder if we're even close. Was there a street sign or anything that–"

"Shhh," Mark said.

I heard it too.

"What?"

"Shut UP. Listen."

In the stillness of the night, over the din of the crickets and frogs, we could hear something approaching. "What is that?"

Footsteps. Fast moving, like someone was running. My heart down-shifted, and I strained my eyes, realizing we truly were in the middle of freaking nowhere.

"Holy crap," Mark said and leaned forward. "Look."

I started breathing heavier and leaned over the steering wheel. After a few seconds the sound materialized into a figure running towards us at what appeared to be a record pace. He was on the right side of the road just barely outside of the lights.

"What the hell? Roll 'em up!" Mark and I both started whipping the handles as fast as we could. Hop leaned up to push down the lock buttons. Right about the time he reached mine, the three of us all looked up, and the person – clearly a male – was almost on us. I let out a little yelp and started to honk, but before I could react, he split left just in front of the truck and continued down the road, never breaking his stride.

We were speechless, and when Hop tapped me on the shoulder and pointed, I nearly came out of my seat. Seeing a stranger running at you in the middle of the night while you are miles from civilization is enough to give anyone the willies. That wasn't the weird part. In the second he cut in front of the Milk Wagon lights, I recognized him. He had on the same blue Polo, the same khaki pants, and the same pair of Nikes from earlier.

But it wasn't the clothes that got my attention. It was the expression on his face.

His eyes were wide open and his mouth drawn into an oval. Tears were streaming down his cheeks, and spit was dripping off his chin.

Nate looked terrified.

CHAPTER 23

The three of us were shocked into silence. We all realized it was Nate, but it took a bit of time for our brains to process what we had just seen. Try as we might, none of us could come to a satisfactory explanation. Hop banged the back of my seat. "D-did you, did you see that? Did you see that?" His voice squeaked like he was thirteen. "That was Nate right there. What the hell?"

"I don't know, man," Mark said "What is going on? Was someone chasing him?" The three of us turned our heads and looked down the road to see if anyone was in pursuit. Other than the gnats, mosquitoes and the occasional moth flying in front of the headlights, we saw nothing – thank the Lord. If anyone had jumped out of the woods, we would have passed out right there. One thing was clear: we had to get out and get out quickly, so I slammed the Milk Wagon into reverse and started to turn around.

"Where are you going?" Mark asked.

"I don't know. Anywhere but here. This creeps me out."

"Me too," Hop said, still leaning over the front bench, his eyes peeled on the woods, "but we can't leave. Not yet."

"Oh, we most certainly can," I said. "We are done."

"Right on," Mark said. "Punch it."

"No, we can't," Hop said. "We have to check on Nate."

"But –"

"C'mon Matt, what if it was you?" Hop asked, his voice returning to a more normal level, although his eyes were still wild. He was talking a mile a minute. "Or me or Mark? Wouldn't we want – or expect – our friends to at least try to catch up with us? What if he was running for his life – which is not outside the realm of possibility, odd as it seems? You have a vehicle. There are three of us. At a minimum, we have to make a few passes."

Hop was often the voice of reason, and to some extent the moral compass of the group, so long as we weren't talking about girls, and as much as I wanted to disagree with him, I couldn't. The fact that Hop was sticking his neck out for Nate, of all people, spoke volumes; of the three of us, Hop was the most reluctant to bring Nate into the fold. Even so, Mark was also spot on when he said earlier it felt like we were in a horror movie. Seeing Nate like that in the middle of the woods late at night with no discernible light source in any direction made me weigh Hop's concerns against Mark's observation. If it was a movie, now would be about the time Jason or Freddy would rip through the roof and pull one of us out for a stabbing or a lopping off of an extremity. Upon reflection, though, it couldn't have been a horror movie, at least not a good one, because none of us had ever had sex, much less got naked with a girl, and the best slasher flicks begin with some kind of hanky panky before the first kill. Mark didn't say anything, and I figured he agreed with Hop in principle, but if I voted to go home, he would totally be on board with that as well.

"Okay, guys, here's what we're going to do," I said. "First, we have to get out of this general area. If there is someone else out here, odds are they are watching us, and I want to get as much pavement between them and us as possible. We do our best to check things out and then get back home."

"Fine. Let's just get this done and get out of here."

"I hear you. Now did anyone see where Nate went?"

"Nope."

"Nah."

"Great. Helpful as usual. Best we can do then, is follow this road in the direction he was running until it ends or we go too far. If we see any side roads or turns, we can double back and explore them as well. And if we don't see Nate, we're done. Fair enough?"

"Let's do it."

I turned the Milk Wagon down the road and clicked the brights back on. A summer fog steamed up the ground, mirroring the lights and increasing the creep factor tenfold. The radio was off, and all of us had our eyes peeled – me looking straight, Hop looking to the left and Mark to the right. We drove at least three miles without seeing anything other than an old mama possum that hissed at us before scooting out of the way. Hop and Mark pointed out side roads and turns, and we spent another twenty minutes running those down, but didn't see Nate – or anyone – for that matter. We did see some signs of civilization when we came on some neighborhoods and a few cars on the road, but other than that, nothing. The adrenaline we were running on when we first started had worn off, and the initial fear was transitioning into fatigue, if not boredom.

"Zilch," Hop said after we dead-ended on our fifth side road.

"Is that all?" I asked.

"Uh, I think there's one more up here," Mark said. "You see it?"

"Yeah. If this isn't the one, I say we head home."

"Agreed."

"Yep."

I headed in the direction Mark pointed out and started to slow down after a mile of not seeing anything. I hated to admit it, but I was a bit turned around, and I thought we might need the extra time to find our way back to Highway 49. I was about to throw in the towel when Hop popped up.

"Look! There!"

"What?"

"I don't see anything."

"Matt turn a hair right."

I did as Hop suggested and sure enough, the edge of a brick column peeked around a magnolia trunk. I drove another ten yards and parked right in front of the gate leading to Nate's house. Of course, it was closed.

"Did we ride by this before?" I asked.

"Probably three times. Any of y'all see anything up at the house? Lights? Anything?"

We squinted down the canopy of trees, and all we saw was a murky black.

"Nothing," I said, "but even if they had every light on at the manor, I'm not sure it would get through this thicket. Certainly not with all this fog."

"So, what do we do?" Hop asked.

I pulled up a few more feet and rolled up next to a post with a keypad on it. On top of the keypad was a circular metal screen and a call button.

"Here we go, fellas. Looks like they do have an intercom. So, do we check in or not?"

"I hate this place," Mark said. "Why don't we just throw the wallet over the fence and haul ass?"

"I would agree with you on any other day, but considering we saw Nate outside the compound, we should at least check in. Hop, what do you think?"

"I'm no fan of staying, either, but we should probably give them a buzz. His dad's a total asshole, but asshole or not, if Nate's in danger, we need to let him know. You're driving, Matt, so I vote you do the talking."

"Second."

"Hold on, guys. What do I say? Hello, sir, have you seen your son tonight because we have and he didn't quite look himself, you see he was running down – "

The box squawked, and a tinny voice cut through the air, causing us all to jump. "Can I help you?"

Mark mouthed an exaggerated 'what?' and pointed to the speaker.

Sounded like Nate's stepmom to me. How did she know we were out here?

"Hello, can I help you?" the voice said again. Mousy voice with a bitchy edge to it. Definitely Vicky.

"Uh, yes, uh, sorry to bother you Ms., uh Maye – Vicky is it?" I wasn't doing too well.

"I asked you a question. Can I help you with something? I don't know who this is, and if you don't identify yourself, you're going to be in trouble."

She swallowed the last word and it came out "trubbah." Vicky had been drinking.

"Yes ma'am, my apologies, this is Matt Frazier, and I'm here with Hop – Jason Hopkins – and Mark Ragone."

Not a word.

"We're Nate's friends. We –"

"Nate's not available right now."

"N-not available?" I turned and looked at Mark and Hop, and they shrugged their shoulders. "Is he there, because, we, uh, we saw –"

"Did you hear me? He can't come out right now. He's asleep. Do you even know what time it is?" For Vicky, alcohol was neither a mellowing agent nor a mood lifter. She sounded like a mean drunk. She was a mean sober, too. Not a good combination.

"Are you sure he's there, because –"

"Dammit, how many times do I have to tell you? Nate is not available, Nate is asleep. Why are you here at this hour? Go home." Lovely lady. Her tone reminded me of Mr. Mayes, which made me wonder why he wasn't joining in this colloquial exercise.

Hop tapped me on the shoulder and pointed at Nate's wallet on the dash. He mouthed 'ask her about the wallet.' I nodded my head and cleared my throat.

"Yes ma'am, but the reason I came by is I have Nate's wallet. He left it in my truck, and I recall him saying he needed it first thing in the morning, so, that's – that's why we're here." It got quiet for a few seconds and then Vicky muttered a few things under her breath I couldn't hear, but it sounded like cursing. I don't think she meant to leave her hand on the microphone. The weird thing was, when she did get back on the horn, she sounded cool, and not nearly as dizzy as earlier.

"Why thank you, boys," she said. "When he got home this evening Nate mentioned to us that he lost his wallet, and he will be glad to know you retrieved it. He was . . . most upset."

"Do you want us to come up and drop it off, or . . . what?" That didn't come off as smooth as I had hoped, either. Of course, none of us wanted to drive up to the house, but all three of us kind of wanted to see Nate to confirm that he was, in fact, back home. The veracity of the shrew's testimonial regarding Nate's current whereabouts was not exactly reliable.

"No. There is a drop box built into the column on the right – just next to the mail slot. Just slide it in there."

"I don't see it."

"Of course you don't. Look to the right, I said. It's behind those bushes."

"Got it. Listen, can I holler at Nate real quick? I need to ask him –"

"That will be all, gentlemen. Thank you. Good night."

"That's it?" Mark said. "Thank you and good night? What a crazy-ass bitch."

"Shhhh." I said to Mark, and pointed over at the receiver. Hop was giving the slice throat signal as well. For all we knew she was still listening. He tossed me the wallet, and I slowly crept toward the post. I fully expected some type of serial killer to jump out of the bushes, and each step felt like my last. When I finally got there, I was a twig break away from dropping a load.

I found a brass slot big enough for several magazines, and I pushed the wallet through. Once it was in, I planned on making a dash for the Milk Wagon, but when the wallet thunked its way to the bottom of the box, something caught my periphery that sent a ripple of goose bumps from my shoulder blades to my fingers. Just a few feet away in the bushes was the yardman. I don't think he expected me to see him, but he gave his position away when he jumped after I dropped the wallet in.

I stepped back, foot over foot, until I could feel the Milk Wagon's bumper, then guided myself around the truck and into the driver's side door, never taking my eyes off the man. The blood pounded through my temples, and I struggled to keep from hyperventilating as I slid into the seat. Hop was confused about my behavior, but when he followed my line of sight, I heard his breath jerk to a stop as the angle of the headlights illuminated the man's profile. Mark saw it too and pointed towards the gate, too shocked to even curse.

We were being watched the entire time.

CHAPTER 24

B ack when she was a college student, Kathryn Cooper considered herself a bit of a free thinker, and even pondered majoring in art studies during her younger, idealistic days at Tulane. It took only one summer interning at a painters' colony in the French Quarter, however, for her to realize that washing her hair, regular baths and a reliable source of income were legitimate life goals. She came to this crossroads at about the same time a female FBI recruiter approached her during a job fair on campus. As a teenager, she hated being an Air Force brat, and swore she would never join the military, but her father's influence was strong, and something about the opportunity to serve called her. She switched majors, and shortly after graduation, found herself at the FBI Academy in Virginia. She loved Quantico, hit the field running, and other than the dark year after her father's death, never looked back – which was good and bad in her eyes. She was happy to have an occupation with real opportunities to advance, but missed those days when she was able to exercise the left side of her brain.

She tried to make up for her creative dearth by volunteering at the Holden Gallery on 27th Avenue in downtown Gulfport. She liked the gallery because it offered a good mix of local and national artists, and on Second Saturdays, the gallery brought in live music, set up a cash bar, and turned the place into a laid-back, funky lounge. As a volunteer, she helped with painting, exhibits, and occasionally worked the bar. Eventually, someone recognized her artsy side, which led to her consulting with visiting artists to plan their shows. Over time she was elevated to a staffer, which paid a small (very small) stipend for her work, did two rotations on the board, and eventually was asked to serve as chairman.

One of her pet projects was a student outreach endeavor called Campus Creatives, where high school volunteers came in to help with shows, exhibits, or parties that the gallery hosted. She always had a large contingent of kids from St. John High School because they had to get ten mandatory service hours per semester.

Kat scheduled the first meeting with the new group to discuss the fall events, and to start planning for the big Marty Deen exhibit, which was to kick off in December and culminate in a big party on New Year's Eve. She got off work early, and after taking a quick shower to freshen up, arrived in time to set up chairs and put out cookies and lemonade. The kids eventually filed in, and by six o'clock, twelve of the fifteen had arrived, which was par for the course. She absolutely had to be done by seven, so she went ahead started without the others.

"Good evening, everyone. Thanks for coming out," she said, adjusting her seat so she could see better. "There are some faces out there I recognize, and some I don't, so I'll introduce myself so we can get started. My name is Kathryn Cooper, and I serve as chairman of the board here at Holden Gallery." She continued with a brief history – her education, the FBI, and how she got to the gallery, then handed out a sheet listing upcoming events and assignments. She also passed around a legal pad to get the attendees' personal information, and had them fill out name tags for the first meeting.

"Okay," Kathryn said, looking down at her notes, "looks like we have a pretty good mix." Kathryn enjoyed this part because she used it as a litmus test to see if her analytical skills were on point. Right or wrong, she made snap judgments of every kid based solely upon first impression and documented her thoughts. At the end of the year, she would look back over it to see if her instincts had proven true.

By the time she reached the end, she had four from Gulfport High, one from Long Beach, two from Harrison Central, and five from St. John. Of these she noted about one: '*bored stiff/ate nearly all the cookies*,' two: '*slouchy disinterested types*,' two: '*great potentials*,' one: '*hilarious and loud*,' and one: '*shy but engaging*.' Just as she turned to address the group, the door chimed, and two latecomers walked in. She could tell by the crowd's response that they were from St. John.

"Glad you could make it. Please have a seat. Eagles, right?"

"Yes, ma'am."

"Good. My name is Kathryn Cooper, and I'll be working with you two throughout the year." She turned to the girl. "Now let me hear about you. Your name?"

"Emily Miller. Nice to meet you."

"You too, Emily. And what brings you here?"

"Well, I needed to get my hours somewhere, and like to paint. I've known Marty Deen since I was a little girl, so working with him should be fun." She looked up at the tall boy next to her. "Plus, he wanted me to come with him." He halfway smiled. "So here I am."

"Certainly glad you are here and I look forward to hearing your thoughts about Marty."

Pretty. Confident.

"You're the last one. Tell me your name."

"Nate."

He carried himself differently from the others. Strapping kid; athletic type – potentially good with the girls at school, but carried himself like he was dragging something. She could see he was intelligent, but had something else going on in his head. She wrote *timid* then scratched it out when she noticed his leg bouncing up and down a mile a minute, which wasn't totally unusual for a teenager in a crowd of strangers. Then she saw a look of panic come over his face, as if a terrible thought popped up, and then in a flash of self-awareness, his eyes darted around the room to see if anyone noticed. His gaze landed on Kathryn and she looked down at her pad.

Cagey.

"Okay, great. Again, thanks for coming. We really couldn't do this without you. As you may know, the gallery's next big event is in a few months, where we will be showcasing the work of Marty Deen. Who in here besides Emily has heard of Marty?"

Most of the kids raised their hands. "Fantastic. We are very excited to be exhibiting Marty. In addition to the drawings we already have on hand – which are fabulous, by the way – Marty is doing a few more. I may recruit some of you to go through these with me to help pick out the best ones." Kathryn winked at Emily and got a thumbs-up. She gave a short spiel on Marty's background and informed the students his exhibit could provide a lot of exposure for the gallery. There was an outside chance of it being covered by the New York Times for a Sunday feature, and to make the night even more extraordinary, a string quartet led by a member of the first violin section at the Chicago Symphony Orchestra would be performing. It was an easy deal since the musician would be home for the holidays to visit her parents nearby in Ocean Springs.

"It will be black tie, so we will need a lot of help sprucing this space up. Because of all the work ahead, we will begin the Saturday after next."

Sammy, one of the St. John kids, raised his hand. "Did you say Saturday after next? What time?"

"Oh, I don't know. How does nine sound?"

"In the morning?"

"Yes. In the morning." Four of the St. John students groaned.

"Is there any possible way you could push that back, Ms. Cooper?" Sammy asked. "Our homecoming dance is the night before and we – uh, we may want to sleep in a bit." He laughed like a hyena through the last part.

Kat remembered those days, and she knew that if she didn't take it into account, attendance would be sparse. "For you, Sammy, sure. How about eleven, then?"

He looked at his friends. Most shrugged their shoulders with a nod, and the deal was struck. Eleven it was.

They spent the next twenty minutes scheduling another workday over the holidays and looking at potential dates to meet once school got back in session. She then had the boys move some of the temporary walls and pull out the risers and start blocking the stage. The girls unloaded four bolts of muslin out of the storage room in the back, and Emily took point laying it out. Kat planned to drape it throughout the gallery and turn the place into a winter wonderland.

Just before seven, she rounded them up, thanked them for coming and reminded them to be on time for the next meeting. When they left, she went to the bathroom to freshen up and brushed her teeth with the toothbrush she kept in her purse. When she was rinsing her mouth, she heard the door chime. She listened, and when she heard footsteps, her heart skipped a beat.

She hurried out and saw a man standing in the middle of the floor staring at her. He had a funny look on his face.

"Um, hello," she said. She could barely breathe.

Yes, she was expecting him, but not like this. Seeing him all cleaned up out of uniform was almost too much for her. And he was carrying a rose.

"You look amazing," he said.

"Why, thank you. You don't look too bad yourself." She took Rick Papania's arm and locked the door on the way out. It took all she had to keep from leaning up and giving him a peck on the cheek.

It was her first real date in over three years.

CHAPTER 25

According to legend, the unofficial St. John homecoming week kickoff party known as "Fish Feeders" began one chilly weekend in October 1977, when a group of St. John seniors gathered for a night of drinking and bonfire gazing at Gulfport Lake. It was essentially a public boat launch and picnic area – a perfect spot for a late-night party. Out of the way, no neighborhoods nearby, and very little police presence to speak of. The boys stacked old warehouse pallets fifteen feet high and ten wide on the beach, doused them with gasoline and lighter fluid, and lit a bonfire that could be seen from planes taking off at the airport two miles away. Ford and Chevy pickup truck beds served as mobile beer coolers while 8-track stereos blared licks from the Stones, the Allman Brothers, and Jimmy Buffett for the benefit of those trailblazers who kicked off their shoes to dance in the sand. They started calling it Fish Feeders after a few lightweights puked in the water after taking on too much Thunderbird.

For the first couple of years after the inaugural event, the date was chosen randomly, but over time everyone settled on the Friday before homecoming week, which was a great way to rouse school spirit, if not other things. The Chief and the rest of the hounds quietly looked the other way – not that they could do much anyway because it was an off-campus event. One of the cooler teachers, Ms. McGuffee, actually attended Fish Feeders '78 as a student herself, and my oldest brother, Will, told me that one year Father Tommy, our school chaplain, showed up with a shillelagh in one hand and a bottle of Jameson in the other. He blessed the fish and then got canned with everyone else before challenging Timmy Sneed to a bareknuckle fistfight. The bout never happened, and Father Tommy settled for warbling a mumbled version of *Danny Boy* by the fire, using his stick as a conductor's baton.

Hop, Mark, and I did not have liquor, but we did come stocked with beer Mark bought from the lackey who managed the warehouse where his band – Wombat Revolution – practiced. Mark was going through his INXS phase and thought the name had a good Aussie ring to it, although I had yet to hear them play a song. We had to give the dude five dollars for his efforts, but it was worth it. Unfortunately, my mom watched out for such things, so Mark and I thought it would be a good time to actually test the capacity of the Trapper – and it passed with flying colors.

My discovery of the Milk Wagon's best kept secret was purely by accident. I had barely been driving it for two days before the radio started dropping out whenever I hit a bump, and I took it upon myself to see if I could find the problem. I opened up the ashtray halfway to create some space to access the speaker cable, but instead of finding the wire, my finger hit a latch, and with a click, two linear feet of bottom trim dropped open from the radio to the glove compartment, revealing a storage area about six inches deep.

It had been retrofitted with a hidden piano hinge, and the interior of the box was treated with some type of spray-on velveteen to muffle anything that might bang around. It was clearly not part of the original vehicle, and I would have never noticed it had I not come upon it by mistake. When I showed Mark, he thought some of the city boys might have been using it to run weed, but I wasn't sure, and I never found out. The only time I actually used it to conceal something was one morning on the way to school when Hop showed up with the Madonna Playboy he bought at the fart mart on O'Neal Road. It was not his first purchase of the gentlemen's periodical, and wouldn't be his last, but it was the first time he tried to bring one to school, which I thought was a bad idea. Of course, I checked it out, and after a detailed review I ultimately concluded he had wasted his money. Like a virgin? Not even close.

As predicted, a twelve pack of Bud Light lined up side-by-side fit just about perfectly. It was actually a can short of a dozen because Mark wanted a road pop so he grabbed one for the ride over. I was planning on drinking a few myself once we got there. It was our first official Fish Feeders, and I had arranged to stay at Hop's that night –

as had Mark, which meant we would probably end up sleeping in the Milk Wagon. Once we hunkered down, none of us would be driving.

By the time we arrived, the festivities were just getting under way. I could hear the hum of generators off in the distance as a DJ ran his sound check from the back of a pickup. A pointy-elbowed senior with her hair pulled back into a ponytail sat on the tailgate selling t-shirts at eight dollars a pop. I pulled up under the streetlight by the main gazebo with the rest of the juniors. Bursts of laughter, talk of girls, and stories from Fish Feeders past could be heard all through the parking lot. Music from car stereos rose and fell in the background, giving the place a festival vibe. It was exciting for all of us, and to me it felt a lot like the first day of school combined with the last day of school mixed in with a bit of Christmas Eve. We were heady with the euphoria of being amongst friends – and the feeling of anticipation as to what lay ahead was palpable.

"Frazier! Get over here!"

Sammy Mallette was perhaps the most animated of the group, and I heard his cackling well before he called my name. He already had his Fish Feeders t-shirt on, and I estimated he had been there for a while based upon his condition. Somehow, he had managed to get a keg and set it up in the trunk of Freddy, which was lined with plastic bags and filled with ice.

"What's happening, my brother?"

"You, baby," he said, handing me a plastic cup. "Gonna be a good night."

"You know it," I said, taking over the pump, "how in the world did you get ahold of a keg?"

"Borrowed it from the yacht club." Sammy's dad was a charter captain, and Sammy spent a lot of time on the docks. "They had 'em stacked ten deep outside for a party tonight, and I figured they wouldn't miss it. That's where I got all this ice, too."

"Good for you, man."

"No, good for us," Hop said, grabbing a cup. Soon most of the juniors gathered around the old Cadillac, and at first, it was mostly guys. We took advantage of Sammy's illicit haul and felt the cloak of invincibility start to materialize as we reloaded. The lack of female presence was noted, but we were enjoying our hang time, so no one really complained. We knew they were coming, but we didn't know quite when. About an hour later Mark sounded the alarm.

"Well looky there," he said, pointing behind us. A string of headlights a dozen deep bounced down the road like a nighttime Mardi Gras parade, and when we realized it was the girls, we waved them over. By the look in their eyes, they were equally stoked to be there, and it was clear by the way they poured themselves out of their cars that they, too, had started early.

I saw Chrissy first and worked in a little early evening flirting, but we eventually broke off to mingle with the rest of the crowd. If nothing else, I set it up for a circle-back in the event it looked like I could end up solo. I strolled over to the senior section, and after taking a little hazing, drank a round with Andy Tanner, who had always been cool to me, even if some of the other upperclassmen were turds. I made a couple more social stops and headed back to Freddy for a refill and found Sammy crawling out of the trunk. He had just hooked up a new one. Chad and Trey were using the empty as a makeshift bench.

"Two?"

"Freddy's back seat is huge. I got one more in there for good measure. Stood them on their side and used a seatbelt to keep them from tipping." He paused to wipe the sweat off his brow. "This is Fish Feeders, Matt. Our first one. We need to do it right. Set the standard for next year."

"That we do, Sammy." I double checked the connection on the tap and started to prime the pump. When I reached over to grab a fresh cup, a hand holding an empty appeared from behind.

"Fill it up, sir."

Emily snuck up on me yet again.

She was wearing a miniskirt with tights and a thin knit sweater that bunched up at the sleeves. A slight breeze had her tucking and retucking her hair behind one ear. She had no idea what that little move did for me. It also didn't hurt that she had knee-high boots on.

"Well, well. I didn't see you in the caravan."

"Rode with Marcia. Not planning on driving tonight," she said with a smirk and a head bob.

"Why, Emily Miller," I said, "I believe you've been drinking."

"Yup," she said, giggling. "Don't judge me."

"Oh no, I'm not judging," I said. "I'm just glad to see you out letting your hair down for a change."

She put her arm around my neck and leaned in, crushing the good parts of her left side against me and whispered, "you ain't seen nothin' yet, Matt Frazier." Then she pulled away, slammed her beer, and said "another."

I had never before been in the presence of such a perfect human being. I had spent nearly half an hour talking with Chrissy earlier, and I barely felt my heart rate go up, much less anything else. Now, one minute with Emily, and I was a mess. Her proximity alone made everything around me brighter, and suddenly thankful to be wearing jeans.

"Talked to Nate lately?" I knew I shouldn't have asked – at least not at that moment – but it was a fair question. I figured he would show up with Emily, but now that she was here and he wasn't, I started to get concerned, if not interested.

"Nope," she said, exaggerating the "-ope" into a popping sound with her lips.

"Do you know if he's coming?"

"I hope so, but we haven't talked in a few days. It would do him some good to hang out with us tonight." I agreed. Nate had become increasingly withdrawn, almost to the point of silence, since we saw him running that night. The one time I was able to corral him, he reassured me he was okay but that he still needed to work some things out. We hadn't spoken since. Emily squeezed my hand then leaned in. "Just being here is already doing me some good," she whispered. She gave me a kiss on the cheek and walked off.

And just like that, thoughts of Nate disappeared into the night. I must've let half a beer pour out onto the ground before Mark jabbed my side to let me know the tap was still running.

Chapter 26

As the music played, the crowd grew, and little by little, people started congregating towards the beach. Per tradition, the lighting of the bonfire happened at ten straight up, and as I turned to make my way up to the mountain of pallets, logs, and boards, something akin to an air horn sounded and caught my attention. When I looked up the road near the entrance, I saw a new row of headlights coming down the trail; these sat higher in the air, and there were a lot of them, probably fifteen or more. The DJ killed the music as they lined up in the parking lot, one jacked up four-wheel drive after another, some with whip CB antennas bouncing around the back.

I knew right away they weren't from St. John, and I had to shield my eyes to read the license plate on the front of the lead vehicle. It was the West Harrison Red Rebels. Our homecoming opponent.

Somehow, they had gotten wind of our little kickoff soiree and thought they would pay the home crowd an early visit. The driver's side window of the lead vehicle rolled down, and a big green stream of spit shot out and splattered on the concrete. He hit the horn again, and it was so loud up close, my hair vibrated, and one tooth way in the back started to hurt. The door swung open, and the biggest redneck knuckle-dragger I'd ever seen stepped out just as Hank Williams Jr. twanged out something about a family tradition. This guy had more facial hair than the Pittsburgh Steelers' front four, and I estimated, just by the way he was standing, that he could have fathered one, maybe three kids, all probably more closely related than they should be. He pulled a lacquered piece of wood out of the bed, slapped it in his hand a few times, and spoke.

"This here's 'Cousin.'"

It was an axe handle, and sure enough, the word "cousin" had been roughly etched and burned in the side. The business end where the blade should have been was nothing but splintered wood and dark stains.

One by one the other trucks parked, and more good ol' boys got out flanked by the occasional good ol' girl, and even though it was chilly, most had cutoffs on. I checked them out, and I would say a respectable third of them were dateable in a farmer's daughter kind of way. I looked over at Andy Tanner, and he had stepped from around his Camaro to size up the new arrivals as well.

My first thought when I saw how big they were was that they were going to beat our ass on the gridiron next week. My second thought, which was not nearly as pleasant, was that they were going to beat our ass right then and there. We were outnumbered, outgunned, and really had no means of retreat. The Frazier family might have been known for a lot of things, but fighting wasn't one of them, and if we were going to come to blows, one thing was for sure.

It was not going to end well for me.

The standoff continued as more trucks parked and more people got out. I wouldn't have thought that many people would come all the way out to Gulfport Lake looking for trouble – as a rule, most schools played in their own back yards unless there was a personal affront of some sort. When there was an offense, it usually involved someone jumping the fence and snaking on someone else's girl, but I had heard no reports along those lines. Not saying it didn't happen, just saying I wasn't aware of it.

As fate would have it, most of the St. John crowd moved closer to the beach when the convoy rolled in. Except for my dumb ass, that is, and when Big Boy surveyed the scene like a field commander on the front line, his eyes landed on me. I had a penchant for talking myself out of situations like this, but at that time I was rendered mute. No icebreaker, no insult, no utterance of any sort came to mind. So there I stood, cup of beer in one hand, suddenly conscious of the very different sartorial choices he and I had made in preparation for our night out. I had on a Members' Only jacket, faded jeans, and Sperrys, and he looked like he was dressed for a day of interning at the taxidermist.

The only thing I could think to do was make a peace offering, so – being careful not to make any sudden movements lest I startle the bear – I motioned to the keg and grabbed an empty cup. Before I could hand over the proverbial olive branch, however, a laugh erupted from behind the line and broke the silence.

"Matt Frazier, you drunk son of a bitch," the voice said, still laughing. It had a nasally country twang that would have been good for telling jokes. "We drive our ass all the way out here, and all you offer us is some stale beer served out of a trunk of – what is that, a Cadillac? And you call *us* rednecks?"

All eyes turned to me from both sides, and I wasn't sure whether to smile or run. Even though he called me by name, my mind pulled a blank, and it wasn't until the heckler stepped into the light that I started to breathe again. He had a bottle of Jack in one hand and a good-looking Winston Cup-type blonde in the other. He pointed at me and winked. "I told you we was going to party down one day. Tonight is the night!"

It was one of my old friends from Lyman, Lance Glenn. He walked up and gave me a hug.

"You old country bastard," I said. "You scared the nuts off me." I reached over and shook the hand of the bouncer, who introduced himself as Hayden. He smiled, revealing a gap-toothed grin that took the edge off his menace.

"Don't listen to Lance," Hayden said (he pronounced it *Laynce*). "I like me a good beer. Even better if it's draft." Sammy had one poured for him before Hayden finished the sentence, and Hayden finished it before Sammy could pour him another. Even though everyone took a breath, people were still watching us. Lance felt it too. "So what now, Frazier?" he whispered out of the side of his mouth.

I tapped Hayden on the shoulder and pointed to his truck.

"You mind if I jump in the back for a second?"

"All yours, buddy."

Just the fact that he let me get in told me things were going to be okay.

"Hey, everybody, my name is Matt Frazier. This idiot down here who won't shut up is my good friend Lance Glenn. You may wonder how Lance and I know each other, and I'll tell you. I went to Lyman – up in West Harrison territory – from third to sixth grade – probably was there when some of you were there – and I didn't have one single friend for about three months. Lance must have felt sorry for me, because after a while he let me sit with him at lunch, and before we knew it, we were ruling the school." A few snickers but still no converts. "He saved my ass, actually, and I have good memories from back then. But now he shows up here wanting me to pay him back by drinking our beer and stealing our women." More laughter and a few whoops from the West Harrison side. It came to a head when Lance yelled out, "Damn Right!" and racecar girl pushed him away "So, to my classmates, I say – at least for tonight, treat these folks like they are one of our own." I raised my cup, and I saw Andy and his circle of seniors follow. "And to the Red Rebels – welcome to Fish Feeders."

On cue, the music started, and within fifteen minutes, there was backslapping, laughing and dancing going on – the cease-fire had been declared. The bonfire brought everyone together, aided in no small part by the West Harrison boys emptying out whatever it was they had been carrying around in the back of their trucks and throwing it on the fire. Up until then, I had no idea people actually picked up road kill, much less kept it for special occasions.

At around eleven-thirty, people started disappearing into back seats, and I went on the hunt for Emily. When she came over earlier and introduced herself to Lance, he about fell over himself trying to talk to her. I had to explain to him that no, she was not my girlfriend, although it wasn't for lack of effort, and he was visibly disappointed. I continued to watch for her throughout the night, and every now and then, I caught her looking my way. I found her over by Marcia's Celica, swaying to the opening riff to "Just Like Heaven" with her eyes half closed. I couldn't have timed it better.

"Hey, there," I said.

"Well, hello. I was hoping you'd make it over this way."

"I had to finish catching up with Lance. Thank you for coming by and speaking to him."

"He seemed nice. You two had a tense couple of minutes, huh?"

"You could say that. Worked out okay though, right?"

"Matt Frazier saves the day again." When she said that she put both arms around my neck, and her dark brown eyes locked on to mine. She pushed me back against the car and let all of her weight tilt on to me. I realized right then it was going to happen, and I tried to lick my lips without Emily seeing it. Somewhere between "saves the day again" and her pinning me to the car, they withered up. She started to cock her head to the side in that pre-make out turn, so I closed my eyes and put one hand on her cheek to make sure I was on target. My lips grazed hers, and I could feel them part about the same time she squeezed my waist.

Then she stopped me.

"What?" I pulled back and she was looking just over my shoulder. She pushed off my chest with both hands and ran up to the front of the car. When I turned around, I saw why.

It was Nate. He had made it, all right, but he looked like he had been through a meat grinder. One eye was partially swollen shut, the bridge of his nose was misshapen, and his upper lip was puffed up and purple.

And he was smiling ear to ear.

CHAPTER 27

"What happened?" My first thought was that the West Harrison peace accord we had brokered had fallen through, and Nate was the first allied casualty. My second thought was that I should start marshaling the troops in the event our very first Fish Feeders ended up in a brawl.

"Looks that bad, huh?" He licked a cut on his lip.

"Do we need to get you to a doctor?" By now a few other people had come up.

"You need to get me to a cold beer."

Marcia handed him a longneck, and he took a swig using the good side of his mouth, then rested his bad hand on my shoulder.

"I finally did it, Matt. Just like you said." He snorted. "My old man tried to square on me, but I would have none of it. Not this time. I whipped his ass."

Emily looked back and forth between Nate and me. She couldn't figure out whether she should be concerned or mad.

"Guys?"

I was still trying to recover from my almost encounter with Emily and it took a few seconds to get my head around what Nate had said. "Good for you, buddy. I think. Well I hope he looks worse than you."

"Guys? Hello?" Emily wedged herself in between us.

"Oh, he definitely looks worse than me, partially because I got him with this," he held up his hand and wiggled two of the four exposed fingers, and then put his arm around me. Even after getting into a fight, Nate still managed to look cool – like Rocky at the end of his second match with Apollo Creed. "But what really got him is what happened after."

Emily finally had enough. "Nate, what are you and Matt talking about?"

"After?"

He took another swallow, puff-burped, then looked right at me. "The FBI raided his office today."

"The who? The FBI did what?" Emily asked before I could. "I don't understand." I didn't either.

"Raided his clinic and shut it down. Then they sent a different crew to my house and did the same thing."

"For what?" I asked. "I mean, why'd they do a raid?"

"Not sure; I heard someone mention something like fraud, but I didn't get it all."

"What'd your dad say?"

"Not a word. Not much you can say when you're handcuffed and being helped into the back of a cop car."

"They arrested him?"

"Yep."

Wow. Even if Nate's dad was a dick, this had to hit hard. "Sorry, man."

"Oh, no need to be sorry, Matt," he said, "had it not happened, I wouldn't have been able to get here to see all of y'all."

I still didn't fully understand what he was saying, and as much as I tried to look like I was following him, Nate's cavalier approach to it all puzzled me. Nate moved in to explain.

"Remember that control thing you and I talked about?" Nate said, tapping the longneck on his forehead. I nodded, and Emily looked mad now that it dawned on her that she had, in fact, been left out of the loop.

"Other than going to school, I haven't been allowed out of the house. Not once. Nada. Several nights I've been locked in my room. This is the first taste of freedom I've had since we went to the movies."

"Yeah, but —"

He held up his bandaged hand in the 'shush' position and leaned in a little closer, forcing the three of us into a mini-huddle. "Is this not Fish Feeders – the greatest party of all time?"

"Well, yeah," I said, and Emily nodded her head.

He stood up straight and clapped me on the back. "Then quit standing around looking like someone just stole your dog and tell me where I can find another one of those coldweisers."

I pulled another beer out of Marcia's cooler and popped the top. "You sure you're okay?"

He grabbed the bottle and downed the entire thing, then turned his head upward and smelled the air. When he opened his eyes back up, they were as clear as the night sky.

"I'm more than okay, Matt. My old man is in jail; it is a beautiful evening, and I am here for the first time ever with friends – *real* friends." He surveyed the crowd, then put his arms around Emily and me.

"In fact, this may be the best day of my life."

CHAPTER 28

It didn't take long for the story surrounding Nate's arrival to spread through the crowd, and for a short while a steady stream of on-lookers strolled by to check him out. Three months ago no one had even met Nate, and now he was like Bono. Not everyone goobed out on him, though. Andy stopped by with his stacked girlfriend, Janene the Machine, who gave Nate a big full frontal hug. That certainly perked Nate up. Made me want to claim some kind of physical injury or moral victory myself.

After about an hour, the novelty wore off, and everyone continued like nothing had happened. Physical appearance notwithstanding, Nate looked as comfortable as I'd ever seen him. He mingled in and out like he was running for office, the wheels of conversation no doubt lubricated by a full cup and the liberation that came from breaking free from whatever chains that had been keeping him down. As the night grew on, we congregated around Freddy's trunk, telling stories and pumping the kegs until they floated. Soon the girls joined us, and a few of them regaled us with tales of their own, which fascinated Hop to no end – especially when the topic turned to sleepovers. Emily played it cool with both me and Nate, and I wore the same mantle of diplomacy with Chrissy. The moment had passed with Emily, and I was having too good of a time just hanging out to be worried about snaking. If either had thrown it on me, I would have, no doubt, but it didn't feel right to go chasing it. Not really.

Eventually, the parking lot emptied one by one until it was just me, Hop, Mark, Nate – and Lance, of all people. When he heard we were staying, he told Hayden to go on. Throughout the evening, he had progressively shed his clothes piece by piece. By the end of the night, all he had on was cowboy boots, a cowboy hat and a pair of grippers that were starting to lose the elastic around the leg. He said that's how he did it when he went camping.

I backed the Milk Wagon up as close as I could to the bonfire, and we opened up the rear cargo doors so Hop and I could sit with our legs hanging over the bumper. I showed Nate how to access the Trapper, and he was amazed not only that it was virtually unnoticeable, but also by the fact that there were still five beers inside. Mark and Nate wrestled the third-row bench out of the back and plopped it on the sand like a trailer park couch. Lance squatted on an aluminum beach chair with dry-rotted webbing and rolled an empty beer keg back and forth under his boot. By that time, everything was quiet except for the crickets, the bullfrogs and an occasional pop from the bonfire that shot whirling laser beams up in the sky.

Over in the east, the sky was transitioning from jet black to a deep navy, which told me we were closing in on five a.m. Still, none of us mentioned leaving or going to sleep. Maybe it was the beer, maybe it was because it was only the second time in my life I could recall staying up that late, and maybe it was the way the red orange glow from the coals lulled us into a trance, but we were all in a good place. Even Lance seemed to be enjoying his daze, although I suspected he was riding a second buzz, due in no small part to him nursing a dip of Copenhagen the size of a small mouse.

Nate broke the silence.

"You know, I saw y'all the other night."

"What?"

"When I was running down the street outside my house. I saw y'all. In the Milk Wagon."

Hop jerked to attention, and I looked over at Mark. He glanced at Nate and then down at the ground, not quite sure what to say, and wishing he wasn't sitting right next to him.

"I had seen you pass by a few times already, and I tried to avoid you, but when you made that last stop, I had already turned and there was nowhere else I could go, so I kept on trucking."

Nate looked straight ahead, his voice a barely audible monotone. Lance looked the most confused of all, but he was quick enough to pick up on the fact that there was something deep going on, so he didn't chime in. He pushed his hat back on his head and spit a precision stream of slurry onto an ember, sizzling it from pink to black to pink again.

"You scared us pretty bad, you know," Mark said. "At first we didn't know who was coming our way. Looked like a crazy person."

"Then when we realized it was you, we thought someone might be after you," Hop said, "but we never saw anyone else."

"That's 'cause no one was out there but me."

"So why were you running, Nate?" I asked. "We drove around looking for you for a good thirty minutes. Even stopped at the front gate but were told to go home."

"Y'all came by the house?"

"Yep."

"No one told me that."

"Sure did," Hop said.

Nate shook his head. "I was running because I saw something."

"Saw something? Like something in the woods?"

"No, not in the woods."

"What? What did you see?"

He took in a long deep breath through his nose. "Look, y'all know the dark side of my dad – some of you know more than others," he said and glanced at me. "He is a mean, spiteful man who has said and done some things that can't be unsaid and can't be undone. For years now I have hated him. Hated his stupid rules. Hated that he remarried right after my mom died. Hated the fact that he hates me – for reasons even today I still don't understand." He poked at the fire with a stick. "But I never had a reason to be scared of him."

"What happened, Nate?" I asked. "Was he the one chasing you?"

"No. He wasn't even there that night."

"Then what? I'm not following you."

Nate squeezed his bottom lip with the thumb and index finger of his good hand. Then all of a sudden he popped up and walked over to his truck, continuing to talk.

"Let me rephrase it. He was there when I got home from the movie, but he and Vicky were watching TV. As usual, he didn't acknowledge my presence, so I went to the kitchen to get something to eat."

Nate opened the door, and I could see him reach into the glove compartment. "Then he got a phone call in his office near the den – which was weird, because I had never heard that phone ring. Not once." He shut the door and walked back to the fire. "His office is off limits to everyone but him. Keeps it locked. Most of the time."

"Who was on the phone?"

"No idea, but it must've been important because he took off as soon as he hung up."

"Where'd he go?"

"Don't know that, either, but it doesn't matter. What does matter is that he left his office door open. First time ever. So I investigated."

"Vicky?"

"Not a problem. She was deep into the wine by that time. Even if she had seen me, she wouldn't have remembered."

"Okay. So what'd you find?"

Nate stretched out his hand and fanned a stack of Polaroids out like a blackjack dealer.

"I found these."

The dawn sun provided just enough light for us to see without having to rely on what was left of the bonfire. I stood up to get a better look but stopped when the image of the one on top came into focus. It was a snapshot of a man wearing a tie lying on the side of a road. His right arm was extended above his shoulder disco style, and his legs were jacked out to the side. When I leaned in closer to try to see his face, I gagged.

He was missing the back half of his head.

CHAPTER 29

"What the hell?" I flipped to the others. One was the remains of a man sitting on a couch. It was much worse than the first because there wasn't much left above the chin. Blood and meat everywhere. The third was a hand with the thumb and finger cut off. The person in the fourth was beaten so badly you could barely tell it was a man. I couldn't even look at the last one. I had seen enough.

Everyone else pretty much had the same reaction. I had never seen a dead person – in real life or in pictures – and was surprised at how sick it made me feel. Lance was the only one who made it through the stack without commenting. He just adjusted his hat and walked back to the fire.

"You found these in his office? Were they just sitting around?"

"No," Nate said. "When I first walked in, I didn't notice anything. I opened a drawer or two. Nothing too weird. I did find a pistol under a pharmacy book, but I knew he had that anyway, just didn't know where he kept it."

"So where were the photos?"

"You may have noticed when you were over that everything in my house is always perfectly in its place. Silverware, dishtowels, furniture, you name it. It's one of Doc Mayes's many mandates. The one thing that caught my eye when I walked in was this painting he has hanging behind his chair. It was crooked. Not enough for most people to notice it, but I sure did. So out of habit I tried to adjust it, but something dragged on the canvas from behind. I pulled it off the hook, and there was a wall safe. And it was unlocked."

"Damn. This is like a spy movie," Mark said. "I've never seen a wall safe before."

"Me neither. When I first opened it, I was pretty disappointed. No gold or jewelry like I was expecting. At first glance just some medical records and other paperwork. Then I took another look and tucked in the back I found a small, blank folder. I opened it up and there they were."

"Anything else?" I asked.

"Uh, not really."

"Do you know these people?"

"I don't have a clue who they are. Thank goodness."

"Wow," Hop said, taking a closer look. "Do you think your dad, you know, did this?"

"I don't know," he said. "I don't know."

"Does he even know you have these, Nate?" I asked. "I mean, if he is such a stickler for details, he has to realize they're gone."

"Funny you should ask, because I don't think he suspected anything for a few days. I left the empty folder in there. It wasn't until yesterday that he accused me of going into his office. Didn't utter a word about the safe, but he stormed into my room and asked if I'd been in there. He was beyond livid."

"What'd you tell him?"

"I told him I didn't have any desire to go into his office, and I knew it was off limits. It was a lie, but it's not like he's been exactly honest with me through the years. Then he got in my face. He was off the rails crazy. He pushed me; I pushed him, and that's when we fought it out. Vicky had to pull us apart, but not before I started windmilling on him."

"Atta boy," Lance said.

"He can't hit me like he used to. Now that I'm as big as he is. Next time he comes at me, I'll kill him."

"Did you ever tell him about the pictures?"

"Nope."

"You going to give these to the cops?"

"I was going to. But then my dad got arrested. Now I don't need to."

"I'm just saying if the cops or the FBI saw these —"

"I'm not going to turn these in now, Matt." He turned back towards the fire again. "Not yet. Not until I figure this out."

"Figure what out?" Hop asked.

"Trust me, guys," Nate said, looking at me. "I will turn them in when the time is right."

"Hey, it's your call, man. You know the situation better than any of us."

Nate pulled both hands down the sides of his face and closed his eyes for a second. When he opened them, he was staring right at me. "The truth, Matt, is those aren't all the pictures I found."

He reached into his back pocket and pulled out another, older Polaroid. It was yellowed around the edges, and the thick border on the bottom had cracked.

"There's one more."

He looked at it for a brief second and handed it to me. I squinted up at the image. It had darkened over time, and the details were not as clear as the others, but it was not so bad that it had blacked all the way out. I could make out a woman sitting in a car. Her head was leaned over across a seat belt and resting on the steering wheel. Broken glass was all around her and a trickle of dark blood oozed out of her mouth.

"This," Nate said, but stopped when his voice turned husky. He cleared his throat and resumed. "This is why I was running Friday night."

I looked at the picture again, and while it was clearly disturbing, it was not nearly as bad as the others.

"Why this one, Nate?"

"Because this is a picture of my mother."

CHAPTER 30

The Charlotte Gutherz who surprised Kathryn by arriving unannounced at the FBI office the Monday after the raid on Cedar Lake Internists was different from the person Kat and Ethan had interviewed just a few weeks before. When this new and improved version of Charlotte showed up, she exchanged pleasantries with the clerk, took her seat, and waited without any hint of anger or arrogance. Kat studied her and noticed Charlotte did not read any magazines, did not fidget, and only occasionally moved her hands. Judging by her body language alone, she seemed a bit tense, if not concerned.

Kat had her own reasons to be tense, concerned, and if she allowed herself to take it one more step – angry. When her team showed up at the raid, they were met with a television crew – which made Kat so mad she couldn't see straight. For the life of her, she couldn't figure out who tipped them off. It was a harbinger of what would become a very bad afternoon. The team came on too strong, and the waiting room turned into chaos in a matter of minutes once the marshals, guns visibly holstered at the hip, flashed badges and demanded access to Dr. Mayes and his records. Of course, the news crew ate it up, using interviews with crying patients and staff as fodder for their evening lead-ins.

All of that would have been palatable if, at the end of the day, Kat had scored. When they entered, however, they found Dr. Mayes leaning back in his chair with his feet on his desk. He was wearing his white coat reading a *Sailing* magazine, and when they cuffed him, he handed his lawyer's card to the marshal taking point. He didn't look the least bit surprised or concerned, and three hours later, Kathryn found out why. Her team did not find a single record that matched up with any of the Cape Island submissions Ethan had pulled.

Still, Kat got the impression all was not right with the doctor. He was moving slowly and had a bandage covering a cut under his eye and what looked like a bruise under his cheekbone. When she asked him about it, he said he had taken a fall during his morning walk. He was lying.

Kat brought over two cups of coffee. It was Kat's third one of the day, and she had not ruled out the possibility of another. She was exhausted, didn't even take the time to put on makeup, and drew on the influx of caffeine and her simmering anger to power the conversation. "Last time you were here," Kat said, sitting down, "we had a long discussion, and you told me Dr. Bradford Mayes was the one."

"I know. I did."

"And I told you I would help you if you helped me."

"You did. I'm sorry." She wasn't crying, and she wasn't mad. Very direct, though. "I don't know what happened."

"You don't know what happened? I'll tell you what happened. I busted up in that medical clinic with three federal marshals on one side and two FBI agents on the other, and I didn't find a damn thing." Kat snorted. "Not a damn thing."

"Look, I didn't make any of that up. I have known Ford – er, Dr. Mayes, for a long time and, uh, I –"

"Ford?" Suddenly the fatigue dropped off. "Did you call him 'Ford?'"

"Well," she said, "he and I used to be close." Now she took a sip of her coffee. "Real close."

Of course, Kathryn thought. Dr. Bradford – "Ford" (she hated that pretentious sounding name already) – Mayes would go for someone like Charlotte. Young, fit, and beautiful, she was the perfect trophy to feed his insatiable ego.

"Remind me what you do now?"

"I still work in sales, but not for a compounding group anymore. When Cat Island shut down, I got on with a pharmaceutical company - Samantof - mainly detailing statins to internists and heart doctors for their patients with high cholesterol." She paused for a second. "Different than what I was doing for before – for Tom Chrestman."

"I would hope so. You like your job?"

"I do."

"I assume you want to keep it?"

"Look, Agent Cooper, let's don't play the 'gotcha' game again, okay?" Charlotte said. "No threats. I came here voluntarily. Cut the crap."

"You want to cut the crap? Then let's cut the crap. When was the last time you spoke with Dr. Mayes?"

"Probably a year ago."

"Are you his mistress?"

"Was."

"What does that mean?"

"Just as I said it. I was his mistress. We were involved in an affair for almost two years."

"Was he married at the time? To his current wife, I mean?"

"Ugh," Charlotte said. "Yes. What a bitch."

"What stopped it? Why did it end between you two?"

"He ended it cold turkey when things started getting hot up in Hattiesburg last year."

"Hot?"

"You know what I mean. You and your people started arresting pharmacists, nurses, and doctors right and left. Ford got scared. He wanted to cut anything that could remotely tie him to the investigation. I was –" Charlotte looked a little ashen but continued. "I was the first to go."

Kat tapped her pen on the table. Charlotte had essentially just admitted that she was at the least a potential co-conspirator to it all. This could be big, but Kat needed more, so she tried a different tack and dialed it down. Good cop time.

"Charlotte, if you want my help, you have to tell me everything. We're beyond holding back at this point."

Charlotte nodded and bowed her head. "Agent Cooper, you asked me to be honest with you, and I said I would."

"Yes."

"I will do it under one condition."

Kathryn wanted to tell her that she was in no position to be stating any conditions, but she let it ride. "What's that?"

"That you likewise be totally honest with me. Fair enough?"

"Fair enough."

"Okay," Charlotte said, "did you interview Ford? You know, after you arrested him?"

"Briefly."

"Did he say anything about me?"

"Nope."

"Did you say anything about me to him?"

"No. I didn't."

"So he doesn't know I was the one who gave up his name?"

"I don't think so. I certainly didn't tell him." Charlotte closed her eyes, and Kat could see some of the tension melt away. "Why?"

Charlotte stared past Kat, not saying a word. She cracked her neck and rubbed her hands together. "I thought when y'all picked him up, he would be in jail for a long time. Then I saw the news that he had been released, and I got a little nervous. That's why I came in here this morning."

"Nervous? Why?"

"Dr. Mayes is not a nice man, Agent Cooper. He's got a mean streak, and when things don't go his way, he is prone to lash out."

"Lash out? How?"

"He's rude. He's a jerk. I have seen him dress down his employees and publicly shame his son for no reason other than sport. He's a bully."

"What about physical violence? Has he ever gone down that road?"

Charlotte grunted. "I've heard stories."

"What type of stories?"

"Well, for one, his history of domestic abuse is well known in certain circles. As much as I dislike Vicky, I have seen her after a brutal weekend. Black eyes. Busted lips. Jumpy."

"What about his first wife?"

"She died years ago. Freak car accident. Skidded off the road taking their son to preschool one morning. She was killed instantly, but the boy survived."

"You said your reason for being here is out of concern that Dr. Mayes may actually seek you out and harm you, right? If he knew you had given us his name?"

"Yes and no. Do I think he would come after me? Yes. Do I think he would do it himself? No. Considering you presently have him under investigation, I don't think he will step out of line."

"Then why did you come in if you're not worried about him?"

"Who said I limited it to him?"

"Well who else, then?"

"He has a man who will do it for him."

"A man?"

"Yes. Someone to do the dirty work for him."

"Who?"

"His smurf," she said with a head tilt, "a junkie he refers to as 'Fast Eddie.'"

CHAPTER 31

Most of the bank transactions Fast Eddie made for Doc Mayes back in the heyday of the Hattiesburg fix – and there were plenty of them – were done via after-hours deposit. The reasons were twofold; first, no one ever saw his face; and second, doing smurf work at night did not interfere with his day job. He did have one bank, however, where he actually went inside on occasion – and he risked exposure at that bank for the sole purpose of skimming. Sure, Doc Mayes paid him a cut out of every transaction, but the son of a bitch could also be a stingy bastard. Not once during their whole relationship did he throw Fast Eddie some extra change or even offer a kind word for a job well done. Fast Eddie's day job did not support his preferred lifestyle, so he used the Bank of Wiggins when he needed to supplement his base, as it were.

The exposure was actually pretty minimal. He grew up with Rachel Beckett, the bank manager, and knew her family. She was the first one from her bloodline to hold a job that was actually inside a building. She was a single mom with a penchant for alcohol, cocaine, and sex – not necessarily in that order, and Fast Eddie did his best to deliver on all three. He also provided her with a stipend large enough to cover groceries for that rotten ankle-biter of hers. In exchange, she looked the other way and let him move money in and out of the bank as he pleased. She also alerted him if she noticed any unusual activity regarding the account, which is why he rolled up to her office first thing Monday morning.

The meeting started, like they always did, with him discreetly passing her an envelope and a small plastic vial. Her lack of caution bothered him, and he cringed as she tore the envelope open on her desk in plain sight. She slid the vial in her bra, presumably for a quick snort at her next bathroom break.

"Welcome back to Wiggins," she said. "I hope you will make this one an overnight. It's been awhile. It gets lonely up here in Stone County."

He had no such intention. "No can do today, Rachel. Lots of irons in the fire."

She stuck her lip out in a pout. "Well, that's disappointing. I hope you don't make this a pattern. This bank account of yours isn't the only thing that needs servicing."

"Sweetie, you know there's nothing more I'd rather do right now than wiggle you out of those britches right here in this office, but if I don't get back and take care of some things on the homestead, life could get ugly quick."

She studied him for a second. "Well, since you put it that way, I guess I'll have to take a rain check." She winked at him through hooker blue eye shadow and turned the monitor his way. "Now let's get down to business. I've got the account pulled up."

"Yep."

"See where it shows a current balance just north of $275,000?"

"That's the one. I am quite familiar with it."

"Maybe so, but probably not as familiar with it as you think. This time last week, it had a balance of $284,000 and change. Not anymore."

He leaned over and frowned. He certainly hadn't withdrawn any money, and he had never known Dr. Mayes to take any out – and he certainly wouldn't right now, anyway considering he was under surveillance. "Who signed the withdrawal slip?"

"Well that's why I called you. No one. This was a wire transfer."

"Wire transfer? To who? Where?"

Rachel typed something and pointed at her screen. "Went offshore to a bank in the Bahamas. Ring a bell?"

"Nope. Can you follow up? Get any more information?"

"I wish. Most people think only Swiss accounts keep things secret. Not true. Dominican Republic. Antigua. Nassau. Lots of Caribbean banks operate under the radar. We can't touch them."

He leaned over and looked at the screen. "All they transferred was $9,000? Why $9,000? To get around FinCEN?"

Fast Eddie was well aware of the federal reporting requirements – even Rachel couldn't bypass them. Any deposits or withdrawals in excess of $10,000 triggered the filing of a currency transaction report, or CTR, to FinCEN – the Financial Crimes Enforcement Network of the U.S. Department of the Treasury. Which meant bad news for folks like Doc Mayes. That's why they had smurfs making low-impact drops at banks all over the place. So long as they didn't exceed the magic number, the principals remained virtually unnoticed.

"No. We only have to do CTR reports with deposits or withdrawals of hard cash. Not wires."

"Really? What about I.D.?"

"Hmm. Well, if you had the account number, the routing number, the PIN, and could verify some personal information – you know, social security number and whatnot, we can do the transfer in a matter of minutes."

"Over the phone?"

"Yes. Again, we would verify, but yes."

"That quick?"

"Knock the balance down to zero if that's what you wanted."

"So why wire such a small amount?"

"No telling. Maybe she was testing it, you know, to make sure the money would go through."

Eddie leaned up in his chair. "*She?*"

"Yes. *She*. Female caller."

"Did she leave a name?"

"Uh, I'm sure she told me, but I didn't write it down. Didn't really need it, though, since –" His silence caught her off guard. "Did I miss something?"

Of course she missed something, but now wasn't the time to engage the stupid hack. He needed her on his side, at least for the time being. More importantly, he had to get back to Gulfport and fast.

"No. Thanks for the heads up. I got to go, though." He withdrew five thousand dollars on the way out – for his troubles – and headed back to Gulfport. But he wasn't going to his house or his office. He had another stop to make. He just hoped he could get there in time.

CHAPTER 32

Charlotte closed the bathroom door and exhaled a long, slow breath. She had been doing her best to tell her story in a manner that would not arouse suspicion, and as she looked in the mirror, she allowed a bit of a smile. Not only had she been able to frame the narrative like she had originally intended, but she had done it in a manner that seemed almost, well, easy.

Agent Cooper was clearly worn out and near the end of her rope, but even so, Charlotte was surprised by how quickly she bought the lie about the last time Charlotte and Ford spoke, not to mention the way she bit on nearly every affirmative nonverbal move Charlotte made. The wringing of the hands. The long pauses. Looking away before making a 'confession.' Every time Charlotte played an emotional card, Agent Cooper bought it hook, line, and sinker.

Which was a good thing. In fact, the interview – at least to this point – had gone way better than Charlotte had hoped it would. Sure, Charlotte thought she might be able to plant a few seeds and gain some intel, but she had no idea she would get as far as she did – which is probably why she got a little careless with her overtures. Had she said more than she had initially planned to say? Probably, but sometimes you have to improvise, and in this case, she felt like it moved the needle. At least Charlotte now knew Ford Mayes had not mentioned, implicated or discussed her in any way, shape, or form.

Charlotte would not extend that bastard the same courtesy.

* * *

She was surprised when Ford called her out of the blue. He was in an absolute panic and told her it was best she didn't know the details, then asked if she could meet at their old rendezvous point within the hour. The only thing he told her is that things were about to get hot again and he needed her to help him with something.

She had a glimmer of hope that his call meant the fire between them could be rekindled, and when he referenced Paul B. Johnson State Park, it further escalated her expectations. Paul B. was where the two used to go for some discreet after-hours action, and she convinced herself he did not indiscriminately choose that spot. When Charlotte, fresh as a spring morning, drove down the snaky roads through the pines to their favorite campsite, however, she found his wife, of all people, waiting for her. Ford was nowhere to be seen.

Vicky got out of the car and dropped two packages through the driver's side window of Charlotte's car. One was a bound stack of bills totaling twenty thousand dollars. The other was a locked briefcase.

"The money is yours. The bag is Ford's. Keep it locked and in a safe place until he calls on you again." Vicky leaned her head, roots showing and all, into the window and added one additional instruction. "And stay away from my husband."

Charlotte was stunned. Not only did Ford betray her by not showing, but he sent Vicky in his place. Who did he think he was – and did he really think through whether Charlotte would even consider taking instructions from Vicky? If he did, he was wrong. Dead wrong. The first thing Charlotte did when she got back was jimmy the lock open.

Initially, Charlotte didn't know what she was looking at, but as she read the names of the financial institutions on the documents, it all came back to her. Inside were ledgers containing records, deposit slips, and contact numbers linked to banks that Charlotte used to call on – and if the current balances were anywhere close to what they used to be, they held millions. She looked in the mirror and gave it some thought. Had Ford personally come out there and asked her to hide it until he could stick his head up again, Charlotte might have obliged. She had done many favors for him over the years, both personal and professional, and she had been more than willing to do his bidding.

But not this time.

One thing she learned from Birdy's ordeal – once the Feds had you in their grasp, they did not let up until they put you under the jail, and now that she had the ledgers, she hoped to expedite the process for dear old Ford. The smurf, on the other hand, might not be so easy, primarily because Kathryn had never met him, not even in passing, and she had no idea who he was. She hoped if she selectively dropped some facts to this FBI agent, though, there would be enough bread-crumbs for the feds to lock him up, too. She smiled. If both Ford *and* Fast Eddie were off the street, it would be smooth sailing ahead.

It was time to set the table. She put her most serious face back on, fixed her hair, and for good measure, adjusted her boobs so they rode a little higher. You never know, she thought as she opened the door to the hallway.

You just never know.

CHAPTER 33

"Fast Eddie, huh?" Kathryn asked. "His smurf?"

"Yep."

Something wasn't ringing right with the story, and before the break – for the first time that day – Kathryn got the impression Charlotte had veered into fictional territory. "So, you're telling me you were not the one running money for Dr. Mayes? I thought we were being honest, Charlotte. You seem to know a lot more about this operation than one would expect from a mere sideline observer."

"The reason I know a lot about 'this operation' is due in part to the fact that he told me. Remember, I was sleeping with him, and despite his usual discretion with matters associated with business, he engaged in a lot of pillow talk."

"So, let's talk about this 'Fast Eddie' fellow. Who is he? Do you know his last name?"

"No idea. I don't know if Eddie is even his real name. Probably not. Ford liked to put as many layers between him and his enterprise as possible, which is why I never laid eyes on him. That's how Ford referred to him, though."

"Did he work just in Hattiesburg?"

"No. All over the state, but mostly Jackson south."

"What makes you think he would be the one to do Dr. Mayes's dirty work?"

Charlotte sucked the air through her teeth and looked at Kathryn. This would be a good story to tell.

"I know because one night at a hotel, Ford took a call at about three a.m. He thought I was asleep, but I heard everything, although I could only pick up bits and pieces coming through the receiver."

"And?"

"He referred to the guy on the other line as 'Eddie.'"

"Okay."

"This Eddie fellow told Ford he was with the doctor who shorted him."

"Doctor who shorted him? Who? What does that mean?"

"Don't know either. Ford was very upset." That was partially true. Charlotte never found out who the doctor was, but she knew exactly what was going on. The primary way Tom Chrestman grew his scam was to bring in more doctors to feed him with fraudulent prescriptions. Ford was his main point of contact for growing the pipeline, and the Doc expected a healthy cut from the revenue each doctor brought in – and he turned vicious if it was not delivered. The night she heard him on the phone, one of the doctors from a group out of Meridian had been holding out, and whenever Ford got the call, Fast Eddie already had this doctor in his car bound and gagged.

"Really? What did Dr. Mayes say?"

"He told him to take care of his hands."

"What?"

"He said to make sure his operating days were over."

"Did he do it?"

"I can't say for sure, but Ford got a call about fifteen minutes later that put him in a good mood." She left it at that. In fact, he did much more than break that surgeon's hands – he cut off two fingers and shattered his dominant wrist. There were more stories, but it was neither the time nor the place to share them.

"So you do know more than you told me at first. I really don't want to play the 'gotcha" game – as you describe it, but I really need you, right now, to come clean," Kathryn said. "It's time."

"Sure, but I think you're going to be disappointed. I realize now that the son of a bitch had been setting me up all along. I was recruiting doctors all right, but apparently not for the reasons I had been told."

Charlotte had rehearsed this bit before and was prepared. She knew she would have to tell enough to make her story credible, but if she danced the dance just right, she wouldn't have to spill all the beans. She told Agent Cooper that when she was first hired by Joe Birdsall, her job was just as she described it – to market compounding services to new physicians to try to get them to send legitimate prescriptions Birdy's way so he could grow his business. She was then told to look specifically for doctors whose practices were faltering.

"Why those particular doctors?" Kat asked.

"According to Birdy – that's what we called Joe – these doctors were more willing to try out compounding than traditional doctors. So I followed his orders." Truth was, when Birdy realized he could make exponentially more money running a scam on the government, her role expanded – and doctors who weren't making enough money to cover payroll, student loans, fund their entitled wives, and pay their exorbitant mortgages were more than willing to jump into the mire. The more doctors she enrolled, the more Birdy paid her.

She explained she never dealt directly with any of the payments to the doctors – with one exception. Dr. Mayes mandated a personal cash delivery at his house – pursuant to specific directions. As she understood it, at the beginning, Tom Chrestman drove to Hattiesburg and delivered it to Fast Eddie directly, but Dr. Mayes became paranoid, so he added Charlotte for another layer of separation, with the understanding was that she would never interact with Eddie personally. She then told Agent Cooper the cash was placed in a locked drop box built into the fence just inside Dr. Mayes's personal property – accessible on the inside only by a key. Charlotte was generally the one who dropped it off. When she did, she would call or page a number to let Ford know it was delivered. What she didn't tell Agent Cooper was that her call would actually signal the smurf to pick up the drop for deposit. In most cases.

"Then," Charlotte said, "it ended as quick as it started. Ford broke it off with me; he broke it off with Tom, and told us both to never contact him again. Just like that."

"How much money did you drop off for him?" Kathryn asked.

"I never really counted it, and it varied every day, depending on how much Tom got in. I would guess a light day would be five thousand; a regular would be ten to fifteen thousand. Sometimes more."

"Didn't you think that was a lot?"

"Wasn't my job to think."

"What about banks? Did you make any of those deposits?"

"No." A lie. She had personally made deposits at two banks – maybe three – when Fast Eddie wasn't available.

"How many drop-offs a week?"

"Again, it depends," Charlotte said. "Sometimes only one. Sometimes three or four."

Kathryn did the math and shook her head. "When did it stop?"

"About the time word got around that federal agents were interviewing doctors." That wasn't the entire truth, either. She actually made a few drops for him later – in Gulfport, while they were finishing up the renovations on the house he bought. He had a similar drop installed in the fence on his new property for that exact purpose.

"So after all you have done," Charlotte asked, "all of your investigating and interviewing, and even after the raid last weekend, you have no evidence to charge him?"

"Not enough to keep him in jail, no."

"It doesn't make sense," Charlotte said, "Ford was meticulous with his books. What about bank records? Deposit slips, ledgers, anything?" Of course Charlotte knew where the bank records were – safe and secure, thank you – but she still wanted to know what information the FBI had regarding any of those bank accounts, even if she was being a little sloppy by asking.

Agent Cooper's next move surprised her.

Kathryn pulled out a copy paper box and set it on the desk. "These are some things I found that I thought may be worth a second look."

"Where'd you get this stuff?" Charlotte again kept a poker face, but she pulled her hands off the table. Her palms had started to sweat, and she didn't want to leave a mark.

"Some of it at the clinic, some of it at the house. Again, I haven't had time to dig in too deep."

Charlotte pulled out a few files bound by a large rubber band and opened one up. "Why these?"

"I don't know. They were the only medical records at his house, so I figured we could look to see if he wrote any prescriptions for those patients and try to match them up."

Charlotte thumbed through them and set them aside. Nothing there; even if they were cross-referenced with transaction records, there would be no prescriptions documented. She found a Franklin day planner, but it had only a few entries, none of them suspicious. There were half a dozen VHS tapes and what appeared to be a stack of unpaid bills. All in all, she didn't see much that sparked her interest, and she breathed a bit. She picked up a plastic box holding several bottles of prescription medications, and she glanced at the labels. No controlled substances; some stomach drugs – mainly proton pump inhibitors – and prescription ibuprofen. When she sat it back in the big box, she noticed an eelskin checkbook cover in the corner and held it up.

"Oh, yeah," Kathryn said, "I forgot about that. The one and only rogue bank record. Got that out of his desk at his home. I think it's from a bank in Hattiesburg."

"Yep." Charlotte opened up the register.

"Not much there to put Dr. Mayes away on, is it? If memory serves me, there is twenty thousand dollars in that account. While I've never had anything close to that – ever – some would say it's small change for a doctor with a thriving medical practice, wouldn't you agree?"

Charlotte felt relief come over her body and relaxed in her chair. "You are right. Some would say that – if this account was for Nathaniel Bradford Mayes, M.D."

"It is."

"No, Agent Cooper, it is not." Charlotte slid the checkbook over to Kathryn.

She studied one of the checks. "But the name says-"

"The name says 'Nate Mayes.' This isn't Ford's account."

"Is his name not 'Nate Mayes.'?"

"I guess it could be if you shortened it, but it's not. Ford has never, to my knowledge, gone by the name 'Nate.'"

"Well, whose is it, then?"

"Nate," Charlotte said, leaning back and crossing her arms, "is his son."

CHAPTER 34

Fast Eddie parked on a cross street about ten houses down from Charlotte's; far enough away that he wouldn't be seen, but close enough to maintain a visual. He had ridden through the neighborhood twice, timing his intervals about fifteen minutes apart to see if he noticed any activity that could interfere with his plans. He didn't expect her to be there, but he couldn't take any chances, and he thought it best to do some additional surveillance before he made his move.

He had watched the raid unfold on a local TV news station like everyone. It was he, of course, who had called Dr. Mayes at home that Friday night with the heads-up, and when a reporter leaked that the feds came up empty-handed, he knew the Doc had actually taken his advice and gotten rid of the evidence. He also knew that the Doc's love for money would prompt him to secure the football – the briefcase containing the secret bank records – in good hands until he could access it again. It took Rachel informing him that a female had set up the wire transfer before he finally put the pieces together.

He squeezed the lump of cash folded in his front pocket. If he played his cards right and used a modicum of self-control, he could stretch $5,000 out over a month, if not longer, but it was getting more and more difficult to keep his hands off the merchandise. One gram of Peruvian Flake cost him $100 – more if he wanted it on the weekend – but it was *so* worth it. It was unadulterated, pure, and took him to places no other blow ever did or ever could. No way he could go back to the cheap stuff he passed on to Rachel – cut with baking soda, laxatives and who knows what else. If he lost his smurfing money altogether, he may have to go bottom shelf or even worse, crack, which had only recently made it to the Mississippi streets. Or he could just stop. His employer had announced earlier in the year that they would soon be implementing a random drug testing policy for its employees. He didn't know when or if his name would come up in that lottery, but if he did, his career was a goner, which meant he had to have a fall back. He hoped Charlotte would be sympathetic to his situation. If not, their first meeting would most certainly be her last.

She lived in a new subdivision consisting mainly of young professionals. Most of them would have long been out of the house and at work by the time he made his move. Sure, there might be a few yuppie stay-at-home housewives, but he was willing to bet none of them would be active neighborhood watchers, unless they were powerwalking, and even then, they wouldn't be paying much attention to anything but their pace, their distance and how their legs looked.

He picked up a *Sun Herald* at the gas station on the way up to see what the newshounds were saying about the weekend's activities. He saw they had finally moved away from sensationalism and were now delving into backgrounds. The reporter did a good job profiling Doc Mayes, and Fast Eddie wondered who he used as a source. There were pictures of the Doc as a kid, pictures from high school wearing a letterman's jacket, and a more recent headshot from when the Doc served on the hospital board up at Forrest General. The story detailed how a young child from Brookhaven, Mississippi – the son of an alcoholic mother and a deadbeat dad – worked himself out of a life of squalor to graduating first in his class at Vanderbilt University School of Medicine.

He did the crossword, the Jumble, the word find and looked to see what new movies had come out. Nothing he wanted to see. At five after eleven, he stepped out and started to stretch. He was wearing the newest jogging clothes and would have fit in just right with the rest of the exercise freaks who seemed to be taking over the city's streets and sidewalks – assuming those overachievers had a pair of gloves and a gun strapped under their shirt. He made three passes around her block to try to get a feel for the best way to make his approach. Fortunately, her house backed into an undeveloped wooded area that bordered a new road on the other side where they were expanding the neighborhood to add another row of look alikes. At the end of his third loop, he took a detour down the construction road and cut through the woods. Five minutes later he was inside.

It wasn't his first time breaking and entering, and he went about his task methodically, like he had been trained. It was a Kwikset, basic and off the rack, and it took less than a minute to pick. Gloves on, no prints, nothing left behind. It was a fairly simple tract house layout. Front door opened into a den/seating area that connected to a kitchen in the back that overlooked a porch and the woods he just traipsed through. A hall that ran to the right of the kitchen led to what appeared to be four rooms and a storage closet – a converted office/bedroom, a bathroom, a guest bedroom and the master with its own small bath.

He started with the den and went through every nook, every drawer, every possible cubby or shelf where she could have placed, stored, or tried to hide the football. If he could get the ledgers from Charlotte's house, he could be gone and have his pockets full before she even realized he had trespassed.

When he struck out in the den, he continued zigzagging through the house, starting with the kitchen then down the hall and through the bedrooms. When he finished one room, he would return to the den window, surveying what was going on outside to see if anyone had grown suspicious or if anyone had pulled up, then go back to where he left off. The streets were predictably quiet, and there were no interruptions to throw off his rhythm.

He came up empty-handed after searching the kitchen and thought he would finally strike pay dirt when he got to her office. As he dug, though, all he found was the typical paraphernalia one would expect from a legitimate pharmaceutical sales rep. Boxes of samples, tear pads, posters for doctor's offices, and more pens than anyone should ever need were stacked and sorted on the floor and on her desk. Drawers contained receipts, notebooks, detail pieces, and a few opened packets of gum. He thought he found a ledger under a PDR, but it was only call notes and a work binder.

Eventually, panic set in when it dawned on him that it was not in the house. When he closed the last drawer, his head started to pound and he broke out in a cold sweat. He dabbed his brow with the hem of his t-shirt and went to the kitchen to get a cup of water. He couldn't figure out why he was starting to feel so bad until he looked at his watch. He had been searching without stopping since he got there, and in his quest to make sure the house remained pristine, he lost track of time. He carried the water to the coffee table and got on one knee. He pulled a small packet out of his shorts and fumbled its contents on to the table. He leaned over and snorted the coke until there was none left, bypassing the usual step of cutting and lining it up. He let it take effect and then dabbed and licked the remaining residue until the surface of the coffee table gave no appearance that it, too, had been compromised, then he wiped it down with a cotton ball and some rubbing alcohol he found in the bathroom.

It was only a matter of minutes before the headache disappeared, the shakes abated, and he could once again think clearly. He checked his nose for blood, and his fingers came away clean. He looked around, and it dawned on him that while he had made fun of the neighborhood earlier, he actually liked Charlotte's little abode. It smelled like it had never been dirty -- not quite like a brand new house, but more like his grandmother's house when they would sleep with the windows open in April. He had debated about when he should leave, but the longer he sat, the more comfortable he felt. He went to the kitchen to see what Charlotte kept in the fridge, hoping he would find something more substantive than a salad. He was happy to see real food and grabbed some turkey and cheese to make a sandwich, which he brought back into the den, along with a half-eaten bag of Lay's potato chips and a Barq's root beer.

Along with the munchies, a hit of coke usually brought on a wave of confidence coupled with a side dose of nostalgia, and as he sat there chomping down, he realized he really could get used to living like this. He imagined coming home one day to a house with an actual yard and a guest room. He would have a wife greet him at the front door and a kid or two to tuck in and tell stories before bedtime. He would definitely have a dog and a fence; maybe he'd even start going to church again. In that moment he didn't care any more about the game, the fix, or the score. He could ditch it all, and he would be just fine.

Except he couldn't ditch it all. Before any of his grand plans could even begin to take effect, he needed to find a way to kick his habit. He needed to be able to get out of town on a whim if need be. He needed to have the means to start over. To do any of this, he needed money.

What then, to do with Charlotte? Maybe he had been wrong. Maybe when Doc kicked her out of the sack, he broke all ties with her. Perhaps she wasn't hoarding or hiding the ledgers. Perhaps if he got her face-to-face, he could get a better handle on what she knew and what she didn't know. The prospect of meeting her had its own set of problems, however, not the least of which was what he should do with her after they talked, to put it mildly.

He checked his watch and figured he had one hour – maybe two, tops, before she got home. As he started to put together the beginnings of a plan, he popped in a mixtape he found next to the stereo. He looked around the house as the opening guitar chords electrified the room and asked himself the same question posed by the Clash, recognizing that they expressed it in a much cooler way than he ever could.

Should he stay or should he go?

CHAPTER 35

As Charlotte drove home, she couldn't help but congratulate herself on a job well done. Even when it looked like it might get dicey when Agent Cooper pulled that checkbook out, she maintained her composure; in fact, she couldn't think of one instance where she stumbled. To the contrary, she had checked nearly every box on her list.

She did wonder, however, why the account on the checkbook had Ford's son's name on it and not his. She would look at the rest of the accounts later to see if they were set up that way. Of course, it didn't matter if they were. She was about to drain each and every one of them to zero and move the money where no one would find it – or find her, for that matter. He had made it too easy. It was nice of him to keep all of the account information in one spot – including the passwords. An uncharacteristic move for Ford, but he had probably grown too confident, if not cocky, that it would never see the light of day.

Charlotte knew it was the password because that fine lady at the bank in Wiggins with the three-pack-a-day voice processed Charlotte's little telephonic experiment without so much as a single question. Money transferred – no problem. Now that she knew it would work, all Charlotte had to do was move the full balance from all the accounts. Then she would pack up and get out of the country before anyone knew what had happened.

First things first. She needed a drink. When she got inside, she grabbed a bottle of Cabernet given to her by a horny young cardiologist one night after a company-sponsored dinner. The wine went down smooth, and when she started to wonder how much it cost, she stopped herself and smiled when she realized she would soon no longer have to consider those types of questions. On her way to her bedroom she turned on her stereo and was surprised to hear a tape playing. She didn't recall putting one in, but since it was provided by one of her other M.D. suitors after a very pleasurable overnight visit, she left it in.

She had hidden the briefcase in a storage unit off Pass Road that she used to share with another Samantof sales rep named Christy Warren. At one time, all the sales reps kept their boxes of samples and promotional items in storage lockers, but company policy changed, and all materials were now supposed to be kept at home. Christy had it paid for it through the end of the year, and when her husband got transferred to Texas, Charlotte asked if she could use it until the lease ran out – mainly to store a couch and some odds and ends she was trying to sell. Christy didn't care, and Charlotte had used it for the very purpose she stated. Up until that point.

She set the wine next to her bed, and then changed into some pajama pants and a t-shirt before sprawling out on the mattress. She was going to miss this little house. Of course, she was sure she would get over it after she spent a few nights in her new casita in Barcelona. We all have crosses to bear, she thought as she sat up to stretch. She reached over to get another sip, but her hand never made it to the glass.

A shadow from behind the door moved, and in her haste to get away, she kicked the nightstand, splattering wine all over her carpet.

He was on her before she could even scream.

CHAPTER 36

The St. John High School Class of 1980 will forever go down as the wildest, most out-of-control group of students to ever grace the corridors of those hallowed halls. I blame my twin brothers Chuck and Will and their compadres for a lot of the shadowing we got from the teachers when I did finally make it to the big house a few years later. Word is their class started out their spirit week by setting three pigs loose in the halls – numbering them one, two, and four to make things interesting. Then they took several classroom doors off their hinges and hid them in different parts of the city with ransom notes written on chalkboards providing clues to their whereabouts. They stopped up all the toilets, put Pez dispensers in the tampon machines and spliced a second line into the intercom system, then ran the Bee Gees on a loop for two hours before anyone could figure out how to stop them. It was bad enough they were playing disco, but to add insult to injury, they dubbed "Night Fever" to say "Nice Beaver." Over and over. The night before the pep rally they snuck into our opponents' school – unfortunately named the Trojans – and put rubbers on all the lockers.

After that experience, the junta issued a set of retaliatory rules and oppressive guidelines designed to avoid anything close to a repeat. By the time I rolled in as a seventh grader, they had all but abolished the tradition of spirit week. No more dressing up, no more floats, and no more themed days – unless you counted Spirit Day, which was lame -- a mediocre event, at best, where everyone wore blue and white and attended a tired pep rally that played like a North Korean campaign propaganda film.

Our class went along to the extent we had to, but we were not without means of our own to make the days more bearable. Fish Feeders was one example. The secret make-out corner behind the library trailer was another. The ability to pilfer as many free French fries when Mr. Klein was working the cafeteria was well known. Perhaps the greatest asset we had was our cohesion. We were as tight as seventy-four teenagers could be, and we lived by that bond. No ratting each other out, no infighting, no stealing, and most importantly, if we needed to come together to accomplish an objective, we did. Which was why the Sunday after Fish Feeders, Mark, Hop, Emily, Ben, Antonio, and Sammy showed up at my house for what turned out to be an all-day work session. The school might not have sanctioned any official homecoming events, but they never said we couldn't have any unofficial events, and if the school wasn't going to do its job, we would.

The plan was to start the week off with a parade – and as long as we arrived on time and stayed within the dress code, there wasn't a whole lot they could do. If they wanted "Hooray for Hollywood," then by golly, we were going to give it to them. We broke the class into groups of eight to ten and assigned them a movie with each group agreeing to do their part to give it everything they had.

We drew *Ghostbusters*, and my buddies did not disappoint. When we rolled in to the designated marshaling area near the Winn-Dixie parking lot on Monday, the Milk Wagon looked as close to Ecto-1 as an old tricked out Suburban could. It had everything the original had and more. Two scuba tanks, the housing of a window air conditioner, a radar bulb, part of a bullhorn, and a cardboard carpet roll wrapped in aluminum foil that looked like a rocket tube. I didn't even ask where Sammy got the siren and light bar, but it was perfect. Emily – the artist – put the icing on the cake when she hand painted a near-perfect logo on poster board that we taped to the sides.

Me, Mark, Sammy, and Antonio went as Venkman, Ray, Spengler, and Winston, respectively. Our suits were old painter coveralls, and our guns were made out of converted backpacks and old vacuum hoses and attachments. Hop, of course, went as Louis – typecast to the bone – and Emily about knocked me on the floor when she stepped out as Dana. Sigourney Weaver herself would have been jealous. Travis showed up in a suit and said he was Ray Parker, Jr. The rest of the parking lot was a sight to behold. From *The Empire Strikes Back* to *Pretty in Pink* and everything in between, we had it all. The Chief was going to be so surprised.

It came time to organize the cars, and Emily and some of the other girls, clipboards in hand, started lining them up one by one. Right before we got the signal to go, we heard the screeching of tires, and Ferris appeared from behind the grocery store going at least forty, if not more. Nate wheeled it our way, and when he pulled up next to me and rolled down his window, I couldn't believe my eyes.

Nate's face was green all over and he was wearing what looked to be a latex bald cap – also green, but not quite the same shade. Very much not Nate. He sported a grin so wide it looked like all his teeth were showing.

"I didn't miss anything did I?" He looked at the Milk Wagon and whistled. "Dang, that looks good."

"No you didn't miss anything. But what – who are you supposed to be?"

"Hold on. Y'all got room in there for me?"

"Sure." He pulled over and parked, and when he opened his door, we fell out laughing. Nate was wearing green pants and a green shirt. He reached in the bed and grabbed a green bean bag chair that had all the stuffing out of it. He put it on and poked his head and arms through the holes he had cut and walked over our way, still smiling like he had won a prize.

"What in the world?" Antonio asked, shaking his head.

Mark called it first. "Slimer!"

Nate had nailed it. His homemade Slimer costume was better than any of the others by far. Whether it would survive dress code scrutiny was a different story, but at that moment, he was king of the world.

When everyone started chanting "Slim-er! Slim-er! Slim-er!" Nate started hopping around and dancing – not just around the Milk Wagon, but up and down the line. He was whooping and hollering and high-fiving everyone he could, yelling "Who you gonna call!" each time he slapped a hand.

I was watching a changed man. This was not the same person who showed up in the St. John parking lot that early August morning not knowing a soul. Heck, it wasn't even the same person who went to the movies with us just a few weeks before. By the time he made his way back to the Milk Wagon, Nate had changed his mantra and was now hanging out of the window, hollering "I ain't 'fraid of no ghost!" to everyone we passed on the road. It was a phrase I thought quite fitting.

"You ready?" I asked.

He scratched his bald cap then leaned over and yelled out the window, "I ain't 'fraid of no ghost!" one more time at a car that pulled up next to us and honked. After they passed, he slipped back in his seat and leaned up between me and Hop.

"Do what, now?"

"You ready to roll?"

"You better believe it," he said with a grin, then leaned over to turn up the radio. "Money for Nothing" was playing. "I'm ready for anything."

"Anything?" I asked.

"Anything."

I believed him.

CHAPTER 37

For a bachelor pad, it was quite nice. In fact, it was so well done, Kat would have been happy living there herself. It had been a small hardware store back when downtown Gulfport used to have small hardware stores downtown. Rick bought it at a foreclosure sale when he transferred from Jackson and fixed it up himself, one weekend at a time. He moved in when it was partially livable and slept on the floor until he finished. Now the upstairs had exposed brick on two walls, along with a bedroom, bath, seating area, and balcony. Downstairs had brick on three walls that pulled the open kitchen and living area together perfectly. He hadn't even been in a year, and it still smelled new on the inside.

The funny thing was that Kathryn had never noticed the place, even though she drove by it every day. Now each little detail stood out like a freshly discovered treasure, and she wondered how he was able to afford it. She knew how much cops made, and even with Rick's salary, it seemed like a lot. The New Orleans door with the aged bronze accents. The gaslight out front. Rick even went so far as to preserve one of the old signs that had been painted onto the exterior brick, and if Kat looked closely enough, she could see the faint outline of a Morgan's Hardware logo from two generations ago.

Of course, Kathryn also had ample time to inspect the finer details of the inside – especially the original tongue and groove cypress that ran the whole length of the upstairs ceiling. She had slept there three times since their first date at the gallery, and each was better than the last. Initially, it was a bit awkward, and she felt self-conscious taking off her clothes. She hadn't done that in the presence of anyone other than her doctor in years, but she had no need to worry. Rick was so patient and complimentary, he put her at ease. Now Kathryn could barely contain herself as she waited for him to wake up so she could send him off to work properly.

Kathryn, for once, was taking a day away from the office – the first scheduled time off for her in over a year. It had been a hell of a week, and even though she still had a lot to do, she needed a day to recharge. With Friday spilling into the weekend, it felt like the beginning of a three-day vacation. Between all the paperwork from the Mayes raid and working overtime to try and follow-up on her other leads, Kathryn was exhausted. She hadn't made a lot of additional inroads on the case – yet – but she had Agent Davis and others running down the rabbit trails trying to find more information on this Eddie fellow.

She thought focusing on the gallery exhibit could help clear out some of the work cobwebs, so she had Marty Deen's dad drop his sketchpad off at the office, and she brought it to Rick's. She planned to get a cup of coffee and go through it out on the balcony. She slid over to the edge of the mattress as quietly as she could and reached for her bag, but she wasn't quiet enough.

"You up already?" Rick Papania rolled over and halfway opened an eye. "I thought you were going to sleep in."

"I was," she said, "but even though I'm off today, it's still hard for me to sleep past six. Plus, once I woke up, my mind started racing, and, well, you know how that is. So I thought I could sneak out and . . ."

"Come here."

"Hold on." Mornings in the real world were never like mornings in the movies. Kathryn slid out of bed to go to the bathroom. Not only did she need to tinkle, but she wanted to brush her teeth. She liked the way Rick had made a spot on the counter for her toothbrush and cleaned out one of the cabinet drawers for her girly things. As she brushed, he walked up behind her and put his arms around her waist and then reached around to cup her breasts, his fingers finding her nipples. He was wearing a pair of boxer shorts, and all she had on was one of his t-shirts.

"Good morning, sunshine." He started in on her neck, but she stopped him.

"Your turn." She handed him his toothbrush and he smiled.

"Real cool, Kat."

"I'll make it up to you," she said, then threw the shirt off and crawled under the covers. The cool sheets felt wonderful, and she pulled them up to her chin. She listened to him as he freshened up and giggled when she heard him humming Marvin Gaye. She rolled over to watch him and wondered where he had been all her life.

He was just toweling off his face when his radio popped. The sudden burst of static made Kathryn jump.

"Dispatch to 304, Over." 304 was Rick's badge number.

He looked at her and winked. "Don't go anywhere. This will only take a second." He picked up the radio. "This is 304, over."

"Chief, can you call Johnny at the station? Looks like we have a 187 that you may want to check out."

Kathryn sat up. A 187 was a homicide.

"Will do."

Kathryn knew her chance at a morning interlude was over when Rick picked up his interview pad along with a fresh t-shirt and underwear and started downstairs. He looked over at her as he passed the bed and mouthed, "I'm sorry."

"Go," she said, and lay back down on the pillow. She tried to listen, but the sun coming through the window distracted her, so she slipped on some warm-up pants and one of Rick's flannel shirts and sat out on the balcony to watch the morning come to life. Not a whole lot of people were out, other than those coming in to work early. She couldn't quite see Triplett-Day from her vantage point, but she saw cars parked around it, so she knew they had a fresh pot of coffee on and sausage biscuits baking, if not already out. She would have been content to sit out on the ledge all morning, but she didn't have any coffee herself, so she headed back inside to brew some. When she opened the door, Rick was standing there. His pants were on, and he was buttoning up his shirt. The look on his face told her he meant business.

"Was it a homicide?"

"Looks that way. Female. Strangled, possible sexual assault."

"Suspects?"

"Kathryn —"

"Any I.D. on her?"

"Yes. They were able to identify her. They found her at her house."

"Do we know her?"

"You do."

Kathryn felt that sinking feeling in her gut. No way. "Don't tell me it was Charlotte."

"Yeah.It was Charlotte." He held his pad up and read it aloud. "Charlotte G-u-t-h-e-r-z. How do you say that?" She recited the correct pronunciation and plopped down on the bed. Charlotte had come up in previous discussions with Rick, but Kathryn had never mentioned her last name.

"According to Johnny, she's been dead probably three days."

Kathryn did the math in her head and then started putting her clothes on. That put the murder shortly after her last interview. She looked at her bag as she slid her watch on her wrist.

Marty's sketches would have to wait.

CHAPTER 38

omehow Mark had convinced the homecoming committee to let his band play one set during the dance. Well, maybe not a complete set. They agreed to let them play four songs while the DJ took a break after the first hour. The dance was officially scheduled to run from eight until midnight, but the reality was, no one usually showed up until around nine-thirty anyway, so the powers that be figured no harm done in case the band crashed and burned.

But this was no ordinary homecoming, and our class was no ordinary class, so when Wombat Revolution cranked up the amps at nine o'clock sharp, they had seventy or so of their closest friends crowded around the stage. Mark was no Michael Hutchence, but I'll give him credit. For their first outing, they weren't too bad. Mark played drums and sang backup; Trey was the front man on keyboards; Travis played guitar, and a kid from tenth grade named Jaybird was on bass. I didn't know him, but he could work that axe like a madman.

The girls screamed and hollered like they had never seen live music before. Had it been a real concert, I would have hoped to see a bra or two tossed on the stage, but since we were at a Catholic school, the only lacy thing that caught air was a cheap wrist corsage that someone flung at Jaybird slingshot-style. It cleared him and landed right in front of the hole in Mark's bass drum.

In true Australian fashion they opened with "Don't Change," then brought it back stateside with "Day by Day." They then went back overseas – this time to Europe – for "Your Love," and then brought the house down when they went old school and played, of all things, "Good Lovin'." I didn't see that coming, but I was glad they did it because Emily grabbed me and proceeded to shake the paint off the walls.

By the time the band quit, the rest of the crowd had rolled in, and once the DJ got set up, we danced the night away – well most of it, anyway. For all of his goofy ways, Nate was actually pretty light on his feet and wasn't scared to hang it all out on the floor. Hop was wooden, but not in a cool I'm-doing-the-robot way. He looked more like someone's dad chaperoning a dance at a math convention. Mark was as smooth as you would expect from a budding musician, and I fell somewhere in the middle, although I doubted anyone was watching me, except when Emily happened to be my dance partner – which seemed to happen more and more as the night moved on. It surprised me as much as anyone else, and I was not disappointed with this new development. Nate didn't appear to mind, and Chrissy pretty much disappeared anyway once we got inside, so who was I to argue?

The second surprise of the night was when Lance showed up on the arm of Elizabeth Hyde, a senior. We weren't aware that they even knew each other, but Lance told us Fish Feeders opened a lot of doors, among other things, for him. He was the only one from West Harrison to make the cut. To say his dance style was unorthodox would be an understatement, but he sure looked like he was having fun. We all were.

It helped that we made frequent trips out to the parking lot where we stealthed over to the Milk Wagon for some libations. All cars were subject to inspection by the Gestapo, but we weren't too worried because the Trapper kept everything hidden away and out of sight. We had already been out there twice, but the clock had struck eleven, which was our last predetermined time to meet. Besides, we had heard the parking lot patrols slacked off the closer it got to midnight. We walked out separately so as not to arouse any suspicion, and by the time I got there, the old fireside crew was already passing around a bottle.

"Frazier! Thought you'd bailed on us for this one."

"Nope. Wouldn't miss it." I checked out the booze. "Who brought Mad Dog? That's disgusting."

"Need you ask?" Lance said and turned it up like it was Gatorade. "I keep at least two of these on hand in case of emergencies. Just wish

I hadn't run out of Orange Jubilee." He handed it to me. "This purple stuff's called Red Grape Wine."

It may have been purple, but that's where any similarities ended. A whiff of it made my mouth water and my jaw tense up like I had just eaten a lemon. To call it "Red Grape Wine" was an insult to grapes and wine everywhere.

"Nope. I'll pass." I reached into the Milk Wagon and grabbed the Captain Morgan and mixed it in with my Coke.

"This is better." I licked my lips and raised my cup. "Here's to homecoming, boys."

"To chicks." Mark said.

"To, uh, nights like tonight," Hop said, which was pretty good for him, although he didn't have a glass to raise. He never drank when he was out with Kristin, which made him the default DD.

"I'll second all of those," Nate said. "But I want to add something else."

We all moaned. Since his reawakening, there were few short conversations when Nate was involved, and we needed to get back inside.

"Chill out, guys. I promise this won't take long. What can I say – I like giving toasts, okay?"

"Hurry up already."

"Shut up, Hop. I just want to let y'all know how much I appreciate you being there for me these past months, you know, with my dad and everything." His eye had faded from purple to yellowish brown, and the cut on his lip had almost healed. He reached up to pick at the scab, and two of his fingers were still taped together. "I didn't have friends like this up in Hattiesburg, you know? Hell, I've never had friends like this – anywhere. I promise you I won't forget it."

Mark mercifully intervened before Nate got too weird.

"Well you're stuck with us Nate, for better or worse. Here 'til the end. So, cheers to that." Nate started to say something else, but by then, we had all raised our glasses and commenced to drinking, so he followed suit. I almost spit mine out watching Lance shiver as the Mad Dog made its way down the hatch.

The clicking of heels on asphalt made us all freeze.

"Bust-ed," Hop mumbled. "Y'all hide the evidence. Hurry." We all turned into Benny Hill as we scrambled to put away the bottles.

A voice called out from around the corner.

"Guys?"

I looked up at Mark. He smiled and stopped the fire drill.

"Hello?"

False alarm. It was Emily. She stepped from around the corner still moving fast and doing the loud whisper voice.

"Where have y'all been? People are starting to wonder." She stopped and put her hands on her hip. "Oh, geez, Lance. Mad Dog? Really?"

He straightened up and tried to set the bottle on the top of the Milk Wagon's tire.

"Just look at all of you. Half drunk, hair messed up, shirts un-tucked. Hop, where is your cummerbund?"

"Inside. I spilled ketchup on it."

"Okay, well, we have to go before y'all get caught, but hold on. I have to get a picture of this motley crew first."

"Rock on," Mark said, making the sign.

"That's not what I meant." She fumbled in her purse and pulled out her Canon Sure Shot. "Okay, get together." She looked over the top of the camera.

"Good, now tighten up. Say 'Eagles.'"

True to form, she snapped it before we could get the words out, and the flash temporarily blinded us all.

"Hey, can you get them to print a few extra copies?" I asked. "I want one."

"Me too," Mark said.

"I'll get one for everyone. Now let's go before you all get expelled."

"It's about that time anyway," Lance said. "I got Elizabeth all lath-ered up, and I don't want to keep her waiting any longer."

"Waiting? I thought I saw her leaving with Travis," Hop said.

"Travis?" Mark said. "No, I saw her in the corner mugging on Ben."

"Shut up," Lance said, tamping in a quick dip of Copenhagen, "both of you. She would never leave such a fine specimen as myself."

Hop mumbled something in return that I couldn't hear, and Lance faked like he was going to punch him then put him in a headlock. I stayed back to put everything away and locked up the Milk Wagon. Nate hung back, too, and we watched them turn the corner, Emily shepherding the rest of the guys like a kindergarten teacher on a field trip.

"Looks like you two finally found your groove."

"Yeah, I'm sorry, man. I know we said we'd wait until after home-coming. I guess the booze got the best of me. Don't worry, though. I'm done tonight. She's all yours."

"Nah, dude, I think you should keep it up. What did Hop say? If she needs to roam, don't let her stay home? Something like that?"

"Uh, yeah, something like that."

"Well there you go."

"But Nate, Emily's your date."

"Yeah, but she should have been yours. Wouldn't be right for me to stay in the game at this point."

"You sure?"

"Yep. Let me talk to her. It's all good. Trust me on this."

And there it was. Another surprise, this time from Nate. I didn't see how the night could get any better.

But it did.

CHAPTER 39

When I got back inside, Emily wasn't sitting at any of the tables, Wendy didn't see her in the bathroom, and I didn't see her out dancing, either. I knew I had only a few minutes left before the lights would come back on. I felt a terrible ache and wondered if she left by herself once Nate pulled the plug, but I shouldn't have worried. The DJ announced one more song, and as soon as "Take My Breath Away" began, Emily walked in the door, taking a page right out of *Sixteen Candles*. We met up in the middle of the dance floor next to Mark and Wendy, and a few seconds later, Hop tugged Kristin out there.

"I thought you had gone already. I was worried I missed you."

"No," she said, grabbing both my hands. "Just had to see Nate out and thank him for taking me tonight."

"Did he tell you —"

"Yeah."

"Was it weird?"

"No, not at all. In fact," she said, "I think he was relieved."

"I'm glad you're here," I said.

She leaned into me. "Me too. Finally."

I had never considered shoulders as something that could be pretty, but hers sure were, and whatever magic she had conjured up to turn her perfume into an invisible flowery halo was spectacular. We squeezed together as close as we could get and moved with the music. I grabbed one of her hands and pulled it up to my chest then moved my other hand down by the small of her back, and we glided some more. I looked up and saw Mark and Wendy likewise swaying to the music. Hop was hunched over Kristin like Quasimodo, and she looked as if she had suddenly been stricken with scoliosis.

As the third and final verse started, Emily looked up at me. This time, there were no hidden suggestions, there were no interruptions, and there were no more excuses. There was just the two of us, in the middle of the dance floor, at our high school homecoming, with our hearts cutting flips against our rib cages. She put one hand around my neck, leaned up, and pulled us together.

Everything about it was perfect. It was slow; it was sensual; it was soft, and it was just the perfect amount of wet. It was almost as good as the first time I saw *Star Wars*.

Almost.

CHAPTER 40

Soon after Kathryn unlocked the gallery doors, students started arriving. Some came alone; some came in groups of two or three, and as it got closer to start time, only about half of the students had shown up at all. Kathryn decided she would give it a few more minutes; it was a Saturday morning, after all. A little extra time could do everyone some good.

When Marty Deen walked in at eleven, Emily Miller – one of the few punctual St. John students – made a beeline towards him and gave him a big hug.

"Marty! So glad to see you!"

"Hey, Emmy. I didn't know you were going to be here. Did you come to hear me talk about my drawings?"

"Not only that, but I get to help with your big show. It's a thing I'm doing for school. It's going to be awesome. I'm so proud of you."

He was beaming. "Have you seen my bike lately? I added red, white, and blue grips on the handles."

"Really?"

"Yeah. Just like Evel Knievel's."

"Well, do you have time to show them to me? I bet they make you go faster."

"They do."

The remaining St. John students lumbered in slowly – each demonstrating varying degrees of recovery from the night before. Kathryn welcomed them and checked them off her list. When it looked like she had almost everyone, she asked that everyone take a seat. Marty had already pulled up a chair next to Kathryn, and he made sure everyone knew the other seat was for Emily.

Right before they started, the door chimed and in walked one more student. Kathryn did a double take when she saw him. He had been there at the prior meeting, but that's not what jogged her memory. The fact that he was there when they conducted the raid is what jerked her brain. She ran her finger down the list of names and stopped at the only one she hadn't checked.

Nate Mayes.

When she saw it, she rubbed her temple. Ford Mayes's son. The kid who just stood there watching when the marshals took things out of his house. How could she have not picked up this connection the first time? People called his name out, and he pointed back at them, mumbling a response to some, high-fiving others. He gave Emily a hug and shook hands with Sammy. When he made a joke Kathryn couldn't hear, Sammy buckled over laughing and said something back that made Emily snicker. Nate was working the room like a politician up for reelection.

She was glad he was being social. She needed him to be chatty. She needed him to be strong. While the kids were still getting settled, she stepped outside and grabbed her backpack with the file folders in it. Other than Doc Mayes himself, Nate was her last hope to solve the case.

He just didn't know it yet.

CHAPTER 41

ast Eddie liked to go to Jack's for lunch because the restaurant gave him the option to buy pizza by the slice. When he arrived just before noon, the large stainless-steel ovens were already full with pies at various stages of perfection, the oregano and spices bubbling up into the air through the cheese. He ordered the usual – all the way – which came loaded so deep with toppings he usually had to eat it with two hands to keep it from collapsing under its own weight. He added a side of garlic knots and a half-and-half iced tea. Sweet straight up was just too much for him. His total bill was under five dollars.

That was another reason he liked to eat there. It was cheap – a quality that had become increasingly significant to him as of late. He was already more than halfway through the five grand he had pulled out of the bank in Wiggins, and was considering going back for more. Of course, his fiscal situation would not have been so much of a concern had things not gone off the rails so bad with Charlotte.

He never set out to kill her – he really didn't. Partially because, to his knowledge, she had never deliberately crossed him, but even more importantly, this was the first time he was acting entirely on his own. All prior direction had come either directly or indirectly from Doc Mayes. This decision to confront Charlotte about the bank ledgers had been his and his alone, and if the Doc had gotten wind of it, he would no doubt have taken extreme measures to stop it.

At the beginning, it worked. Kind of. Yes, Charlotte surprised him by coming home earlier than he expected, and when he heard her pull in the driveway, he barely had time to grab his stuff and hide. Plus, she was a lot stronger than he estimated, so much so that when he tackled her, she fought back and gave him more than he wanted. The only thing he could do to stop her from kicking and bucking him was go for her throat. He held on until she was unconscious but still breathing. When she came to, she was absolutely terrified – and rightly so – and he tried to calm her down by telling her what he wanted. She told him she had a briefcase that contained the bank ledgers, but it was not at the house, and if he would let her go, she would take him to the storage unit where she kept it. He thought she was lying, and he hit her a few times to see if she would change the story, but she held fast.

Looking back, he probably should have at least investigated or gotten an address or name. The paranoia from all the cocaine made rational thought impossible, which led to his next poor decision – to try to take advantage of the fact that he was on top of her and she wasn't wearing much clothing.

When he pulled up her shirt, she snapped and began screaming and flailing like a woman possessed. She wrapped her legs around his torso and flipped him over, punching him and ultimately going for *his* throat. In all her frenzy, she got careless and lost her grip. He knocked her hands aside and locked back onto her neck. It was easy, even with her on top, considering how long his arms were. In a matter of seconds, she went from manic to sluggish to limp. When he finally stood up, panting, sweating and thirsty, Charlotte was dead. Which meant he didn't finish any of the tasks he began that day. No bank accounts, no sex, and most importantly, no more opportunity to get his hands on some cash.

This last bit of truth left Fast Eddie with no choice but to go back to the source. Doc Mayes would pay handsomely to access those ledgers once he realized his ability to retrieve them died with Charlotte. It mattered not that Eddie didn't know where they were either; that was beside the point. The old bait and switch was nothing new to him, and while the Doc was more savvy than most of his marks, with a bit of blackmail and some old-fashioned deception, Eddie was sure he could get the doc to believe that Eddie held the keys, if not the map, to the treasure.

The more he thought about it, the more Eddie looked forward to the opportunity to screw *him* for a change. After all, it had been nearly twenty years since Eddie committed his very first crime, and he had never forgiven Doc Mayes for the hand he played in it.

CHAPTER 42

On a good day, Kathryn could expect an hour to an hour and fifteen minutes of their attention – tops. Saturday mornings, even less. So after she ran through the schedule and discussed some assignments for what had to be done over the Christmas holidays, she let Marty speak. She thought he would be nervous, but once he got rolling, Marty couldn't stop. In fact, he wanted to go into detail on every single drawing of his that had been picked thus far for the exhibit. He didn't focus so much on his technique or the challenges of drawing things like feathers and eyes, but instead went off on tangents regarding the species themselves. Where they originated from, how often they appear in South Mississippi, their lifespan, etc. There were so many details that no one could follow him, and what started as a neat meet-the-artist idea devolved into a mind-numbing exercise in boredom. It was so bad, even Kat lost interest, and no matter how hard she tried to redirect, he just droned on.

Eventually, she put a stop to it, and informed Marty the students were only there for a certain amount of time, and they would have to get together again later to learn more about his fascinating work. Marty didn't seem upset in the least and agreed wholeheartedly that he could come back whenever they wanted. Kathryn asked him if she could hang on to the notebook. He agreed, and to much fanfare, grabbed a cookie and had Emily walk him out so she could see him test out the new grips.

Kathryn reminded everyone about what remained to be done and asked the students to sign up on for the various tasks she had discussed with them. As they stretched and made their way to the board, she pulled Nate aside before he got to the door. It was not the ideal place or time to interrogate a potential witness, but her back was up against the wall, and she was running out of options.

"So how was homecoming?"

He turned around, surprised at the contact. "It was fine. No complaints whatsoever."

Up close, Kat saw some of Nate's dad in his eyes, and to some extent his build, but the shape of his face and skin tone differed – in Nate's favor. They sounded almost exactly alike when he spoke. Kat thought he was more handsome than Dr. Mayes, and she fully expected a similar degree of arrogance but was pleasantly surprised to find him engaging and affable.

"Good. Who'd you go with?"

He tilted his head toward the door.

"Was Emily your date?"

His eyes twinkled a bit, and there was that grin again. "Uh, kind of."

"Really?"

"Yeah." He brushed his fingers through his hair, and she saw a bandage on two of them. She also noticed a pink line on one of his lips and a fading bruise above his eye.

"So what'd the other guy look like?" she asked. So far the conversation had been going well, and she was trying to keep it light. "Didn't notice that before."

This time Nate didn't smile. "Sure you did. At my house last week."

Kat's jaw went slack. "Yeah, about that –"

"You do remember, don't you?"

She held his gaze. "I do, Nate. And I recognize it may have been hard on you. That's why I wanted to speak with you now." This wasn't the entire truth, but close enough. "If this is too much for you – you know, working with us here on this Marty Deen project – I totally understand. If you want to drop out, I won't be offended in the least, and in fact, I'll make sure you get your full credit."

He looked back at her but didn't say anything. This wasn't about school credit anymore, and he knew it.

"So, let's set the gallery work aside and talk about what went down last week," she said. "You've figured out by now that I am the lead investigator on this case, right?"

"Yep."

"And you realize your dad – Dr. Mayes – is under investigation for money laundering, among other things."

"I do."

"Do you know what it means to launder money?"

"Yes. I have been doing some research on it, actually."

Interesting. "Then you know it's a serious crime, which is why we arrested your father."

"Yeah, and then you let him go."

This comment surprised her. Nate wasn't upset his dad had been arrested. He was upset his dad had been cut loose.

"Well, we didn't have enough evidence to keep him."

"That's what I heard."

"At the time we believed we had a reasonable basis to conduct a search and seizure."

"Really? Did you have some secret protected witness or something?" He was asking a lot of questions, but in all fairness, they weren't bad ones – luckily for Kathryn, Nate's inquiries were walking him down a path she intended to take anyway.

"Since you asked, yes, I did interview a potential witness who had some incriminating information. This particular witness had been working for your father as an insider."

"Really? Do I know him? Who is he?"

"She."

"She? Hmm. Okay, so who is she?"

Another good question. Kathryn walked over to the desk by the mail and grabbed the photo of Charlotte from her bag. It was a file photo the FBI had retrieved from Charlotte's employer. She looked absolutely gorgeous. Not too slutty like she tended to present in person, but very professional, proper and even upstanding.

"Do you know who this is?"

"No."

"No?"

"I've never seen her before."

"This is a photo of Charlotte Gutherz. Name ring a bell?"

"No. Should it?" He looked at the picture again and shook his head.

"Not necessarily – at least not for you." Kat was surprised that Nate hadn't come across Charlotte at some time or another – considering the relationship with Dr. Mayes. Maybe she was just a hotel thing.

"What about 'Fast Eddie?' Ever heard of anyone with that name?"

"Nope."

"Ms. Gutherz is the witness I interviewed. Said she used to run money for your dad."

"In Hattiesburg or Gulfport?"

"Hattiesburg. This was before you moved."

"Did she say anything else? That doesn't seem like much."

"Well, yes."

"So, what? What'd she say?"

Oh well. No time like the present. Time to get his attention.

"She was your father's mistress."

Chapter 43

Nate looked like he was trying to whistle but no noise came out. If he was hurt by this revelation, he didn't show it, but he sure sounded angry when he finally spoke.

"Figures. For how long?"

"Years."

"Did she tell you anything else?"

"Yeah, Nate, we did discuss some other items of interest, but because the investigation is ongoing, I am not at liberty to tell you all the details surrounding the case."

Nate shrugged his shoulders.

"But I am allowed to ask you about one thing she did say."

"Okay. What?"

"She gave up a name. Someone she believed may have played a role in the crime."

"Someone I know?"

"Most definitely."

He stood up straight. She had his full attention. "Who?"

"You, Nate," Kathryn said, and paused. "She identified you."

"Me? Wait, wait. Are you saying this lady – this Charlotte lady – your 'mystery witness' identified *me* as part of this case?"

"She did."

"Well, I can tell you I have nothing to do with this." He started pacing the room and then stopped right in front of Kathryn. Suddenly, he was talking fast and stuttering. "Ab-absolutely nothing. I need to speak with her," he said, raising his finger to make a point. "I-I need to know exactly what she said abou- about me, and what she knows about my dad. And I want to hear it directly from her mouth."

"You can't."

"What do you mean, I can't? Of course I can. Call her."

"I can't call her, and you can't talk to her." She peered out the front window. Emily was looking down the street, and Kathryn could see Marty on his bike near the corner showing it off. She still had some time with Nate before they came back in. Kathryn handed him another photo. It was one taken by the detectives at Charlotte's house after she'd been cooking for three days.

"She was murdered, Nate. Just shortly after she spoke to me last week. That's why I need to talk to you."

He put his hand to his mouth, and the color in his cheeks faded so quick Kat thought he might pass out.

"Murdered? Who did it?"

"We don't know, but I suspect it's someone who works for your dad who goes by the name of 'Fast Eddie.'"

"Fast Eddie? I already told you I don't know who that is."

"I know, but I think you may know something, Nate. And I'd like to talk with you some more about it."

Nate looked out the window and at a sparrow picking at a piece of crust on the sidewalk. He took a deep breath, and turned back her way, a bit standoffish, but, not totally disengaged.

"Let's talk about it then."

CHAPTER 44

J ack's was set up so that a solo eater could dine in peace without feeling like a leper. In addition to booths and tables, it had a countertop with barstools facing a large plate-glass storefront window that provided a good perch for people-watching downtown. Fast Eddie took one on the left corner so he could see out and still keep an eye on the restaurant.

It was more crowded than usual for a fall Saturday, and he chalked it up to the fact that Southern Miss and State had away games, and Ole Miss had a bye weekend. Some people were shopping, perhaps getting an early start on Christmas, and some were just out and about socializing. He saw a few joggers and watched three young mothers push their strollers down the street before stopping at Coast Roast for coffee and girl sandwiches. He liked the small-town feel he got when he ate downtown. It made him nostalgic for a childhood that never was.

He was halfway through his slice when his eyes locked on a bike leaning against a pole outside the art gallery. But it wasn't just any bike – it was an old Schwinn with a silver banana seat. It had a retro vibe, and while he liked the look of it, something about the bike disturbed him. Had he seen it before? He kept eating and watching it, hoping the kid who owned it would come out and jog his memory.

A few minutes later, his patience was rewarded when the door swung open and a grown man and a teenage girl walked out. They were clearly talking about the bike because the man was pointing to it. He flipped it over on its back and cranked the pedals super-fast, making the back wheel a spinning blur. They used to call that making ice cream back in the day. Then the man eased it back upright, climbed on, and sped around the block, taking a lap. When he returned, the girl was jumping up and down and clapping.

Fast Eddie motioned behind the counter. "Hey, Jack, you got a second?"

"You need a refill?" Jack perpetually wore a bandana tied around his head positioned so his blonde wavy hair stuck out the back. He could have passed for a retired surfer in looks but not disposition. Jack could be downright surly at times.

"No. Wanted to ask you a question. You see over there, by the Holden Gallery?"

Jack finished throwing a pizza and leaned over his workstation. "Yeah. What about it?"

"It's kinda weird. There's an old bike over there – it was leaning on the rail earlier – and I just saw a grown man jump on it and take it for a spin. He's over there right now, still sitting on it."

Jack squinted down the sidewalk and pointed. "Oh yeah, that's Marty Deen."

"Marty Deen?"

"Been a fixture around Gulfport forever."

"How so?"

"Retarded son of one of our councilmen. Been riding that bike since he was a kid. He's probably over at the gallery getting ready for his show."

"His show?"

"He's one of those – what do they call 'em – savants? Can draw and paint like something out of a magazine. Mainly birds and things he sees out in the woods where he works. On some mornings you can see him hightailing it down Pass Road on that bike with his bag strapped to his fender rack."

Suddenly Eddie was not hungry anymore. He knew exactly what show it was. Kathryn had been talking about it a lot.

He turned back to the sidewalk, and as his mind churned, he definitely recalled seeing Marty on the road, but what made him set his pizza down was the very real possibility he had also seen the bike a few months before.

"Where does he work?" he asked, even though he was certain of the answer.

"Over in Archie Park."

His mouth couldn't find the straw to his tea. "Archie Park?"

"Yeah, just off 49. Where they host all of those sports tournaments. It's real nice this time of year. Just gotta' be careful. A fella got killed up that way a few months back. You remember that?"

"Oh yeah."

"There are some crazy folks out there."

"There are," he said, nodding his head.

"Anyway, they have some nature trails and stuff. Not too hot this time of year, you know? May be worth checking out."

"That's a good idea," he said, still looking out the window.

"Right on," Jack said, and got back to laying out pepperoni slices.

Fast Eddie took one more nibble as he watched Marty Deen jump back onto the bike and take off. He drove it right past the window, and Eddie got a good look at him.

Not too tall. Medium build. Looked a bit sluggish. The kind of person they would have called a "soft target" back during training.

If the situation dictated action, he should not be a problem.

CHAPTER 45

When Ms. Cooper told Nate he had been identified as someone who might be of interest in his dad's case, he felt like he had been pushed down an elevator shaft. Sure, the information about Charlotte's being his dad's mistress was tough, but not totally unexpected. Him playing any type of role in the investigation, however, came out of nowhere.

The very first thing that came to mind was the Polaroids. Now that Nate had an FBI agent on his trail, maybe it was time to give them up. He figured she only stopped him because she thought he had them. Before he could respond, Emily stepped back into the door.

"That Marty is something else," Emily said. "He absolutely loves that bike, doesn't he?"

Ms. Cooper sprung to life. "He does, Emily, and he was so proud to show it to you. Thanks so much."

"No problem. Nate, a bunch of us are going over to Jack's for lunch. You coming?"

"Yeah, just give me a second."

"Nate and I are running through some more ideas for Marty's show. I'll send him over when we're done. Probably five or ten minutes."

"Why, Nate, I had no idea you were such an aficionado. You are hiding all kind of secrets, aren't you?"

Nate allowed a weak grin. "I guess so."

"Okay, I'll save you a seat. See you in a few!"

And then Emily was gone. It was a nice reprieve, but it was short lived, and now he was one-on-one again, and there was no way to avoid it. Once the door shut all the way, Ms. Cooper's demeanor shifted from breezy gallery coordinator back to serious FBI agent, and she wasted no time getting to the point.

"You should know Charlotte is not the first person in this case who met an untimely end. A few months ago, there was Tom Chrestman. We found him on the side of the road in Archie Park with three bullets through his head."

"Who is Tom Chrestman?"

"One of the business partners in this little enterprise of your father's. He was actually on his way to the FBI office the day he was shot."

"What was he wearing?"

This was an odd question. "What?"

"Was he wearing a suit?"

"I don't know. Maybe a shirt and a tie. Why?"

"I think I remember seeing this on the news."

"Oh yes, it was. The first death was another partner of theirs they called Birdy. He committed suicide when he thought we were going to cart him off to jail."

As she spoke, Nate clicked off the Polaroids in his head. She had described two of the more terrible ones pretty accurately. He couldn't figure out how she knew. He had been extremely careful and very discreet about the pictures. The only time they had ever seen the light of day was out by the bonfire, and he was certain his friends hadn't told anyone. Now she was baiting him to see who would blink first – and all indications were that it would be him.

"Other than them ending up dead, you know what those two had in common?"

"What?"

"Me."

"You?"

"I interviewed them both. Birdy, the first one, I only spoke with briefly, but I was hoping for a follow-up. Shortly after we met, he allegedly committed suicide before he went to serve his jail time." She shook her head and continued. "The second, Tom, had met with me once before, and the morning he was murdered, he was about to come in for round two."

"But he never made it."

"He never made it. So here we are."

Nate thought he could speed things up by going out to Ferris and retrieving the photos. He started to reach into his pocket for his keys, but before he could get to them, Ms. Cooper pulled a checkbook out of her purse and held it up.

"This is what I want to talk to you about."

A checkbook? He released the grip on his key ring and let his hand slide back out and hang by his side. "I don't understand."

"What does it mean to launder money, Nate?"

"Uh, people who get money illegally in large amounts can't spend it because the government or the IRS will realize they have it. Once they are on to it, they can trace the money back to the source."

"Right. So?"

"So they have to put the money into the system in a way so that when it comes back out, it's clean."

"Clean?"

"Meaning the link between the money and illegal act is no longer there."

"You have done your homework. How do they clean it?"

Nate couldn't figure out why she was having him jump through all these hoops, but he played along. "They form fake companies and deposit it offshore. But that doesn't always work."

"Why not?"

"Putting it overseas is risky, especially if the money is tainted. Who's to keep someone over there from taking it as their own? Not like anyone's going to call the cops if they do."

"Any other ways – closer to home?"

"I don't think so. Corporations can't hide it as easy here as they can elsewhere. Tighter laws."

"What about using individuals?"

"Instead of companies?"

"Yes."

"If a person is on an account, then you're not hiding the money. There would be no point."

"Could be," she said, "if they open bank accounts using fake names or names of family members who are unaware."

He hadn't thought of that. "But how do you get around the fact that a lot of money is still going into a bank account? Wouldn't they still have the same problem?"

"No, not if the accounts are not in their name. And not if there are multiple accounts. Because smaller amounts are deposited over a period of time, no one really finds out."

"How small?"

"So long as each individual deposit remains under $10,000, they will not be reported."

It suddenly made sense to Nate. All of it.

She pointed at the checkbook. "You ever open an account at Hub City State Bank?"

"Up in Hattiesburg? Nope."

"Your dad ever set one up for you? To your knowledge?"

Nate laughed. "Are you serious? My dad never did anything for me."

"Take a look at this and tell me what you see."

He did as she directed and pretended to study the information on the check. "Says here 'Nate Mayes,' and has a phone number I don't recognize." He squinted at it again. "That's our old address from Hattiesburg." When he read the next line, he snapped the cover closed and looked up at Ms. Cooper. "That's my social security number."

"I will tell you that the register on that account says it has just over twenty-two thousand in it – which is a lot of money. Now this account, by itself, doesn't mean anything bad is going on. Who knows, your dad could be putting money aside for you?"

"Would never happen."

"Maybe not, but I have to look at the evidence in the light most favorable to the other side, and this by itself is not enough to issue a warrant."

"Have you found any others?"

"We thought we had a lead – which is why we visited your house, but when we got there – nothing."

"So why are you showing it to me?"

"Because I think this may be the tip of the iceberg."

He shook his head but didn't respond. His hands started to sweat so he put them in his hoodie pocket as casually as he could. But not casually enough. Kathryn noticed.

"I think this could be one of many accounts that are out there in your name. Problem is, I don't know how to access them. I think Charlotte did, but I obviously can't use her anymore, and before I go on a wild goose chase using internal channels running these down, I need to know I'm right." She looked at him and put it out there. "I can't have any more slip ups. I need your help."

Nate tried to hide his emotions. His old man – who never trusted Nate to even sit in his Porsche – had all along been using Nate to hide his money. Which was now, at least according to the banks, *Nate's money*. The irony of the situation was not lost on him, and he almost wanted to laugh, but he didn't, because now that he could see the big picture, things were shaping up differently.

She handed him a business card with her name and number embossed on the front. On the back she wrote two additional numbers.

"If you want to talk about it some more, call me at any of those numbers. Unless I am out, one of these should work." Her face turned serious again. "I would much rather speak informally than formally."

"Thanks." Nate had been thinking about how to get back at his dad for years, but most of his ideas were sophomoric – revenge tales built on emotion and years of simmering anger. But this one was different. This one might actually work. He started to head out the door, but stopped and turned back to her. There was one more thing he needed to know.

"Ms. Cooper?"

"Yes, Nate?"

"Just how much money are we talking here?"

She didn't even hesitate. "Just north of six million dollars."

He gave a responsive nod, doing his best to suppress a smile, then tossed her card in the trash as soon as he hit the sidewalk.

CHAPTER 46

Even after I made the block twice, I still couldn't find a close parking spot. I ended up leaving the Milk Wagon behind a tire and auto shop closer to 25th Avenue, and it took me a good five minutes to walk back to the center of downtown. By the time I got to Jack's, it was slammed. On any other day, I would have not been happy. I don't do well when I'm starving. But this was the day after homecoming, and when I turned the corner just past the fountain drinks, I saw that Emily, Mark, and Wendy had secured the booth over in the corner. When Emily spotted me, she patted the spot next to her.

She had saved a seat. Even better, when I slid on in, she planted a kiss on my cheek.

"Well, hello," I said, and gave her leg a squeeze. "How long have y'all been here?"

"Probably fifteen minutes," Em said, and squeezed me back. "I came straight from the gallery and got here first. As soon as I grabbed this booth, Mark and Wendy came in."

"Where's Hop?"

"He couldn't make it," Mark said. "Kristin wanted him to go shopping."

"Seriously?"

"Yeah, that boy is whipped already."

"He ain't the only one," Wendy said and poked Mark in the side. He gave me one of *those* faces, and I made a note to follow-up with him to see exactly how much progress he had made under the cover of darkness.

"You didn't run into Nate on your way in, did you?" Emily asked.

"No. Is he coming?"

"Yeah. He's doing his service hours with me over at Holden Gallery. When we got cut loose earlier, Ms. Cooper wanted to talk to him some more."

"Ms. Cooper?"

"She's one of the directors. She works there part time. I think she said her full-time job is with the FBI. He's supposed to join us when they're done."

"Cool. We can pull up a chair when he gets here. Y'all ordered yet?"

"Yep," she said, "I went ahead and got two larges when I sat down. One cheese, one pepperoni thin crust. They should be here any minute." If I wasn't in love with her before, I surely was then.

A few minutes later the pizzas arrived, and as our waitress put them on the table, Nate slid a chair across the floor and plopped down at the end.

"That's about right," I said, "showing up just when the food gets here."

"My timing is impeccable. What's up, guys?"

Mark mumbled something back, but no one could understand him because he had half a slice jammed in his mouth. To come from a family of eaters, one would have thought he would have been appropriately trained in the art of consumption.

"You just now getting out?" Emily asked. "What took you so long?"

"Ms. Cooper had a lot to say. A whole lot." Nate grabbed a slice and leaned over to collect the hanging strands of mozzarella into his mouth. Then he looked around. "Anyone order me a D.P.?"

"I had you one, but Mark drank it."

"Nice," Nate said, shaking the empty cup. "If she comes back around, let's get some refills."

"Anyway," Emily piped back in, "Ms. Cooper?"

"Oh yeah. Do you know she is the lead investigator on the case against my dad?"

"News to me," Mark said. It was news to all of us.

"I bet that was awkward."

"Nah, not really. She mainly wanted to let me know I could bail if I didn't want to continue with the gallery gig. So I might."

"You lucky dog," Mark said. "I would. Especially if she was going to give me credit."

"Of course you would."

"So, what are you going to do?"

"I don't know. I'll probably give it some thought. I always do better on a full stomach."

We inhaled the rest of the pizza, and the poor waitress had to re-fill our drinks twice more. Mark covered the tip, and I couldn't tell if he did it to show off to Wendy or if he was just feeling generous. He told me they paid the band forty bucks to play, which meant he pretty much spent his entire take at lunch.

"Nate, we're going over to Mark's to see if we can catch some games on TV. You want to join us?"

"I'm going to pass this time." He looked at his watch. "I probably need to get back home. Where are y'all parked?"

Everyone except me had a spot up close, so Nate offered to drop me off on his way out. I was hoping to catch up with Emily, but I took him up on it anyway. It was easier after she told me she'd make sure we'd get together later that night.

As soon as I got in and shut the door, things turned serious.

"Look, man, I need you to do something for me."

"You got it. What's up?"

"Earlier, when I met with that Cooper lady – from the FBI."

"Yeah?"

"We talked about more than just whether or not I should drop the work at the gallery. She told me some more stuff about my dad's case. A lot more."

"Like what?"

He cut his eyes over to me and shook his head. "Some pretty wild stuff. For one, she thinks he's sitting on a pot of cash somewhere." He looked out the windshield and started to say something but stopped and shook his head. "I would tell you more, but for now, I think the less you know, the better."

"C'mon, Nate. You can't set it up like that and then not say anything."

"I have to do it this way, Matt. Let me just say that I may know who a few of those people are in those photos I showed you."

"Who? Tell me."

"I can't right now. Just trust me on this. For your own good."

This was huge, and I wanted to trust Nate, but he wouldn't give me any more details.

"I need you to hide a few things. Here in the Milk Wagon – in the Trapper. Just for a little while."

"Things?"

"Well, the Polaroids, for one. My dad cannot know I have these, and he's prone to tear the house and my truck apart if he thinks I do."

"I don't know, Nate. Those give me the willies. What else?"

Nate reached behind the seat and grabbed his book bag. In the calculator pocket, he pulled out the Polaroids and handed them to me as if I had already agreed to the deal. Then he grabbed what looked like a small stack of papers, folded in half. When he opened them up, I saw they were deposit slips, but they were all blank, and from different banks. Hancock Bank, Peoples Bank, Magnolia Federal, and others. The last one had some scribbles on the back of it.

"What are these?"

"You probably figured out by now that I took more than just pictures from the safe that day, right?"

"It had crossed my mind."

"Well, stacked in the back was a bunch of financial records – bank ledgers and things. I wouldn't have given them a second look, but there was a weird map on the top with bank names written all over it and circled in red. The names in the ledgers matched up with the ones on the map. That's where these deposit slips came from."

"Did you take the – what did you call them? The ledgers? Did you take them, too?"

"No, they were in binders. I just took these few."

"Why?"

"Check 'em out. You'll see."

I did and they looked just like any other blank checks I might have seen. I shrugged my shoulders.

"Look again."

"Nate, c'mon —"

"Read 'em. From the top."

I took another look. "Okay, so it's a little weird. These are all in your name."

He smiled. "Exactly. Between that map and my name being on these, something didn't feel right, so I tore one out of each check book. Made sure to pull 'em out the back so no one would notice."

I still didn't have a clue what he was talking about. "So, what does that mean? You're acting like this is something important."

He didn't answer, at least not directly. "I just need you to hang on to these — and the pictures. Just for a little while, okay? I need to check some things out, and while I do, these need to stay out of sight." He pulled up next to the Milk Wagon. "Then I'll tell you everything. I promise."

"Does anyone know you have them?"

"No one," he said. "Not even you. Right?"

"Ms. Cooper?"

He made a face. "Eh, she doesn't know I have them, either, but she thinks they're out there. And she wants them bad. Real bad. So to answer your question, yeah, these are pretty important."

"What about the bank records? Didn't she find them when the FBI went through your house?"

"Apparently not, and that seems to be the big mystery. My guess is my dad stashed them away somewhere, but I can't figure out why he hasn't done anything with them."

"Done anything with them?"

"Yeah. Like take the money and run." Nate looked out over the parking lot. "Maybe they are watching him too closely for him to move; I don't know. Still . . ." He looked back over to me. "Anyway, I need to keep what I handed you safe and sound, just for a little while, okay? It's the least you could do."

"The least I could do?"

"Yeah. You and Emily seem to be getting along fine today, don't you? Acting like a couple, even."

Once again, Nate's actions had not been pure happenstance. His concession the night before, while appreciated and somewhat genuine, turned out to be a bargaining chip. I still didn't want to do hide those photos, but he made a pretty strong case, and it did feel like a fair exchange to finally have Emily on my arm.

"Okay, Nate. I'll do it. Just don't leave me hanging too long. I still don't know what you are talking about, but if me putting these away for a bit can help you get where you need to be, I'm in."

He rolled down the window as I climbed out. "Thanks, Matt. If I'm right, the fact that these accounts even exist potentially changes everything." He pointed behind me. "Just let the Milk Wagon be my rolling safety deposit box for a bit. And don't get into a wreck or anything."

I patted the hood. "This old girl has served me well in the past. Rest assured, she'll do the same for you."

"I know she will," he said, sliding Ferris into reverse, "she's the best." As he backed out and straightened up, I heard him yell something else through the music.

"What'd you say?"

He turned down the volume, stopped the truck, and pointed.

"I told you I wanted one."

CHAPTER 47

Now that he had made the Marty Deen connection, Fast Eddie needed to test the water to see if Marty knew who *he* was. If Marty did recognize him, he couldn't be poking his head in and out of the gallery at Kathryn's request, nor could he risk Marty showing up unannounced at the office. After Marty rode past Jack's, he exited the restaurant in as normal a method as he could and was on the road in less than a minute. After a few switchbacks and a couple of turnarounds, he ultimately caught up with Marty near the Green Oaks subdivision.

Eddie knew the area, and once he figured out the general direction Marty was heading, he circled around to a four-way stop half a mile up just past the tennis courts. When he got to the stop sign, he looked left and sure enough, Marty was coming his way. He was wearing his helmet, and he slowed down when he got near the intersection. Eddie could tell Marty had done it a thousand times, because he didn't even look up as he came to a stop. When Marty stood up on his pedals, about to move again, Fast Eddie eased the truck into the middle of the road and rolled down his window.

"Hi there."

Marty inspected the truck, bumper to bumper, his body becoming more contorted by the second. When Marty's eyes landed on Fast Eddie, his face recoiled into a scowl, and he tucked his chin into his chest and started to grunt. The coaster brakes on his bike locked when he tried to backpedal, jerking the handlebars into a Tilt-A-Whirl, throwing Marty to the ground. When he stood up, his hand and elbow were bleeding, and he started slapping the side of his head and shrieking. Eddie started to say something else, but before he could get anything out, Marty broke into a run the other way, helmet on, right down the middle of the road.

That answered that question.

Fast Eddie hauled ass before the car coming up behind him knew what was happening. His hypothesis had been proven to be true. But what to do about it? If Marty was going to shut down around him like that, was he even a threat? Could Marty ever provide a literate word – or description – to the authorities? Even if he did, would anyone even believe him? These were all good questions Fast Eddie was going to have to answer at some point, but they would have to wait for now. He had an errand to run.

He reached into his console and found a picture he had placed inside the sleeve of a CD case. He slid a Sharpie out of the pocket and pulled over into a McDonald's parking lot. After scribbling a few test sentences on a napkin until he got the wording just perfect, he used his left hand to write on the border of the photograph, just in case someone tried to match it to his handwriting.

He blew on the photo until the ink was dry, then turned north on the highway and made his way towards Doc Mayes' house. He knew there were orders in place to keep eyes on Doc Mayes at all times, but he knew those orders could be revised. In fact, he knew the tail that was originally scheduled to watch that day had been rescheduled to a different shift. He also knew the replacement would not be there until after six that evening. He knew all of this before he even left his place that morning.

It was one of the many perks of the job.

CHAPTER 48

H aving secured the package with Matt, Nate felt better about things and was ready to move on. That moment was short lived, however, when he got home and pulled around the driveway to find the front door wide open. The leaves that had blown into the foyer told him it had been that way for a while.

"Hello? Anyone here?" Nate took one step inside and wondered if he should keep going.

"Vicky?" It looked even worse now that he was in the hall. Clothes, paper, and books were strewn everywhere. He wondered if the place had been robbed, but it didn't make sense because the gate was closed when he arrived. No way to get in or out without a code. Plus, the grounds themselves looked normal. Even Creepy Carl was going about his business trimming the knockout roses.

The other weird thing Nate noticed was the garage. His dad kept the doors closed all the time. He opened it only to get in and out, but when Nate pulled up, the door on his dad's side was up, and the Porsche was gone. Vicky's Cadillac was not.

"Vicky? You in here?" By now Nate made it to the game room, and it looked to be intact, other than a red wine stain on the wall and broken glass all around the baseboard. He walked over to check it out, and when he leaned down to get a better look, he heard a noise coming from the kitchen.

He spun around cocked his head. Then he heard it again. Sounded almost like a chirp. He picked up one of the pool cues and unscrewed it so he could use the handle end in case he needed it. He eased up toward the kitchen door until he was just outside the opening. He took a breath, raised his arm, and stormed in.

Vicky screamed so loud he nearly hit her as a reflex.

"Good grief," Nate said, lowering the weapon. "Are you okay?"

Vicky was slumped over the island, sitting one-cheeked on a bar-stool, using her hanging down leg as a prop. Nate took another look at her face. What he thought was blood turned out to be the remnants of mascara. Vicky had been crying. And Vicky was smashed.

"Your father," she said.

"What?"

"Your father!" She screamed, mushing the words and drawing it out in a drunken slur. Then she made a shaky sweeping motion around the room. "Made all this mess. All of it." She knocked over her glass, and the contents rolled off the side of the counter onto her lap. She didn't even move.

"What are you talking about? What happened?"

"I don't know," she said, and this time she bypassed the glass and went straight for the bottle, wiping her mouth with a dishtowel. "Everything was fine when we woke up. Normal morning. Then we had breakfast. I rode the golf cart out front to get the paper like I always do." She was swaying as she talked, and her eyes had progressed from half-moons to slits.

"Then next thing I know I'm heatin' up a English muffin, and Ford starts cursing like I've never heard before. Sayin' all kind of foul things." She burped and put the dishtowel to her mouth. Nate thought she might be sick, but she held it in.

"Did he say why?"

"No, but something set him off. Then he storms into his office and starts tearing it apart. I ran in there and asked him if he was okay and – and –"

"And what Vicky?"

She resumed her crying. "And he hit me. Right across my face." She pulled back her hair and sure enough, she had a bruise on her cheek that followed her jawline. "So I walked out. I don't put up with that crap, no sir, not anymore. So I went to my room and locked the door, and for the next hour or so he made all kind of racket. When I came back down, he was even more crazy and pushed me out of the way onto the floor. Then I threw a glass at him, and he's been gone ever since." She started to raise the towel again, then set it down. "That was two hours ago."

Nate did his best to appear concerned about Vicky, but his mind was elsewhere. Even for his dad, this behavior was uncharacteristic, and Nate wasn't sure what triggered it. One thing he did know – Vicky wasn't going to be upright much longer, so he had to get what he could from her before she passed out.

"I'm sorry he hit you," Nate said and for a second or two he really almost kind of felt sorry for her. But it passed. "You said something might have set him off. Any idea what it could have been?"

She looked around the room and closed one eye to try to focus. Then she pointed over at the breakfast table. It still had one plate, a half-eaten English muffin, two coffee mugs, and what looked like the morning edition of the *Sun-Herald* on it. "Maybe he was in the paper again. Last time, they didn't say very nice things about him, and he got mad – but not this mad."

Nate walked over and picked it up. The first section was turned inside out, and he refolded it so he could read the front page. He looked over at Vicky to see if she had anything else to add, but her head was down. Out cold. He sat down to read the article. The headline blared *Gulfport Resident Found Slain in Home*. Smiling up from the middle of the article was a picture of Charlotte Gutherz. It was the file photo from her work that he had seen not three hours before. There she was again – pretty, fresh, and alluring – just the type of siren a middle-aged man would be attracted to. The parts of her Nate could see, that is. He searched around the table for the rest of the paper.

The page had been torn in half.

CHAPTER 49

N ate found what remained of the ripped-off section on the floor and pieced it together with the other half to finish reading the article. He was surprised there was not a single reference to Charlotte's role in the money-laundering investigation.

Not one.

Nate continued down the hall to see what other damage had been done and found the door to the office ajar. He walked in and found it chaotic and disturbed much like the rest of the house, but to a greater degree. Drawers pulled out and dumped on the floor, cushions off the couch, and the painting that had been covering the safe – which was now wide open – had been thrown across the room like a Frisbee. It sat resting beside the couch with the corner of its frame splintered into pieces.

Nate sat down in the big leather chair and put his feet up on the desk – another act that would have been forbidden in the real world, but he was living in a new normal. He closed his eyes and ran through the litany of events leading up to this meltdown. The phone call a few weeks before. The fistfight after his dad accused him of pilfering the office. The raid on the house. Agent Cooper told him nothing was there, but Nate knew something *had* been there. Sure, Nate took the photos and the deposit slips, but he left the ledgers, the map and the other things. Then Charlotte was killed, and his dad absolutely lost his mind – and it wasn't because he was missing her. His dad was passionate, but not in that way, and certainly not prone to fall apart over a woman. Money? Yes. Power? Absolutely. Ego? Maybe. There must have been something else about her death that pulled on one of these factors, but Nate couldn't quite figure out what. If only he could –

Something leaning in the corner distracted him, and when Nate got up from the chair and walked over to investigate, he came across a relic he probably hadn't seen in eight or nine years.

"Well, I'll be." It was the gold hilt of a Civil War Confederate officer sword poking out of its scabbard. He picked it up, and the pulled blade out, making a *ching* sound when the tip finally freed the cover. The weight of the sword felt good in his hands, although holding it again after all these years made him sad. As cool as it was, it would always remind Nate of the day his dad transitioned from a run-of-the mill poor excuse for a father into an all-out tyrant.

CHAPTER 50

What nine-year-old boy is not fascinated by a real sword -- especially one with silver and gold engravings of horses and soldiers in battle? Nate certainly was, and he saw the sword for the very first time one evening after school. He was in second grade – Ms. Cecilia was his teacher – and he had been eating a grilled cheese sandwich with Doritos for supper on a TV tray by himself. Pretty much like every night, except *Happy Days* was on, which meant it was a Tuesday. Nate could specifically recall the details of the evening because his dad came home in an unusually blissful mood.

"Vicky? Hey, come check this out! I got it, I finally got it."

Vicky ran downstairs, pulling her hair back in a clip. She was in a sundress, and she, too, was bouncy – happy to find an amiable spouse at home for a change.

"What? What is it, honey?"

"This." He pulled out a long slender box and opened the top up.

"Oh, my goodness. Is it the one?"

"It is. The presentation sword of my great-great grandfather, Nathaniel Bradford Mayes. Word is General Lee himself was at the ceremony when he got it."

Of course, that got Nate's attention, so he hopped off the couch and walked to the cased opening that led from the kitchen to the hallway. He knew not to cut in. Adults were talking.

"Oh, it's beautiful, Ford. Even better than I imagined. How'd you get it?"

"I had an antiques dealer in New Orleans run it down for me. They've been hunting it for three years now."

"Can I hold it?"

"No, you can't hold it," he snapped. Then Nate watched his dad lift it up and wave it around like Luke did in Obi-Wan's cave. "This thing is priceless. I'm going to hang it up in the –" He let his arm drop down when he saw Nate standing at the door. "Hey, what are you looking at?"

Nate didn't answer. He didn't think they would see him with all the excitement, but he was clearly busted. "N-nothing."

"Oh really? You'd better tell the truth, son, if you know what's good for you."

"I-I heard you come in and talk about a sword. I wanted to see it."

"Here it is. Now you've seen it."

"Yes, sir."

"This is not a toy, do you understand?"

"Yes, sir."

"And if I ever catch you anywhere near this, you will be in big trouble. Big trouble."

"Y-Yes, sir."

Nate went back to the Fonz and for a little while, forgot about the sword and the scolding. He stayed up for *Laverne and Shirley*, but when *Three's Company* came on, it was time to go to bed. They never let him watch *Three's Company*, which stunk, because he could usually hear Vicky watching it and laughing out loud. It made him mad that he couldn't laugh, too.

He made his way down the hall to the stairwell, trying to remember if he had brushed his teeth the night before. He made it upstairs, and for some reason glanced into his dad's and Vicky's bedroom – and there it was, just sitting on the bed.

He stood at the door wringing his hands, knowing he shouldn't go in, but also knowing he had to. He leaned over the balcony and could hear Vicky and his dad talking through the television noise. He tiptoed in, picked the sword off the bed, and lifted it up.

Suddenly *he* was Luke Skywalker, and the blade was no longer folded steel, but a pulsating blue beam. He pretended to be in the Millennium Falcon, training under old Ben while Han and Chewie sat off to the side, watching. He waved it a few times, making humming sounds with his mouth as he deflected the laser shots from the floating trainer ball. Then he grabbed one of his dad's baseball caps and put it on backwards so it covered his eyes, just like the blast shield Luke used. The ball fired up again, and as it spun through the air the first laser hit Nate on the leg, awakening his senses. Soon the Force took over, and Nate blindly deflected and dodged the next three shots. He jumped on the settee at the end of the bed, and two more lasers glanced off the blade, popping and hissing. Satisfied he had proven the Force was real, he ripped the hat off so he could gloat to Han and get the approval from Obi-Wan that he had unknowingly been seeking all of his life. Unfortunately for Nate, the Jedi Master was not standing there.

But his dad was.

The impact of being caught in the act jolted Nate so much that he lost the grip on the sword's handle. Time slowed down as he watched the blade tumble out of his hand, completely invert itself, and hit – point down – on the marble floor, making a dull clank, then a large crash as the hilt bounced on the travertine.

He had no idea his dad could move so fast, and before Nate could retreat even a step, the back of a hand hit him broadside across the face, knocking him into the bedpost and on the ground. He saw blood pool on the floor from his nose and tried to get up. His dad looked stunned – still angry, but stunned – and hit him one more time before storming out of the room, screaming at Vicky, scooping up the sword on the way out and cradling it as he turned the corner.

* * *

That had been the last time Nate had seen it. His dad put it away after Nate "ruined it," as he was reminded on numerous occasions. It was not the last time, however, his dad hit him. It was the first of many, many beatings to come.

As Nate inspected the sword a little closer, he marveled at how something so beautiful could signify something so horrible. He took a close look at the tip and scraped it lightly with the pad of his thumb then eyeballed the blade and the hilt.

"That bastard," he murmured, "I didn't ruin it. This thing is as pristine as the day it was made."

Nate held it out, and for good measure, swung it back and forth a few times, making the signature strobing noise – which he could now do much better as a teenager.

He was so into it, when the phone on his dad's desk rang, he almost dropped it. Again.

CHAPTER 51

Nate slammed the sword back into the scabbard and tossed it into the corner by the couch. Out of pure instinct he turned to dart out of the office just in case his dad came barreling down the hall to pick up the phone and find him there. The memories of being nine years old and back in that bedroom returned like a flood, and the bowel-loosening feeling of being somewhere he shouldn't be kicked him square in the gut. Then he remembered his dad was gone. He waited a beat to see if he heard Vicky stir, but nothing came out of the kitchen. He put his hands on his knees and took a deep breath. The phone rang a third time and he stared at it. He had heard the office phone ring only once before. It was the only other day Nate had ever been in there. The sheer coincidence was uncanny, and it made him wonder if he should pick up. He looked over at the sword again. If it was his dad calling, he would skin Nate's hide for being in the office. But why would his dad call this line? He rarely even let Vicky in the office, so he certainly would not expect anyone to be in there, much less answer. Nate made the command decision and picked up the receiver before it rang a fifth time.

"Hello?"

"Hello, Dr. Mayes."

Dr. Mayes? "Uh, yes. Yes. Who is this?" *Dammit. Too stiff.*

"I warned you they were coming after you. I am glad to see you listened for a change."

"What do you want?" Nate wasn't sure if that was the right response either, but it must have been good enough since the guy hadn't hung up yet.

"You appear to be in a difficult spot right now, just like me. I think for once, we can help each other out."

"Go on." Nate said, and shrugging his shoulders to himself. *Better*.

"Check the drop and you will understand."

What? What drop? A thought came to mind and before he could even ponder it the implications of it, Nate spoke.

"Uh, Eddie?"

"Yes."

"Why don't you come by here and –"

"I will contact you when I am ready."

The line went dead.

"Hello? Hello?" Nate slammed the receiver down.

So Ms. Cooper was right. There *was* an Eddie out there working with his dad. But what was he talking about? Nate stood, his heart thumping so hard he could feel his neck pulsing against his collar. He breathed until he calmed down, and ran and reran the conversation in his head. He still had no idea what the guy meant. After a few minutes, he gave up and went back out in the hall to start the cleanup process. His dad would make him do it eventually anyway when he got home. Might as well get a head start. He pulled the office door closed. He wasn't going back in there.

He put on his Walkman, and pushed play. He had just picked up the new Cult tape, and as he stepped over Vicky to get the broom out of the kitchen closet, "She Sells Sanctuary" kicked on. He looked at her, passed out on the ground looking puffy and nasty.

Probably not the way she intended to spend her day, either.

Chapter 52

Sundays in November in the South meant two things: church and football – and not necessarily in that order, especially for the Catholics. Priests had been known to cut their homilies short if there was an early kickoff time. Depending on who was playing, it was not uncommon to head out to evening Mass after the start of the second quarter and be back on your couch before halftime was over.

For me and my buddies, the inevitable bitterness of knowing we had to go to school the next day was balanced by the fact that we had Sunday afternoons together. If there were no good games on, we'd usually watch a quarter or two of whatever teams were on the gridiron and then go outside and play two-hand touch until the sun went down. If the Saints were on, it was a marquee event, and we rarely left the TV for more than a few minutes. If it happened to be one of those extra special days – when the Saints played the Falcons – then we pretty much planned the whole weekend around it. A lot of bragging rights hung on the outcome of those games, even though we technically didn't know anyone from Atlanta. It was good to have the win, anyway, just in case we happened to run into any of them.

Every now and then the stars and planets would align, and the whole entire weekend would elevate to a higher plane. Homecoming weekend happened to be one of them. Not only was the Saints – Falcons game the perfect bookend for what had been a pretty awesome three days, but Mark's mom had invited all of us over for a game day feast to rival anything they were serving in the French Quarter. Any one of those events, standing alone, would have merited our undivided attention. But a homecoming-Saints-Ragone meal trifecta? A rare event indeed.

I picked up Hop just after one o'clock, and when we pulled into Mark's driveway, we saw Wendy's car. It shouldn't have bothered me, but it did. Not counting moms, we had never had a chick attend one of our football game watching parties, and I was kind of surprised to see her there, although I couldn't blame Mark for the invite. According to the details he dropped on us Saturday, when he and Wendy went parking after the homecoming dance, he entered the zone of mystery and breached a few layers of rayon, cotton and whatever they made bras out of. Still, I didn't want Wendy to become our Yoko.

When we arrived, Mrs. Ragone was cooking the entrees, but in true fashion, she had not left us hanging either. A tray of fresh prosciutto and cut pears, gobs of buffalo mozz and beefsteak tomatoes, and stacks of cut muffalettas greeted us when we walked in. Longneck bottles of Barq's and Coca-Cola were icing in her old metal cooler, and the smell of seafood, pasta and fresh bread warmed the entire kitchen. Hop and I started going to town, and it wasn't long before Nate and Lance showed up. Lance couldn't believe his eyes, and he must have "yes, ma'amed" and "no, ma'amed" Mrs. Ragone a hundred times in between challenging Nate over who could eat the most food.

After we had our fill, we went outside for a short game. We needed to run off our gluttony, and pregame didn't start until three-thirty, so we had plenty of time. Some other kids from the neighborhood had already gathered in the lot so we ended up with a four-on-four. We had to wait a few minutes for Mark to come out, but it was okay because he was telling Wendy bye, which made everything right in the universe again.

"I pick Nate." It was my turn to be captain, and although Lance had the potential to be a ringer, Nate was a sure thing.

"Lance," Hop said.

Dangit. I thought Hop's loyalty to Mark would force his hand to pick him, but he went for Lance. It was not that Mark was a poor athlete. It's that Mark had just eaten, and even in his best days he had deceptive speed – he was slower than he looked. I rounded out my team with a tow-headed ninth grader named Randy. He was long and lanky, which I thought might help on the receiving front, but sadly, his coordination had not caught up with his body, and when he ran, he looked like pipe cleaners twisted together. Hop picked two brothers who had played with us before, and the game was on.

First team to get to ten – counting by ones – could claim victory, and we went at it. I would like to say it was an epic performance, culminating in a Hail Mary to give my team the win, but it was nothing even close to that. Between Mark and Randy, we didn't have a lot of depth, and at the end, Nate and I just couldn't carry it. Okay, so maybe Nate couldn't carry it. It's not like I was a ringer myself. Final score: ten to four, other guys. Only one allegation of cheating and only one almost-fight, so even with a defeat it was a good afternoon. I just hoped the Saints would have a better showing than we did.

We made our way back to Mark's and sat on the back porch to rehydrate with big stadium cups filled with ice water. Even though it was November, we were hot, sweaty, and starting to stink. Hop and Lance decided to relive their victory and ran some plays in the yard, which gave me and Nate some time to chat.

"Milk Wagon still guarding my treasures?" he asked, not too loud.

"You know it. I haven't touched them since. Remember, I don't even know I have them, right?"

"Right."

"You ready to talk about 'em?"

"Not yet." Nate took a few gulps and wiped his face with the bottom of his shirt. "Getting close, though."

"Good. Just let me know. Things better at home?"

Nate looked at me sideways. "Not really. The Doc went totally berserk yesterday morning over something he read in the newspaper. About some lady he knew."

"Wow."

"Ever heard of Charlotte Gutherz?"

"No. We don't get the paper."

"She was killed this past week, and something about it set him off."

"Killed? Like murdered?"

"Yeah. Sounds like it."

"No shit? Another one. How'd your dad know her?"

"Another story for another day. Anyway, when he found out about it, he tore up half the house looking for something."

"For what?"

"Not sure, but something in the back of my mind tells me I should know. Just not there yet."

"Any clues?"

Nate nodded his head. "Yeah, one weird one that I can't figure out. I went in his office yesterday –"

"You're a brave man."

"Nah, he wasn't home. While I was in there, the phone rang, and when I picked it up, the guy on the other end mistook me for my dad. Started saying things like he had warned me in the past, and that we could help each other out."

"Really?" I sat up. "That's bizarre stuff, man."

"Then he said something I can't figure out at all. He said to 'check the drop' and I will understand. Any idea what that could mean?"

"The drop?"

"Yeah? What do you think about that?"

The first thing that came to my mind was the night we saw Nate running. "Could he have meant a drop box?"

"A drop box? I guess, but where would I find a drop box?"

"At your house. When we brought your wallet back, Vicky told us to put it in the drop box." Nate looked at me like he was confused. "I didn't know what she was talking about, either, so she directed me kind of over by the mail slot, behind some bushes. Near the gate."

"Is that where you put it?"

"Yeah, just like she told me."

"That's weird. Was she actually out there talking to y'all?"

"Oh no, she was on the intercom. But speaking of weird - your yardman was, though."

"The yardman was . . . what?"

"Just standing there by the fence. Not saying a word. Like he was staring at us or something. I didn't even see him until after I put the wallet in. 'Course we were all creeped out anyway that night because, you know, we had just seen you running down the street. I don't know, maybe looking back, I am overthinking it, but – "

Nate put his water down and stood up.

"That's it," Nate said. "That's got to be it." He looked at his watch and grabbed his keys. "I got to go."

"You sure?"

"Definitely."

"Okay, but come back if you want to watch the game."

He gave me a wave and took off, which was a shame, because had he stayed, he would have enjoyed a plate of softshell crabs, a pot of shrimp creole and the best cannoli this side of Sicily.

And, I might add, one heck of a football game.

CHAPTER 53

The first thing Nate did when he pulled in was to jump out and see if there was, in fact, a drop box hidden behind the azaleas. He worked his way between the shrubs and the bricks, and sure enough, there it was: newly built in to the facing – a bronze square that butted out about two inches on the yard side. He gave the handle a pull, but it didn't budge. He yanked it again, but it held tight, and when he ran his hand across the top lip, he saw why it was not giving – it was locked. He felt around to see if he could find a key near it in a box or under a rock, but again came up empty handed. He looked over to the house and realized the key would have to come from a different source.

At first he thought Vicky might have one, but he couldn't recall her ever going out front to do anything but get the paper, and she did that only on the weekends. It would have been highly unusual for Vicky to even step foot out of the golf cart unless she absolutely had to. She was not outdoorsy, and Nate could not ever recall her doing anything remotely related to manual labor, much less pushing her way through branches and wet leaves to check out a glorified mail slot. But according to Matt, she knew about it, and Nate figured his dad must have told her. The Doc was probably the most likely one to have a key, but trying to get it from him was not really a feasible option. The risk just was not worth the reward. If Nate got caught digging around in their bedroom, it would make his prior unauthorized entry into their space seem like a cakewalk.

There was one other option: Carl. The yardman delivered the mail every afternoon from the road to the little table in the foyer. It made sense that he would have been the one to retrieve packages or other things on occasion. Plus, Matt did say Carl was standing there when they dropped the wallet off, which, Nate agreed, was weird.

Nate walked through the house to make sure no one had seen him by the fence, and it didn't take him long to pick up the chill that still lingered in the air. His dad and Vicky were still not talking. The television was on in the game room, and the Doc looked small sitting by himself in the middle of the big couch. He had come back home late the day before – well after Nate was asleep. When Nate hung around a few seconds in the kitchen after breakfast the next morning pretending he was looking for milk, the bastard acted like nothing happened. Once Nate realized there would be no comment on the house, or even a minimal acknowledgment of Nate's unsolicited efforts to clean the mess up, he went to his room until it was time to go to Matt's.

He was beginning to wonder if he was invisible.

Vicky was in the kitchen, telephone in one hand and a glass in the other, blabbing away. Self-medicating was becoming a daily coping routine, and while Nate wanted to feel sad for her, he just couldn't. He actually preferred her a little blitzed because it meant she would keep to herself. She didn't notice his arrival, either, so after he took a quick leak, he slipped out to the potting shed.

If Carl had an office, this was it. The potting shed itself looked ancient, and one time Nate heard his dad say it used to be a slave quarters. Several ligustrum trees, a wise old camellia that was probably twelve feet tall, and runners from two established Carolina Jasmines had grown in and around the building so much that it looked organic, but for the panes of glass breaking up the camouflage. Nate always thought it would make a great Hobbit house if the door had been round.

It was not locked, and when he stepped in the little one-roomer, it was dark, dank, and smelled of peat and topsoil. Roughhewn wooden cabinets and countertops skirted two of the walls, and tools hung on imperfect nails that looked hand forged. Two pairs of rubber boots stood guard to the left of the door, and pots of various sizes were stacked in a corner. An industrial stool with a leather seat was tucked under the workshop area, where a treacherous-looking electrical outlet sat next to a plugged-in fan. Nate pulled the chain on the pigtail light and began rummaging through the shed's two drawers. In them, he found gardening gloves, a Farmer's Almanac, several empty tobacco pouches, and a bunch of other miscellaneous junk.

He sat down on the stool and looked around. Hanging on the walls was just about everything one would expect to find in such a place. Shears, coffee mugs, clippers, weed-eater spools – all there, but nothing of real interest. A wasp's nest had survived up near one of the eaves, and he could detect some winged activity up in the shadows. But Nate didn't see keys anywhere. Not a single one.

The cabinet looked like it hadn't been opened for decades. Humidity had wedged it so tight that Nate thought he would pull the handle off getting it open. He finally did but found nothing but spider webs and an owner's manual from a 1970s lawn mower. He shut it back and reassessed his surroundings.

The one shiny thing that drew his eye was a framed 5x7 photo sitting on the countertop. It was a black and white picture of a couple at the beach taken during either the World War II or Korea era. Nate squinted at the picture. She was pretty, and the man was wearing a uniform. Was that Carl? Nate dusted off the glass but still couldn't get a good look, and when he picked it up, he was greeted with a surprise.

A single key connected by a ring to a patinaed Irish Cross lay there behind it.

Nate squeezed it in his hand and closed his eyes. Could this be it? And if so, did he really want to know what was in the drop box? He took another look at what had to be a picture of Carl in better times and thought about the life Carl had lived that no one knew about – much less asked about. How does one live a life forgotten? What decisions had Carl made that left him living his Golden Years raking leaves and working alone out of a dilapidated building – for a terrible man, no less?

Nate set the photo down. He had already made some choices that had, for the first time ever, put a bright light on *his* horizon. Call it fate, call it timing, call it divine intervention – whatever it was, it gave him a reason to keep going. No way he would stop now. He had to check that box.

Nate trudged out to the fence, and sure enough, the key was a match. He yanked on the handle, and the box creaked open on its hinge. Inside was a singular unmarked small envelope.

Nate slid it in his pocket, returned the key ring to its rightful place, and eased back into the house and slipped up to his room. After locking his door, he climbed onto his bed and opened the envelope. He blew into it, then peeked inside and took a deep breath.

It was another Polaroid.

"Oh, crap."

Looking back at him with one eye open was Charlotte Gutherz. Pasty, bloated, gray, and grotesque. It was a near duplicate of the one Ms. Cooper had shown him, but taken from a different angle. Scribbled on the bottom in barely legible handwriting was a message.

I have the ledgers.

Nate rubbed his temples with his free hand. Now the call made sense — it all made sense, actually. His dad hadn't gone on a tirade because he was mourning Charlotte's death. He was upset because she had the ledgers. Now Fast Eddie had them, but without Doc Mayes, he had no way to access the cash, and without Fast Eddie, Doc Mayes didn't either.

The fact that these two parasites needed each other to carry out their illicit ways made Nate chuckle, but he didn't allow himself time to gloat. Eddie would soon follow-up with his dad to complete the transaction, and Nate had to move quickly to stay ahead of them. He glanced at the clock on his nightstand.

He would call Matt as soon as the Saints game was over.

CHAPTER 54

When I got home from Mark's, my mom told me I had two calls. One from Nate, and one from Emily. Of course, I called Emily first. I needed some privacy, so I stretched the cord of our hall phone as far as I could, and it was just long enough to make it into my room – with the door closed. Granted, I had to lie on the floor with my head jammed near a baseboard so the cord could slide under the door, but with some adjustment, it wasn't all that bad.

We talked for three hours straight.

I don't remember exactly what was said, but we learned more about each other that night than we had ever known, and the more we talked, the more I wished I could morph right through the line to be next to her. I wondered how cool it would be if they ever made video-phones, but the more I pondered it, the more I concluded it could be a mixed blessing. A little mystery was good.

By the time we hung up, it was long after ten, and I thought about calling Nate. They were so squirrely over there, though, and I didn't know how they would react, so I grabbed some Doritos, took a shower, and hit the sack.

* * *

It was raining cats and dogs when I woke up, and even though I ran through the parking lot, I still got pretty wet by the time I made it inside the hallway, and was cutting it close for class. But I didn't mind. I was still riding high from all that yarn spinning the night before with Emily, and just as promised, she was waiting by my locker wearing a J. Crew rain anorak. I tried to act cool and pump the brakes, but I just couldn't hold back, and when I got up next to her, I gave her waist a little hug. She leaned up and gave me a quick peck on the cheek – a huge violation of St. John's PDA rules – but the fact that she risked it told me everything I needed to know. I stepped in a little bit closer to talk, but, as if on cue, Nate butted in.

"Frazier! Hey man, why didn't you – oh. Hey, Em."

"Hey, Nate," Emily said. "You're mighty spry for a Monday morning."

"Yeah, well. Got a good night's sleep for a change. What up, Frayz?"

"Nothing, Nate." I rolled my eyes over toward Emily and raised my eyebrows. "Dude, we got to stop meeting like this." Nate clearly got the hint, but he continued talking.

"Did you get my message? I called you last night."

"Yeah, but it was late, so –"

"Look, uh, do you have some time to chat?" He was almost whispering, and he kind of tugged on my shoulder to get my attention. I did not appreciate the interruption.

Emily squeezed my hand. "Talk to you later." She winked. "Looks like you got a better offer." She turned around and gave me the thumb and pinky 'call me' sign.

"Real cool, man."

"I know, I know. I'm sorry. It was a borderline cockblock, so I get it."

He was babbling and almost manic. "What's so important, Nate?"

He held one finger to his lips and dropped his voice. "Remember that drop box we discussed?"

"Yeah?"

"Well it was legit. More than you know. You've been asking when I was going to fill you in on the details, right?"

"Yep. Shoot."

He looked up the hall and back to me. "No. Not here and not now. How about after school? Can we meet up at Gulfport Lake?"

"Fine." Emily had cheerleading practice anyway. "Three-fifteen?"

"Yep," Nate said. "I'll see you there. Oh, yeah, be sure and bring Mark and Hop."

"The whole crew, huh?"

"The whole crew."

As I walked to class, the rain hitting the roof escalated from a pleasant hiss to a whirring roar and made me wish I was back at home in my bed.

Safe and sound.

Chapter 55

Marty Deen had never been happier to see rain. When it stormed, he didn't have to work, which meant he could spend all day inside. On any other day, he would have curled up with his blanket and played his Atari – a recent birthday gift from his parents. He loved Space Invaders and hoped to get Pac-Man for Christmas. It was supposed to be awesome.

Ever since he saw that man on his way home, however, even videogames didn't interest him. He didn't play anything when he got home from the gallery, and he didn't even turn it on after church on Sunday, which was his usual routine. He stayed over at his daddy's house next door, pretending he liked football, and he didn't go back to his apartment until bedtime. Even then he barely slept.

Seeing that man again was Marty's worst nightmare coming true. It made Marty wonder, though. If he was really the same bad man, then why didn't he shoot him? Maybe he didn't realize Marty had seen him do those terrible things that morning to Mr. Tommy. Maybe it was just a coincidence.

Or maybe it wasn't, and if it wasn't, that meant the man was following him. Marty chewed on the corner of his pillow, weighing his options. It might finally be time to tell his daddy what he saw, but he didn't want to do that because if he did, his daddy wouldn't trust him anymore.

Suddenly, he stopped rocking and smiled. He had the solution. The lady who was doing his gallery show – Ms. Kathryn – said she worked for the FBI. Marty wondered if she was a secret agent because when he asked her if she had a gun, she wouldn't tell him. If she did work for the FBI, maybe he could explain to her what happened, and he wouldn't get in trouble.

Marty clapped his hands in the air and congratulated himself for coming up with a solution. The realization brought a surge of relief, and things started to feel right again. He hopped out of bed, turned on the TV, and popped in an Asteroids cartridge. He was soon flying through space, breaking big rocks into smaller rocks, and shooting at spaceships that happened to get in his way.

Yeah, he would definitely talk to Ms. Kathryn. They had another meeting at the gallery in a couple of weeks. A real FBI agent. Wow. How cool was that? Maybe he could work undercover one day, too.

After all, no one would ever harm an FBI agent.

He was sure of that.

Chapter 56

It was one of those dank, gray November afternoons that always makes the day feel later than it actually is. It didn't help that the temperature had dropped from brisk to downright bitter in a span of about six hours. Our blue jean jackets provided very little by way of protection or insulation, and when the final bell rang, we walked to the parking lot with our hands jammed in our pockets and our heads down, trying to make ourselves as small as possible.

The Milk Wagon might not have had a lot of amenities, but the heater that came standard blew like a blast furnace, and shortly after Hop and I climbed in, we went from cold to warm to comfortable in a matter of minutes. It actually worked too well, and by the time we pulled into Gulfport Lake, we had to crack a window and knock the fan down a few notches to provide some much-needed circulation. I parked over by the pier next to a truck we recognized but weren't necessarily expecting.

"Lance, what are you doing here?"

"I was about to ask you the same thing. Nate called me this morning before school. Said I needed to meet him. Said it was real important."

"Before school?"

"Yeah." Nate got me again. He had this meeting planned and blocked out long before he approached my locker.

"Well, climb in and wait with us. Here comes Mark."

Mark pulled up next to Lance and piled in, too.

"It's cold as balls outside," he said, settling in and pulling his cap off. "So, what's this all about?"

"No idea. Nate said he wanted to meet with everyone, so who knows?"

"You think something else happened with his dad?"

"He didn't say, but it seemed pretty urgent."

"I saw you and Emily chatting after chemistry this morning," Mark said. "That seems to be going well."

"Better each day. In fact, I'm going to meet her for a slice tonight after we leave here."

"Be careful, she'll burn a hole in your pocket."

"Money well spent, dude." Mark was right. I was going to have to get a job over the holidays. Maybe at Bookland or Thornberry's. The mall stores always needed people at Christmastime, and it was fairly easy money, even if I did have to go to Biloxi. We chatted for a few more minutes, and just as we began to question whether Nate was going to show, he pulled up on the other side and got out. He slid into the second row holding a large Burger King sack and a fully loaded drink carrier.

"Well, this certainly makes the afternoon a little brighter," Hop said, reaching in and pulling out a cheeseburger.

"It's the least I could do." He passed out the food, but I noticed he didn't eat.

"Guys, look, I know this is weird meeting like this, and I appreciate y'all coming here on short notice, but things are moving fast – real fast – for me right now." We kept chewing. "And I may have finally come to the point where I could use your help."

"Hold on. You got any ketchup?" Mark asked. Nate threw him a couple of packets, and after he squeezed two onto his burger, he turned back to Nate. "Sorry. So, what's up?"

"I think you'll understand better once I explain everything. Matt, can you pop the Trapper?"

I reached under the dash to hit the switch, and the compartment fell open. Nate leaned up from the second row and pulled out the photos and the bank papers. He laid out two of the gory photos on the dash where all of us could see.

"Nope," Hop said, "not gonna look again. Especially not while I'm eating. Matt, how long have you been keeping these?"

"Just for a few days now."

"I asked him to – and for good reason. Remember the other afternoon at Jack's when I told you Ms. Cooper told me she worked on my dad's case?"

"Yeah."

"Well, she told me a lot more than that – she got real deep into the investigation. That's the reason I was late. Take these two guys," he said, tapping the photos. "They were business partners of my dad's – and I don't mean at the clinic. Earlier this year, they had been busted red-handed for defrauding the government as part of this whole money-laundering enterprise."

"You know who they are?" I asked.

"I think so. According to Ms. Cooper, the first one – this guy that's barely recognizable – was going to work something out, but before his final day in court, he killed himself. At least that's what was reported. The second – his name was Tom – was shot on the way in to the FBI office to meet with Ms. Cooper. Three bullets to the head, mob-style. Boom. Just like that, two snitches out of the picture and –"

Hop put his burger down. "This is starting to freak me out. Now I kind of wish I had never seen these. Period."

"Chill, Hop," Mark said. "Go on, Nate."

"So, here's where it takes another turn. Remember that box at my house where y'all left my wallet?"

"Yeah."

"This weekend, I go to clean it out and find another Polaroid. Take a look at this." He slapped another picture down on the seat.

"*Another* one?" Mark asked, and we all leaned in.

"Victim number three."

The lady in this photo was sure enough dead, but she wasn't bloodied and mangled. She looked like a piece of meat that someone forgot and left in the grocery bag overnight. Tainted. One eye was open, but it was milky and made her stare look vacant. A zombie.

"Nasty. What happened to her?"

"Strangled. In her own damn house. Name was Charlotte Gutherz. And like the other two, she was involved in the fraud scam – although she wasn't as big a player. She also had another connection to my dad, which should not come as a total surprise. She was his girlfriend."

"Girlfriend?"

"Um hmm." He cleared his throat. "Setting that little gem aside, just like the two dead guys, she was cooperating with Ms. Cooper. He got her the same day she gave her statement, right after she got home."

"He? Do you know who did it?"

"I think so," Nate said. "Maybe."

"You *think* so?"

"They know there's another player out there, they're just not sure who it is. They believe his name is something like 'Fast Eddie.'"

Hop couldn't resist. "Look, I know you didn't want to go to the cops before, Nate, but don't you have to now? I mean, this sounds dangerous for you. If I'm hearing you right, everyone that spoke to the FBI about this has died. What if they find out *you* talked to an FBI agent? Or that *we* know about these photos? We should go right now before we end up on the wrong end of the camera."

"You're absolutely right, Hop, and in any other world, I would agree with you. But here's why I can't – at least not yet. The only people who have any idea that Charlotte Gutherz even gave a statement are the people investigating the case. In fact, no one outside of law enforcement has made the connection between Charlotte and my dad."

"So?"

"If Charlotte Gutherz's role in all this is not yet public – then how'd this photo turn up in that box?"

"I don't know."

Nate must have seen me nodding my head, because he called me out.

"Matt does," Nate said. "Tell 'em, Matt. Tell 'em why I can't go to the cops."

"If the cops are the only ones who know about the link between Charlotte and Nate's dad –"

" – then a cop had to drop that photo off." Mark said.

"That's right," Nate said. "There's someone dirty on the inside."

CHAPTER 57

Hop closed his eyes and ran his fingers through his hair. "You really think the cops are in on this?"

"Yep. Has to be, and for all I know, Ms. Cooper could be one of them. She was mighty interested in speaking with me."

This revelation didn't exactly do much to ease Hop's angst, and I thought he was going to go off again, but he didn't say anything. He just put his food back into his bag and stared out the window. Not before Mark grabbed the rest of his fries.

"It actually explains a lot," Nate said.

"How so?"

"Someone in the know – probably this 'Eddie' fellow – has been providing tips all along. Think about it. This second guy there – Tom – was murdered on his way in to a confidential meeting with the FBI. This Charlotte lady barely made it home before they silenced her. And my dad, well, he walked scot-free after his arrest. Someone had to give him the heads up as well."

"Damn. This is getting thick."

Nate picked up the photo. "Speaking of my dad, here's where it gets interesting."

"I thought it was plenty interesting already," Mark said, his mouth full.

"Ms. Cooper thinks he has a lot of money holed away in secret bank accounts somewhere, but she doesn't know where. She thinks that before he got arrested, he handed off the bank info, probably to Charlotte. You know, once he was tipped off."

"How much money we talking about here, Nate?"

"Millions."

"Millions?" Mark let out a low whistle. "You said *millions*. Plural?"

"Plural."

"Well no wonder she's so interested. So why doesn't your dad just go to the bank himself? Withdraw the money and move on?"

"Because he can't."

"Why not?"

"Well, he's still under investigation, so I doubt he can just march into a bank and withdraw a bunch of dirty money without setting off alarms. Plus, I think he gave everything to Charlotte. He doesn't have the means to get the money now even if he wanted to risk it."

"Why doesn't Fast Eddie just go get it himself, then?"

"The accounts are not in his name. He can't access it either."

"Whose name are they in?"

Nate took a breath to let the question settle. "Mine."

For the first time since the food arrived, Mark stopped eating. "You got to be shitting me."

"Yours?" Hop asked. "Then what are you waiting on?"

"Good question. It's kind of complicated." He dealt out the deposit slips. "Looks like there are seven banks total. Two in Hattiesburg, one in Wiggins, and four others here on the Coast – Ocean Springs, Gulfport, Biloxi, and Pass Christian. My plan is to go to each bank, one by one, and withdraw fifteen thousand from each location."

"Just fifteen thousand? Why not gut 'em?"

"Because I don't need to take out any more," Nate said. "First, the greater the withdrawal, the greater the odds of it getting someone's attention – we don't want anyone calling the cops, right? Second, any withdrawal over ten thousand sends an alarm to the IRS – bypassing the local authorities. So to your point, Hop, doing it this way does get the authorities involved, but on a much higher level, bypassing any local corruption."

The more he talked, the more it made sense, but there was one important factoid missing, and I got the impression Nate was tiptoeing around it on purpose.

"Nate, this is all well and good, but you said you needed us to help. If you're withdrawing this money, where do we come in?"

"That's another great question." Nate explained that while one withdrawal may trigger a singular alarm, it had the potential to get lost in the red tape, and of greater importance, potentially trigger a call to the local cops. To avoid that, he needed to have the money withdrawn from all of the accounts at or near the same time, to prompt an immediate, emergency action from the investigators at the IRS. Nate would personally light the fuse by calling each bank manager once the withdrawals were done to tip them off about what was going down. He planned to identify his father as the culprit behind it all, and once Doc Mayes got back on the radar, the authorities would really start swarming.

"Well," Mark said, "if I'm looking at all these banks, you're going to need to cover several hundred miles back and forth. Could take three or four hours. How are you going to do that all at once?"

"I'm not," Nate said. "You are."

CHAPTER 58

If the air in the Milk Wagon felt oppressive before, it turned down-right suffocating when Nate threw down that gauntlet.

"What do you mean *we* are?" Hop asked. "You're the one who is on the accounts. If we do it, we could end up in jail." There were some murmurs from Mark and Lance as well, but we all quieted down when Nate held his hands up.

"Settle down, guys. I get it. You're not going to go to jail, okay? If anyone does, it's me. First off, nobody – not a soul at any of these banks – knows who I am. I have never set foot in a single one. So any one of you, armed with the proper I.D. and basic information – account numbers, passwords, whatever – can get in and get out, no questions asked."

"Fake I.D., you mean?" I asked.

"Yep."

"That sounds like even worse. It makes more sense if you person-ally do it. Even if you can't get them all done in one day, you can hit up at least three or four, right?"

"You're right, but I have to stay put – for two reasons. I already said I need to be on the phone calling these bank managers once I get confirmation that the withdrawal has been made. But that's not the most important one. I made some calls after school pretending to update some of the accounts with our new Gulfport address – just to test the water. I learned the contact number the banks have on file for questions relating to the accounts happens to be the phone at the house in my dad's office. If someone from the bank calls to verify the withdrawal, I need to be there to take it."

"Your house? Are you crazy? What about your dad?"

"My dad and Vicky go to Destin each year over Thanksgiving weekend. And no, I'm not invited. I've never been invited. I will have the place to myself."

"You sure? We thought they were gone a few months ago when we went over there to play pool, but that didn't end well."

"You're right, but that was different. They'll be out of town this time; I guarantee it."

"But aren't we still committing a crime?"

"In theory, perhaps, but no one will ever know you were involved. Plus, I'm hoping all sins will be forgiven at the end of the day." Nate didn't waver and he didn't appear the least bit rattled by our pushback.

"How so?"

"I have reached out to Geoff Clarke, the lead reporter at the *Sun Herald* who broke a lot of the earlier stories. I told him who I was and shared with him some of the details he had not been privy to. He and I are scheduled to meet on Monday, where I'll give him the full scoop – and I'll get to tell my story, for once. My *entire* story. I will give him the photos and will tell him that I – me, Nate Mayes – withdrew the money from the banks to trigger the alarm, and that I am prepared to take full responsibility for that. Frankly, I think he and the public will be more interested in uncovering the corruption inside the investigation than in my actions. Especially if I give the money back."

"You plan to give it back, then."

"Most of it, Hop," Nate said with a wink. "After a long day of work, we could use some of the funds to meet up at Gulfport Lake for a cold beer or two to celebrate."

"But it's not your money to begin with, Nate," Hop said. "That's the flaw in this whole thing."

"At the end of the day though, the money is going to end up where it's supposed to be. Speaking of which, I think once this is all said and done, we'll get a reward"

"Reward?" Mark and I both looked up.

"FBI is already offering $50,000 for information leading to the arrest of those responsible. That puts us at $10k and change – each – if it goes down right, if not more."

"Seriously?" Mark asked.

"Yep."

Reward money was certainly a new concept for me. Ten thousand dollars was a *lot* of dough. Certainly enough to finish out my senior year at St. John's – and get a start on college.

"No argument from me, brother." Lance said. "If we do want to party down that night, just let me know. I'll have my buddies get a fire started."

"Plan on it. Sounds like Lance is on board. Anyone else?"

"I don't know, guys," Hop said. "Even if y'all are right and there is some fishy stuff going on with the police, that doesn't mean it's right. My dad knows a judge. I bet Nate could reach out to him. Just seems like there are other alternatives out there we should consider other than a backdoor bank robbery. I need to sleep on it."

"Okay," Nate said, "but let's keep the judges out of it for now. I understand this may not be for you, Hop – and no hard feelings if it's not. But we've got to make a move and make it soon if we're going to do this thing. Even though I bought a little time by picking up that call in my dad's office, it won't be too long before he and Eddie connect, so I have to stay ahead of them. Mark, Matt, – in or out?"

Mark looked up at me, and I could tell he was thinking the same thing.

"I don't know, Nate. I just think, uh, there's a lot at stake here, you know."

"Mark?"

"Me too, Nate. Makes me nervous."

Nate leaned in. "You're right. Both of you. There is a lot at stake, and I recognize that. I wouldn't ask you if I didn't think it was the right thing to do. I admit, nearly all of my motives are selfish, and other than the reward money, there's not a lot of payoff for you."

I agreed with him. The reward money was nice, but it would do me no good if I were locked up.

"But if I do nothing, then my dad – and this man who killed Charlotte Gutherz – will walk off with a fortune they stole. That by itself is bad enough. But it gets worse. I've got skin in the game now, and when my dad eventually connects the dots and realizes I know everything, well, I don't need tell you how that may end for me.

I shook my head but didn't say a word. No one did.

"Look, guys, bottom line, I'm going to try it whether you are on board or not. Frankly, I'm not too worried about my well-being. What happens will happen, but if I don't at least give it a shot, well, I will do wrong by her." He pulled out the picture of his mom. "Although I'll never know if my dad was involved in mom's death, I certainly have my suspicions. Whether he was or wasn't doesn't matter, because he has made my life hell ever since. And I owe it to her to do what I believe is the right thing here." We all sat there with our mouths closed. "So, win or lose, I'm not going down without trying."

I remembered the advice I gave Nate way back at the locker that morning about taking a stand. What would it say about me if I backed out now? There was not a better example of someone acting simply on principle, and I was not about to let Nate and Lance go at it alone. I rapped my knuckles on the table.

"Let's do it."

Mark looked over at me and then back at Nate, then got a little throaty. "I hear you. I couldn't live without my momma. I'm in."

Nate smiled. "I can't tell you how much this means to me, guys. Let's meet up tomorrow after school at Justin Harrison's house to get our documents in order."

Justin Harrison was the best fake I.D. maker on the Coast. His handiwork had been used at bars and convenience stores from the Flora-Bama to Pat O'Brien's, and not once was anyone busted.

"I'll cover his fees. After we get that box checked we can circle up for more details."

"When do you plan on doing this, Nate?" I asked.

"Like I said, I've got the house to myself over the holiday. I'm thinking the day after Thanksgiving. Crazy busy. Shoppers everywhere. Maximum distraction."

"That's next week."

"Indeed it is," Nate said, collecting the papers and the photos. "We'd better get rolling."

As I drove home, I had mixed emotions. Thankfully, they were more on the positive side than negative. A bit nervous, but glad to be on a team I really believed was doing the right thing. Plus, the more

I thought about it, the more Nate's plan sounded pretty solid. In and out in a few hours. No harm done. Bad guy put away. Retribution. Reward money.

What could go wrong?

CHAPTER 59

It had been just under ten days since Kathryn Cooper stopped Nate Mayes in the gallery to discuss the investigation, and frankly, Kathryn was surprised and a bit disappointed Nate hadn't called back. When they first spoke, he seemed eager to talk and even asked some questions, but she hadn't heard a peep since.

She thought she had one more chance of getting a private one-on-one with him before having to take a more formal – and perhaps adversarial – approach. There was another follow-up meeting with her gallery students coming up on Friday. Yes, it was the day after Thanksgiving, but schedule-wise, it worked best for most everyone. She had planned on pulling Nate aside during that meeting and asking him straight up if he was going to help out with the investigation.

But all that was before the real story behind Charlotte Gutherz's murder broke, and when the above the fold headline – with a full color picture of Charlotte – hit the front page of the *Sun-Herald*, the world suddenly knew there was more to the case than originally met the eye.

It absolutely blindsided Kat, because there was no pre-publication buzz or chatter from her usual reporter contacts. When she arrived at the office the previous Wednesday, Geoff Clarke was holding a fresh copy. The story, citing an anonymous source, linked Charlotte Gutherz to the money-laundering case, and the accompanying multi-page story tied her to Ford Mayes – both professionally and personally. It also linked her to Joe Birdsall and Tom Chrestman, and in so doing, called into question whether their respective deaths came at the hand of the same individual. Although Kathryn repeatedly told Geoff she could not and would not talk, he was relentless, and by Friday, a whole gaggle of reporters, along with several cameras on tripods, made camp outside the FBI office. She knew it was bad when they catered lunch.

She hoped that once Thanksgiving week started, they would back off, but they were still there when she pulled in on Monday. She couldn't blame them, really. After all, a third death in a money-laundering scandal triggered all of the usual questions and headlines – each one a bit more salacious than the other. Was Joe Birdsall's death really a suicide? Who killed Tom Chrestman? Is the mob involved? Was Charlotte Gutherz Dr. Mayes's mistress?

All of them except the latter were questions she, too, wanted answered. Of course the biggest question that remained was what were the Agency's next steps to move the investigation forward? Charlotte Gutherz's death cast a serial killer pall of danger over the community, and everyone was looking to Kathryn for some relief and assurance that she was on top of it.

She had delayed putting out to her team what she had learned from Charlotte about Nate's name being on the bank accounts. It was the one thing the press didn't know about yet. Kat had hoped – through Nate – to run that lead down privately, but she could delay no longer.

It was a holiday week, so she didn't want to overload anyone too much before they peeled off for a day or two with their families, so she scheduled a meeting on Wednesday morning. That way, she could lay out what she knew, field the inevitable questions, and let everyone have a few days to let everything percolate before they got back on Monday and started to drill down – yet again.

She thought about who should attend the meeting, and initially intended to limit it to her coworkers in the agency. In addition to Ethan, she would bring down some of the team from Hattiesburg, as well as some of the federal marshals who had assisted thus far. They had been publicly shamed, too, and would appreciate another chance in the box.

Kat had also kept the information regarding Nate Mayes and the bank accounts from her new favorite person for what ultimately was the same reason, except this time, it was a little more personal. She didn't want to look like a fool in front of him, either. If, however, they were going to go all hands on deck for one more push, the more eyes she had on it, the better.

In the memo she drafted regarding attendees, she added one more line.

Rick Papania, Chief of Police, Gulfport Police Department.

She smiled and folded up the paper.

He would certainly want to know about this.

CHAPTER 60

Fast Eddie left the FBI office a lot more anxious than when he came in. When Kathryn called the meeting, he expected a general update and some planning guidance to cover the gap between Thanksgiving and Christmas. He had no idea she had another name in mind and was frankly surprised she waited until then to spring it on him. The fact that she held back on him pissed him off, so much so that he was cursing out loud as he backed out of the parking lot. After all, she had shared everything else about the investigation ever since they got together.

Or had she? He was also upset that he hadn't thought of the young Nate Mayes as someone who could have pertinent information. He certainly should have because he was the one, a rookie cop at the time, who pulled the boy out of that old Cadillac DeVille when he was just a toddler.

Memories of that day still haunted him, and not just because it was the first fatality he ever worked. As horrible as it was, he could have dealt with the death of Mrs. Mayes. What he didn't expect was his supervisor making him change the accident report after the fact. Eddie was sure her husband, Dr. Ford Mayes, had been driving under the influence, and switched out Mrs. Mayes's body for his after he wrecked the car. But Eddie was a naïve rookie, and when his sergeant told him to toe the line and keep his mouth shut, he did. When he later failed to protest after the Doc put a one hundred dollar bill in his pocket and thanked him for his service on the way out, he unknowingly and unwillingly took his first steps into a life of crime and cover up that he had labored under ever since. Now that he had finally stumbled on a potential way out, he certainly wasn't going to let Kathryn blow it.

She wanted to wait until Monday to make a move. He understood she was set to meet with the boy again on Friday at that lame-ass art gallery, and was going to put the screws to him then if he wasn't helpful. He didn't blame her for taking her time to try and bring young Nate Mayes around. That always seemed to work better with juveniles who were naturally suspicious of adults anyway. Fast Eddie was not, however, bound to her schedule, and he saw a fine opportunity to advance his own interests, but only if he moved quickly. If this boy, in fact, had pertinent information, Eddie could get everything he needed from him without Eddie even having to meet up with Doc Mayes. He could finally be free.

No, Nate Mayes would most certainly not be making it to the Friday afternoon soiree with Kathryn. Not if Eddie got to Nate first.

CHAPTER 61

Thanksgiving was without a doubt the Ragone family's favorite holiday. Food was, and always had been, an integral part of their lives, and when they weren't eating, they were talking about eating. The fourth Thursday in November gave them a legal excuse – federally recognized, no less – to engage in their favorite pastime. It was un-American not to, Mrs. Ragone used to say, and we had no intentions whatsoever of dampening her patriotism.

It had become their practice, much like a movie preview, to have multiple epicurean lead-ups to the big day. Mark's mom started cooking the Saturday before, and she never stopped until the bird hit the table five days later. We, of course, were acutely aware of their schedule, which is why we happened to land there on Wednesday night hoping to gorge on debris po-boys served on French bread from Leidenheimer's.

We were sitting on the back porch, away from the rest of the family, admiring the fake I.D.s Justin had just made. They were masterpieces, wholly indistinguishable from the real thing. He even had bootleg copies of the sleeves used by the DMV that he laminated over his handiwork. All we had to do was show up and take a picture in front of a blue poster board. We provided Justin with the information we wanted on the license itself – including Nate's signature done in our respective scrawls – and he took care of the rest. It was a good thing too, because Nate had the weirdest, loopiest handwriting I had ever seen. The hardest part to me was memorizing Nate's social security number and address. When I looked at his date of birth, I did a double-take.

"Nate, is this right?"

"What?"

"According to this, your birthday was Monday."

"Yep."

"Dude, why didn't you tell us? We would have thrown a party. You can't have a birthday and not tell us."

"It's really no big deal. Certainly not at my house."

"Not this year, for sure," Mark said.

"Not any year."

"What?"

"I haven't had a birthday party since before I can remember."

"That's wrong."

"Sure is," said Mrs. Ragone, walking up behind us. "I'm going to have to do something about that."

"No, Mrs. Ragone, you've done plenty. Please."

"You sit tight, now."

"This means we're getting extra dessert," I said. "I'm glad we brought Nate along after all. Happy Birthday." We all clinked our bottles together.

"Thanks, guys. You may also find yourself surprised at the birth year."

"Huh?" Mark looked at his I.D., then tilted his head up toward the light, calculating in his brain. "If this is right, it makes you . . . eighteen?"

"One would think so, right? I was surprised when I saw it the first time, too. I don't know if he did it on purpose or not, but when my dad opened up these accounts, he got the year off by one. He probably has no idea what year I was born. Par for the course, right?"

"Uh oh," Mark said. "I don't know if I can pass for eighteen."

Lance piped in. "I can."

"Lance, you could pass for thirty," I said, "you have a beard, for Pete's sake. Just be glad Hop's not doing it. He barely looks old enough to be driving."

"Hey, y'all talking about me?" The screen door popped open, and Hop stepped out. "Again? Well, I must be important, then."

We all shouted his name, and he pulled up a chair. I was glad he came out after all. He had been laying low. I was even happier to see Mrs. Ragone trailing right behind him carrying a pound cake that had previously been designated for the Thanksgiving table. She jammed a handful of candles into it and lit them in one pass using a long wooden match from a box she pulled out of her apron.

As we sang Happy Birthday, Nate grinned like a cheetah and blew all the candles out on the first try, which just made us cheer louder.

"Did you make a wish?" Mark asked.

"I sure did," Nate said, giving us a wink. I could tell Nate was pleased. And we were, too. Every kid should have a birthday party.

When it got down to just a few crumbs left on the plate, we turned back to business, starting with logistics. Nate had assigned us by region. I was covering the two banks in Hattiesburg, Mark had a bank in Saucier and a bank in Wiggins, and Lance had the Coast run – one bank each in Gulfport, Biloxi and Ocean Springs. I was kind of hoping I would cover the Coast, but since Lance lived up in the county, it made sense for him to be the one going to banks where we had the greatest risk of running into anyone we knew.

"There is a method to my scheduling, Matt. I think this works best."

"I see what you're doing, and I don't disagree, it's just that the Milk Wagon has been acting real squirrelly lately. I'd hate to drive an hour or so up to Hattiesburg and not be able to get back. The last thing I want to be is stuck on the side of the road with thirty thousand in cash riding shotgun."

"That's a good point," Nate said. "I'll tell you what, you take Ferris and leave the Milk Wagon here. I'm manning dispatch at home base all day, anyway."

"Lucky," Mark said. "What if my car breaks down?"

Nate turned to Hop. "Does your presence here tonight mean you are back in the game?"

"Depends on what you mean by 'in the game.' I still don't plan on going into any banks, if that's what you're asking. But y'all know I can't let you do this alone. I figured you may need some brains to pull this off. It's not a stretch to say this isn't exactly a Mensa meeting."

"What?"

"Shut up, Mark."

"You in, then?"

"Somewhat. I guess."

Nate grinned. "Well . . ."

Mark put his arm around Hop and gave him that old shit-eating grin of his. "You feel like being a driver?"

Hop looked like he was going to be sick.

"I'll take Hop's silence as a 'yes', so problem solved."

"Where do we go once we have the money?" Lance asked.

"That's the next item on my list. Bring everything back here, and I'll start putting things together for that reporter. If we get through soon enough, I may get him to come over Friday afternoon."

"What if you can't give it to him then? That's a lot of dough to carry around over the weekend."

"True, but if I have to wait until Monday, I know where to keep it. I found a spot outdoors in that old potting shed out front that hasn't seen the light of the day since before all of us were born. None of the staff is working this weekend with the holiday, so no one will touch it. Meet at my house just before noon." Nate said. "We can go from there."

And that was it. Everyone was on board. Seeing all of us there together made me feel like Jake and Elwood after they persuaded Blue Lou and Matt Guitar Murphy to join the band.

Probably not the best analogy, in retrospect.

They all ended up in prison.

CHAPTER 62

Rick Papania tried to reassure Kat that her decision to bring everyone in to discuss Doc Mayes's son was the right move. While she appreciated his efforts, she was not totally convinced. What if she dropped the ball on this one, too? What if the press got wind she had been sitting on it all along? What if whoever remained out there got to Nate before she did? Kat didn't think she could handle another call informing her that one of her witnesses had died. Especially one involving a minor.

Of course, Rick's methods of persuasion were not limited to talking. He drew her a bath, and afterwards, she unleashed a week's worth of frustration on him in the bedroom. She was glad he didn't live in the typical cop apartment, because the neighbors certainly would have gotten an earful. When they were done, she rolled off and passed out cold – exhausted in the best way possible – and slept solid throughout the night.

She and Rick celebrated Thanksgiving lunch together, and the event was, at best, bittersweet. She was happy they were spending the holiday together, but it was the first time since her father's death that she hadn't done Thanksgiving with her mom. She had moved to Nashville over the summer to be near some of her girlfriends, and between Kathryn's work meeting Wednesday night, and her gallery obligation on Friday, she just couldn't make the sixteen-hour round trip. She missed her mom's cornbread dressing, done-buttered biscuits and fudge pie. Not one to beat herself up too much, Kat countered her melancholy by devouring Rick's smoked turkey breast, sweet potato casserole, and bacon-wrapped green beans – not a bad meal itself – before sprawling out on the couch to watch NFL. It wasn't too long before the tryptophan kicked in and pulled them both into a deep slumber. When she woke up, Rick had already slipped out to go to Baton Rouge to have dinner with his mother, who also lived alone. Kathryn hoped he would ask her to go with him, but he said the timing was not yet right. He promised Kat she would meet his mom over Christmas, which was fine. What difference would a few weeks make in the big picture, anyway? He would be back by Friday lunch, and he promised he'd come that afternoon to help with any heavy lifting she might need for Marty Deen's show.

Kat drove back to her place and curled up on the couch with a plate of leftovers and her cat, an old gray tabby named Patty that showed up on her doorstep the day after she moved in. She popped in a rented copy of *Splash* just as the sun disappeared below the horizon. She liked the movie a lot more than she thought she would, but she wouldn't go so far as to say she had an enjoyable evening. She used to watch videos by herself all the time, but on this particular night, she felt the pang of not having Rick by her side. It kind of surprised her. Just a few months ago, she existed, quite contently, in her own world – work, the gallery, and the cat, pretty much.

Now she couldn't imagine her life without him.

CHAPTER 63

Kathryn fully intended to wake up early Friday morning to get a head start on some of the early bird Christmas sales, but when her alarm went off at seven she bypassed the snooze and shut it off completely. A few hours later, she still wasn't dressed, and she really didn't care. She poured herself a cup of coffee and sat on her front porch, wrapped in a robe and a blanket, stroking Patty's back and thinking about what she should buy Rick for Christmas. She really wanted to get him something special, but she had no idea what a man like him needed, and shopping for something so personal in the company of a thousand other people was not something that appealed to her. She went inside and pulled out the Mayes file, making some more notes in the margins in preparation for her talk with Nate. When she came up for air, it was eleven-thirty, so she called Rick to see if he was home. When he didn't pick up, she left a message, pulled on a sweatshirt, and went on a run to work out the kink in her thigh from sitting cross-legged on the floor. When she got back in, her answering machine was blinking, so she rewound the tape and played it back.

"Hi, Ms. Cooper, this is Grant Deen – Marty's dad. I was wondering if you could give him a ride to his meeting at the gallery today? His mother and I have to leave for a few hours this afternoon. I'm sorry this is so last minute, but Marty would be so upset if he couldn't attend, and I'm in a pickle. We should be back no later than five-thirty or six and can pick him up then. Thanks; please call if this works."

Kathryn called and let them know that, yes, someone would get Marty to the gallery. They told her that on any other day, they would have let him ride his bike, but they usually didn't allow him to be on the road if at least one of them wasn't home. She was glad to do it, but it kind of put her in a spot. She needed to get there early before everyone showed up so she could get everything arranged. She picked up the phone, dialed, and once again, the call rolled over to an answering machine. It was one of those days.

"Hey, it's me. Can you pick up Marty Deen on your way in to the gallery this afternoon? He needs a ride. His address is 3860 Hawthorn Drive; over in Green Oaks. Thanks. See you then."

Kat jumped into the shower, and as she was rinsing her hair, the perfect gift idea came to her. She was surprised she hadn't thought of it before. She was so excited, she decided to brave the crowds after all, and as she left the house, she laughed to herself.

It was not the type of Christmas present she would want him opening in front of his mother.

CHAPTER 64

Marty had a wonderful Thanksgiving. It was his second favorite holiday, due in no small part to the fact that it meant that his most favorite holiday, Christmas, was just around the corner. He had spent the morning helping his mom get the house ready for company. He was in charge of setting the table and putting the ice in the glasses, and his Nana, who had come down to eat with them and spend the night, told him he did a splendid job. After they ate, everyone loaded up in the car – even Nana – and went to the Village Cinema to watch *Rocky IV*. When they got home, they popped popcorn on the stove, then drank Cokes and played spades until bedtime.

It was a perfect day. So perfect that Marty could not imagine how the day after Thanksgiving could equal it, much less be any better, but boy, was he wrong. After breakfast on Friday his parents loaded him up and took him to Wilson's to look at toys and remote-control cars. They had a display set up, and Marty tested out a red and yellow one. Then they all had a fancy lunch at Vrazel's right on the beach where Marty had to put his napkin in his lap and keep his elbows off the table. He ate one whole loaf of hot bread before they even brought out the food. His parents had trout and spinach soufflé. He had a cheeseburger, then a chocolate chip cookie and ice cream for dessert. The cherry on top, however, was when Marty's daddy told him after lunch that Ms. Kathryn or one of her friends would be picking Marty up to take him to the gallery, because they had to take Nana back home early. He could barely sit still in the car. He was so excited that when they pulled up, he went straight to his apartment to pack up his supplies, even though it was still several hours before his new partner would show up.

Who would it be? Was it Ms. Kathryn? What if it was someone else? Probably was, if she was a secret agent. He packed two walkie-talkies, several pens and magic markers, as well as a Kodak disk camera in case they let him take pictures in the car. He sat down in front of his TV set and pushed in the *Spy Hunter* cartridge on his Atari, then looked at his calculator watch. Only two more hours. When the "Peter Gunn Theme" began to play, he scooted up closer to the TV and started driving his Aston Martin, shooting at the bad guys as he passed them. When he made it through the first level with no deaths and a personal high score, he thought to himself that the day could turn out to be the most exciting day of his life.

He couldn't have been more on target.

CHAPTER 65

Nate's plan sounded reasonable when we were talking about it back in Gulfport, but when I pulled into the parking lot of the Magnolia Federal Bank in Hattiesburg shortly after noon on Friday, my hands were sweating so badly, the steering wheel looked like it had been wiped down with Armor All. I stayed in the truck for a few more minutes, cut the radio off so I could be in total silence to concentrate, and ran Nate's personal information in my head again. Full name, date of birth, address and social security number. Repeat. I must have done it at least eighty times on the way up.

I eventually got out, checked my wallet to make sure I had switched out my regular driver's license for the fake, then made my way to the door. When I walked in, I felt like I was in a Stanley Kubrick movie, and things did not appear to be what they seemed.

Was everyone in the bank staring at me?

Did they know what I was up to?

What was that lady over there whispering to the other lady?

What is that kid looking at?

Is that a manager standing right behind the teller?

How many here are undercover cops?

I grabbed a checking withdrawal slip from one of the cubbies out of the big waist-high table in the middle of the lobby. My mind had not yet stopped racing, and I started to get second thoughts. To get my focus back, I did what I always did when the stress becomes too much to bear.

I slowed down. I breathed – in and out – five times.

In a matter of seconds, my perception changed, and instead of just looking at everyone, I started to *see* them. Yes, there were a lot of people in the bank, and there was some whispering and pointing going on, but the more I took it in, the more I realized no one had noticed me. There was a manager behind the rail, but he was leaning up against a counter, talking to one of the older ladies. Most of the office doors off to the left were closed, and the open ones were vacant.

Things were going to be okay.

I filled out the withdrawal form just as Nate had said and signed his name like a champ. The one cheat we allowed was the account number, and I had it written on a sheet in my wallet. Made sense since no dude my age would have known his own bank account number anyway.

Now I had to choose the right teller. There was one elderly lady with her hair pulled back tight. She had probably been there since back in the days when a free toaster came standard with a new savings account. Translation: she was an old-fashioned rule follower. A pass for sure.

The next prospect was a complete opposite. College student, but not at USM. Probably William Carey. Remarkable in just how odd she was. It looked like she got her fashion guidance from the clothing section in a JC Penney catalog, but altogether skipped the pages offering grooming or hygiene implements. Add to the mix side-parted oily bangs and runaway teeth, and I knew she was a pass as well. I don't do well with bad smells from girls, and she looked to be potentially off the charts.

The next two were housewife types, one a divorcee who was looking, and one still in the happy throes of a young marriage. I almost went to the more seasoned one, but they were so chatty, I was concerned the two would want to consult on the merits of my case. A teenager seeking to withdraw an amount that probably eclipsed their collective annual salaries was certainly fodder for discussion. No good either.

Then I found what I was looking for. The last lady in the line was a slightly overweight middle-aged black lady with a Tina Turner wig on. For some reason, I have always gotten along with black women, especially older ones. I've always been drawn to their kindness and the fact that they laugh at anything – really laugh. Most love to hug, and as a kid, I can recall being happily enveloped in many an ample bosom when I visited my mom during her shift at the hospital. She saw me and waved me over.

"Hey baby, what you got?"

"I, uh, need to make a withdrawal."

"You got your slip all filled out I see."

"Yes, yes I do, uh, . . . Yvette?" Her blouse was partially blocking her nametag.

"That's me, honey. Give it over here, now." She motioned at my hand and I slid the slip across the marble counter and watched her eyes. They flickered, but not for long. Her hands flew across the keyboard, unencumbered by her long fingernails.

"Dang, boy, you kind of young to be swinging this much gold, huh?"

"Old enough," I said, watching her look at the account history. "My dad made some investments that turned out in my favor."

"I would say so," she said, "good for you." She chuckled. "I wish I had a daddy like that."

Oh the irony.

"Planning on buying a big gift today, huh?"

"Yes ma'am. Buying a car."

"For real?"

"Yep. For my birthday." She was starting to get a bit too comfortable with the situation, and I was ready to move on. "It was just a few days ago."

She stopped typing and looked up at me with one eye squinted. "Whatever you do, don't spend this kind of money on a girl, now, you hear? Unless it's your mama."

"My mom would love a gift, for sure." Now there was some truth.

Someone got in line behind me and cleared his throat. Yvette put the back of her hand to her forehead like she had a fever, then stood up out of her chair to see over my shoulder. "We're doing business here, aight? You see them other lines?" The man moved on.

"Some people," she said, shooing him along. "You got any I.D., baby?"

This was it. The real test. Could I keep cool enough to not blow it? I slid the drivers' license across the counter and then pretended like I was looking through the Dum-Dum jar. Actually, I kind of was really digging in there. I like the root beer flavored ones. Everything was fine until she said, "hold on" and walked away.

My legs turned to jelly, my hands started shaking, and I no longer wanted a sucker. I just wanted to get out. I looked over at the door. By my estimate, I was ten to fifteen paces away in case I had to sprint. Add to that another ten seconds or so, since I parked on the side and –

"Son?"

I turned back, and standing next to Yvette was a prematurely balding man in his thirties wearing a short sleeve dress shirt and a striped tie with a grease spot on it. The tie was seven years too old and three inches too high.

"Yessir?"

"Is everything okay?"

I had no idea what he was talking about, but he didn't look mad, and he wasn't motioning for security to come and haul me away, so I stood as firm as I could. I wonder if he could see my hand clamping on the countertop. If this was going to work, I had to pull it together, so I took a deep breath, stood straight up and looked him in the eye and tried to channel Abe Froman.

"Yessir. Is there a problem?"

"I certainly hope not," he said and smiled, holding out his hand. "My name is Patrick Ladner. I'm the branch manager."

I gave him a good grip in return. "Nate Mayes. Nice to meet you."

"I haven't seen you here before. You are . . . younger than I would have imagined."

"Good genes, I guess."

"Uh, yes. I just wanted to come follow up with you and make sure you are happy with the services Magnolia Federal has been providing. We sure hate to lose a good customer like you."

"Thank you."

"Any particular reason why you've taken such a large amount out today?"

This was the second time they got a little too personal with the questions. Yvette got a pass, because I don't think she meant anything by it. This cat, however, was probing. I didn't know much about banking etiquette, but even I knew he was crossing a line here by asking me why I was taking money out. Even if I looked like I was ten years old, he had no right to ask me about my intentions.

"Mr. Ladner, I don't discuss my business publicly, and frankly, I don't see how it is any of your business why I'm making a withdrawal. Now I would just like to get my money and go, please."

He looked around to see if anyone was listening before he spoke. "I'm sorry, Mr. Mayes, I didn't mean to imply that I was asking about what you were going to do with the money. Not at all." He leaned in and whispered. "I just wanted to see if we had done something wrong that made you want to clear out your account. Between your call earlier for the wire transfer, and now this withdrawal, you are down to your last few hundred dollars."

Wire transfer? I stared at him and he stared at me. I, of course, had no idea what he was talking about, but he didn't know I had no idea what he was talking about. I got short with him again.

"Sure, there's a reason I made that call, Mr. Ladner. But now is not the time or the place to discuss. Especially in front of all of these people." I motioned grandly, but not too grandly. "Is your manager here? I don't know what he would say about this inquiry you have begun."

He straightened his tie. To my surprise, it was not a clip on. "Inquiry?"

"Yes, I feel like I'm being interrogated."

"I am sorry. Again, that was not my intention –"

"Good." I had probably pushed it as far as I needed to, and it seemed to have worked. All that was left was to move in for the close, get the money and get out.

Then he tested the waters.

"Just for security purposes, can you remind me of the number you called in from earlier today, Mr. Mayes? The one associated with the account?"

We had memorized Nate's full name. We had memorized his social security number. We had even memorized both of Nate's most recent addresses – Hattiesburg and Gulfport. And of course, we memorized his date of birth.

We barely even looked at the phone number.

CHAPTER 66

I could hear the blood swishing by my ears with each heartbeat. It was acceptable to not know your own bank account number, but not knowing your phone number was unforgiveable. I tried to buy some time.

"You mean my social security number?"

"No, your phone number. The one we have here on file."

I froze, not sure what to do and puffed up a little bit, thinking I was going to have to bluff my way out. I looked down. The account number could be my saving grace after all.

While none of us memorized the phone number, Nate did actually give the office number to us in case we needed to reach him while we were out. I still had my wallet open with the slip of paper containing the account number, and the phone number was written below it in pencil. I pulled it out, scowled and shook my head – all for show, of course.

"You mean for this account number?" I asked, and read the account number out loud – very loud, so much that people were starting to look my way. Mr. Ladner moved closer to the opening, and that was all the time I needed to get a full read of the phone number.

He leaned over and checked her screen for confirmation, and by the time he responded, I was ready to go.

"Yes, Mr. Mayes, that one."

"Okay; my bad. I got confused. Since we moved to Gulfport, some numbers have changed." I figured talking about the move would give me a bit of credibility and get things back to center. I tucked the slip back into my wallet, got one more glance, then recited the phone number to him verbatim.

He looked at me and didn't say anything else. I raised my voice just a bit – one more time.

"Is there anything else, Mr. Ladner?" A slight sheen had started to develop where his hair had once been.

He allowed a conciliatory smile and patted Yvette on the arm. "Please take care of Mr. Mayes here," then reached over the bars to pass me his business card. "I am the manager, by the way." Then he gave a curt "my apologies again," and walked off to answer a question from college girl teller. I was glad to see him go.

Yvette grinned at me. "You making people nervous up in here. You want this in large?"

"What?" I still had no clue what was happening.

"How you want this? Large bills?"

"Uh, sure." I stood there, feeling even more paranoid, as she counted out fifteen thousand dollars in cash. It took way longer than I thought, and when she finished, she put it, along with the withdrawal slip, in a manila envelope with the Magnolia Federal Bank logo in the corner. Mr. Ladner was two stations down now, but I noticed he already looked at me twice since he walked off. I took a chance anyway and had one more request.

"Yvette, do you mind printing out the other withdrawal slip - you know, the one from the wire transfer earlier? I need it for my records."

"You got it, honey." The dot matrix printer brapped out a small piece of paper. She tore it off and added it to the envelope.

"Have a good one," I said.

"You too. Don't forget your sucker."

I walked out as naturally as I could and pulled out of the parking lot, cool and collected. I checked my rearview mirror at least ten times to be sure no one was following me, and once I felt safe, I pulled over at a Ward's and looked in the envelope. I still wasn't used to seeing that much money, but it wasn't the cash I was looking for. It was the withdrawal slips.

Sure enough, the first one I grabbed was the one I had filled out for the cash. Showed a balance of two hundred twenty-eight dollars and five cents after the withdrawal. I then took a look at the one from the phone transfer earlier in the day to try to get a handle on what exactly Mr. Branch Manager Patrick Ladner was talking about.

I let out a slow whistle. It showed a transfer to an account number I hadn't seen before. It certainly wasn't one Nate showed us. The amount: five hundred forty-five thousand dollars.

It was time stamped just twenty minutes before I got there.

CHAPTER 67

Eddie deliberately did not answer his phone. He had a full day planned and really did not have time for anything – or anyone – else, especially prior to three p.m. So when he played back the message, the first thing he did when he heard her voice was curse.

Of course, it was Kathryn, and, of course, she wanted something. She always wanted something. But as he listened to her message, he softened his stance and grinned. He listened to it again and clapped his hands together.

He had been wondering just how he was going to get this Marty idiot out of the picture. Snatch-and-grabs were tough, especially in the daylight, and Marty was no child. Eddie had read *Of Mice and Men*, and if Marty was going to be his Lennie, he might have had a fight on his hands. To make matters worse, apparently most folks in Gulfport knew Marty, and some considered him the city's adopted son, so he wouldn't exactly be low profile if someone happened to witness the act – especially by Fast Eddie, who was not exactly a private citizen himself.

Thanks to Kat's message, such concerns were all behind him now.

He called her back and confirmed. Yes, he could pick up Marty Deen and get him to the gallery. It was the least he could do. She had just made his life a whole lot easier, and as he played back the message one more time, he shook his head in amazement. He had never seen anyone bungle a case so bad, and he had never, ever had a target delivered so innocently right into his hands. By the time she figured out who he really was – assuming she ever did – he would be long gone.

Much like her career.

CHAPTER 68

I drove off feeling a bit conflicted. Happy and relieved to have completed the first leg of my mission without incident, but concerned and confused about the telephone transfer. How in the world did that happen – and who did it? When Nate said these accounts had a lot of money in them, he wasn't kidding. I figured it was several thousand – but half a million? Something was wrong here – very wrong, and I felt like I should call Nate and give him the heads up. I couldn't though, because I didn't have enough change for a pay phone, and I dang sure wasn't about to make a collect call, considering all that was going on with his dad. I might have been paranoid, but my voice was not going to be on any police recordings or phone taps. I decided to go ahead and hit up Hattiesburg First Bank & Trust, per the plan, then hightail it back to Gulfport.

This time I felt a lot more confident going in. I knew Nate's personal info like it was my own. I had survived the experience of not only making the withdrawal at Magnolia, but did so in the presence of a manager. It was well after lunch by now, and as I walked in, I noticed this bank was more crowded than the first one. It was Friday afternoon, and everyone either needed cash for the long weekend, or were desperate to transfer money to pay for the outrageous purchases they made earlier that day in the name of giving. I found a young teller named Chrissy. She had a cute grin and an ever-so-subtle floating eye that made her look even more like a blonde whenever she smiled. I walked right up, not sweating a bit.

She took the withdrawal slip, keyed it in then bit her bottom lip. I didn't start to pucker up until she looked over to her left, not sure what to do.

She tried to get the attention of what looked like her manager. He was young, too, probably a few years out of college at his first real full-time job. Fortunately for me, he was dealing with an irate customer about a declined check. Their back and forth kept getting louder, and soon the other employees stopped what they were doing to see how things would turn out. The top part of his blue button-down collar had started to turn navy and he wisely asked the man to step into his office before things got too heated.

Crisis averted. For him, at least. The manager suddenly disappearing did not help my teller's situation. She tapped on the lady next to her and asked her to take a look. The lady – whose customer line was four deep now that the commotion had died down – looked put upon by the intrusion. Clearly, Chrissy had called on her neighbor before, and the relationship was not what it once was. Her colleague looked at the slip, looked at my driver's license, then looked at me.

"Do it," was all she said and got back to work.

Chrissy counted out fifteen thousand large as she laid them down. I considered asking for a withdrawal history, but once I had the cash in hand, I didn't want to push my luck and got on out of there.

It's a good thing, too, because after I jumped into Ferris and started to pull out of the parking lot, Chrissy pushed the door open and pointed my way. Next to her was manager boy. When he saw me turn and look, he tried to wave me over. I acted like I didn't see him and moved out into traffic before he could get any closer.

It was a potentially close call, and I was glad to have it behind me. The sooner I got back, the better, and it wasn't just to drop the cash off. I hoped Nate wouldn't be too offended if I didn't hang around.

He wasn't the only one waiting for me back home.

CHAPTER 69

Ever since she turned thirteen and really got into shopping, Emily and her mom had a tradition of getting up early the Friday after Thanksgiving and going to Edgewater Mall. This year was no exception. They were first in line at Gayfers, and once the door opened, she and her mother mobilized to their pre-agreed upon departments and loaded up. They then went through the rest of the mall methodically, stopping at Casual Corner, Hobbyville, Goudchaux's and then planned to reconnect at the Walgreens café for lunch.

Once it got past ten-thirty, the chaos started to subside, and by eleven-thirty, the crowd felt to Emily a lot like it did the Saturday before school started. Crowded, but not crazy crowded. She covered the entire mall twice, just to make sure she didn't miss anything, and was happy to finally take a break. She still had a few hours before she had to meet up with everyone at the gallery, so she took her time and chatted with her mom over club sandwiches and fizzy fountain Cokes. Her mom reminded her she needed to get something for Matt. Like she needed reminding. She played along anyway.

"You think so, Mom? I mean we just started officially dating a few weeks ago."

"It's up to you, but if you think he's going to get you something, you don't want to be empty-handed, right?"

"I guess so," Emily said and picked at a French fry. She wouldn't eat the ones that were slick with ketchup. Truth was, she didn't want to let on how much she liked Matt, so she played it down as much as she could. She already bought him a Swatch watch. It was a new thing from Switzerland and super cool — and only cost twenty-five bucks.

Talking about Matt made her miss him. She had hoped he would meet them for lunch, but he was dodgy when she brought it up. Now his absence made sense. He skipped out on lunch because he didn't want to let on he was doing some shopping for her. If so, she hoped he wasn't going overboard. Money was tight around his household, and he wasn't scheduled to start working again until they got out of school for the Christmas holidays.

She thought about it some more, and by the time she finished her meal, she changed her mind. He probably wasn't out doing any shopping after all.

It wouldn't be like him to have any extra cash on hand this early in the season.

CHAPTER 70

I pulled into Nate's driveway with thirty thousand dollars sitting in my lap. It didn't feel as heavy as I thought it would. More like a large paperback book than a brick. I parked next to Lance's truck, and since the front door was unlocked, I started towards the game room, but Nate called me down the hall.

He and Lance were sitting in his dad's office. Considering everything that was going down, Nate looked surprisingly relaxed, and almost cool. He was wearing his Fish Feeders t-shirt, an old pair of jeans, and what looked like a pair of Vans he borrowed from Mark. Lance, true to form, gave the impression he was on the way to a backwoods rodeo. I gave them each a slap and plopped down across from Nate, who sat in the captain's chair, resting the checkerboard shoes on top of the desk. He had the radio on and I could hear Sting singing in the background, making me even more paranoid about every step I had taken over the last several hours, and just who, exactly, had been watching me.

"This is the inner sanctum, huh?"

"This is it, brother."

"Feels weird in here." I looked around. Other than the trash all over the floor, it was about what I would expect from a man Doc Mayes's age. A framed diploma. A few pictures of him and some celebrity types at a golf course. The infamous wall safe. Some mediocre art – prints only; no originals. Right across from the desk above the couch was a canvas picture of the Doc and Vicky wearing leis on a beach somewhere in Hawaii. Propped up on the credenza were four of five more framed photos of the two of them frolicking in various exotic locales.

I didn't see a single picture of Nate anywhere.

"I thought it would be, you know, neater."

"My dad hasn't touched this room for days. Not since he found out Charlotte died."

I tossed the Magnolia Federal envelope on the table. "There it is. Two banks' worth. More money than I have ever seen in my life."

"Any problems?"

"No, not really. Just a lot of nerves on my part and some questioning looks from one of the managers.

"From First Bank?"

"Yep."

"He called me right after you left," Nate said. "Panicked. Worried he was going to be fired. Had his regional manager coming in the office who wanted to talk to me about the account. I told him I had just been there, and everything was A-okay."

"Were you able to make any calls to any of the other banks?"

"Calls?" Nate looked at me weird when he said it – frowning and gritting his teeth.

"Yeah. You know, to get the managers on your dad's trail."

"Oh yeah," Nate said. "I made some calls."

"Good. That reminds me. There was one other thing. At the other bank I went to – Magnolia Federal – the manager there told me my withdrawal wasn't the first one of the day –"

"Yeah, I, uh, spoke to him. Ladner was his name, maybe?" Nate looked at a notebook to confirm. "Yeah, that's him. I called Magnolia Federal." He stared at me, unflinching.

"But Nate, this was before I got there, and he wasn't talking about my fifteen thousand–"

"I got it under control, Matt." I started to speak again, but Nate redirected the conversation.

"Lance, tell Matt what happened to you." As Lance started to speak, Nate looked at me and made a 'chill out' gesture. I almost chimed back in, but I backed off. We could cover it later.

"Well," Lance said, thumping a Copenhagen can. A fresh dip usually meant he was winding up for a long story, and he was true to form. He walked through more details than I cared to hear – some of them pretty hilarious, and at the end of the day, he was able to get out with few problems.

"Only thing," Lance said, "was that I flubbed the social security number at my first stop, but I guess they forgave me."

"With all that, Lance still made it through all three banks in record time."

"Yep, and I used one of those hundreds at McDonald's. Big Mac meal. Kept the change."

"So other than the social security number, no one questioned you?"

"Not a one. I tell you, them fake I.D.s did the trick. I got some funny looks, but there wasn't a whole lot to be said."

"That's two out of three," I said. "So where's Mark and Hop?"

"Good question," Nate said, "they should be here by now."

"Yeah," I said. If it was just Mark, I wouldn't have worried. He was always late. But not Hop.

Hop was never late for anything.

Chapter 71

Hop checked his watch. Mark should have been in and out of the bank in five, maybe ten minutes max, but now he was closing in on twenty since he walked in the door. If they had been in Gulfport, Hop would have left to get Nate or Matt, but Wiggins was just too far away.

A few times he thought he should drive to a 7-Eleven and make a call but that didn't feel right, either. What if Mark came out and needed to leave quick? A teenager walking out with several thousand dollars in cash with no visible means of transportation would surely throw up some red flags. Hop cursed himself for caving in and agreeing to drive and wished he'd stayed at home like he said he would when he first heard of this screwed up idea.

Who was this Nate Mayes, anyway, to put them all in such a bad spot? Just four months ago, no one had even heard his name, and now he had Tom Sawyered Hop and all of his friends into doing his whitewashing while he sat back waiting for the spoils to come in. Nate might have had a rough time at home, but who didn't, and there was more than one way to skin this cat – Hop was sure of it. Hop was going to give Nate a piece of his mind when he saw him again, and his fury grew with every passing minute.

He stared at the door, willing Mark to come out, and when his watch alerted him to the half hour mark, Hop's anger started to swing the other way and turned to nerves, then to panic, then to a borderline freak out. He didn't know whether to leave, to stay, or to just say screw it and walk in. The only thing he did know was that Mark had been in there too long, and whatever was holding him up could not be good.

Not good at all.

CHAPTER 72

ark didn't give the Bank of Wiggins a whole lot of thought on the ride up, and was happy to have a wingman driving. Hop was not nearly as relaxed as he could have been, but it was understandable. The very real fact that Hop was going to be a get-away driver had finally dawned on him, and he wasn't taking it well.

Mark cut a few jokes and talked about their girlfriends to loosen things up. He even gave a few first-person details of his last date with Wendy, which seemed to draw Hop out of his funk, but his change in demeanor didn't last long. Once they saw the light at the Frosty Top that heralded the entrance to town, Hop reverted to his old self. Mark wasn't going to give him time to think about it, so as soon as they parked, he strolled right in.

There was only one teller working, which made sense, because there was no one else in the lobby other than an old lady wearing a pink muumuu and house slippers murmuring to herself as she dug through her purse.

The teller took his drivers' license and deposit slip, typed in a few numbers, and without emotion, called another lady over to check the screen. This woman seemed bored too, but when she took a look, she perked up and went so far as to move the teller out of her seat. This new lady looked like she stepped out of a poor man's Whitesnake video, her hair burnt and strawy from losing one too many battles with the curling iron. She hopped on the computer and typed away, going back and forth between Mark's fake I.D., the deposit slip and the computer screen. She even wrote down some numbers on a note pad. She folded it up and finally spoke to him.

"Hi, Mr. Mayes?"

"Yes, ma'am."

"My name is Rachel."

"Nice to meet you."

"So, we usually don't get a request to withdraw this much money all at once, especially on a holiday weekend like this one."

"Okay. So?"

"So, I'm going to need a little bit of time. Would you like to take a seat while you wait?"

"The money's in the account, right?"

"Yes, but we are a small bank, and we don't have it on hand – at least not in large bills, so I'm going to need to have a transfer brought over from our main branch."

"You have a main branch? I mean, this is the Bank of Wiggins, right?"

She put her tongue in front of her teeth with her lips closed the way people do when they want to say something they shouldn't, then sucked in some air before speaking again.

"The money will be here from Hattiesburg shortly, Mr. Mayes. Please sit down, and I will call you when it is time. This shouldn't take long."

"What if I reduce the amount? Do you have eleven thousand on hand?"

She squinted her nose. "No. Please have a seat."

Freaking po-dunk banks. Mark turned and sat down in the waiting area two seats down from grandma who was now asleep sitting up. He looked outside and could see Hop in the car. He wasn't pleased.

After ten minutes passed, Mark started to doubt Rachel and decided some private sleuthing may be in order to put his mind at ease. He approached an office cubicle with a yellowed sign hanging on the outside that read *Want a new car? Come see me for a loan! Grrrrreat Rates!* A Tony the Tiger knockoff was in the bottom right corner holding a wad of cash.

Mark walked through the opening and found a man with a beer gut wearing a yellow short-sleeved shirt, polyester gray pants and cowboy boots. He was leaning back in his chair facing the wall reading a Louis L'Amour paperback. He didn't notice his new visitor, so Mark knocked on one of the plastic dividers that held the panels together.

The man turned, his chair squeaking in response, and peered at Mark over greasy government-issued glasses flocked with specks of dandruff.

"Can I help you, son?"

"Yes sir, sorry to bother you. I'm new in town, and my mom wants me to open a bank account. She told me to go the Bank of Wiggins, and I wanted to make sure I was in the main branch."

"The main branch?" The man rested his book open-faced on his belly and started to laugh, making it bounce up and down. "Son, this is the main branch, the satellite branch, the home office, and the executive branch, if you want to call it that. We are in Wiggins, Miss-ippi, boy. This is the only branch. There ain't no others. Heck, there's only one other bank in town – and trust me, it ain't ours. I should know 'cause my cousin works in it." He said that last part to the wall, then grunted at some far-off memory.

"You're not affiliated with a bank in Hattiesburg?"

The chair cried out for mercy when he leaned up and put his elbows on the desk, making Mark wonder how anyone else got any work done whenever this fella moved – which by the looks of him, was not very often. "Where'd you say you was from?" He had quit laughing now. Mark had already wasted too much of his time.

"Uh, Picayune."

"Naw, we don't have no banks in Hattiesburg, Jackson, Gulfport, or New York City, in case you're asking. And I ain't the new accounts person, so unless you're wantin' to take out a loan for a Chevy or Ford pickup truck – which you clearly ain't, I think you and I are done here." He squealed the chair back to its original position and returned to his book.

"Thank you, sir. Sorry to bother you." So much for small-town hospitality.

Mark looked back toward his teller. She was staring past him, chewing gum. The loan guy had confirmed what Mark had begun to suspect. Rachel was lying. Mark almost bought her lack of funds excuse, and if she had just stuck to that, he would have hung around. But she overplayed her hand by making up the story about the other bank.

She needed him to stay. But why?

Mark wasn't sure he needed to wait for the answer. If he cut out right then, he and Hop could have several miles behind them before Rachel even realized they were gone. There was no way they could track him anyway after he was out of sight; all they had was Nate's information on the withdrawal slip, not his, and –

He froze and patted his pockets, then looked up at the counter. The teller was still staring, except this time, she was looking directly at him and had quit her chewing. He watched the corner of her mouth turn up into a tiny little smirk.

They still had his fake I.D.

CHAPTER 73

When he woke up that morning, Eddie had no idea that not one, but two special gifts would be laid at his feet that day. In fact, when his phone rang a second time, he got mad because he thought it might be Kat calling back telling him he no longer needed to pick Marty up. But it wasn't Kat. It was Rachel – and she let him know some kid with the name of 'Nate Mayes' had shown up at the bank down in Wiggins wanting to withdraw fifteen thousand dollars from 'their' account. She had taken to calling it that.

Nate. Mayes.

With the siren on and him going full throttle, he could get there in half an hour, tops – maybe even less if he could bypass the traffic. Should give him plenty of time to get back and take care of that retard. He threw his tactical bag over his shoulder and slid his badge in his front pocket.

This was going to be too easy.

CHAPTER 74

M ark sat down and tried to figure out what to do. He had already asked the teller if he could get his I.D. back. Of course, she said she didn't have it, and that he'd have to wait for Rachel. Problem was, Rachel's office was behind the counter, and the door had been closed ever since she walked away. He went back up and said he was pressed for time and needed to ask Rachel a question. She told him again that Rachel was busy working on getting his money and would be with him shortly.

He glared at her and then reassessed the situation. Even if they kept the I.D., the only information on there that could peg Mark personally was his photograph. If they chased down the address, it would lead them to Nate – who was planning on speaking with them anyway, so what was the big deal? Mark concluded once and for all they could keep his I.D., picture and all.

He needed to get out of there.

He picked up a checking account brochure and slowly backed out of the waiting area pretending like he was reading it. When the carpet under his feet turned to linoleum, Mark spun and speed-walked to the exit.

He never made it.

Just as he started to push on the bar, the door flew open, and a stout man wearing cargo pants, a snug long-sleeved t-shirt, and sunglasses stood before him. He was gripping Hop's arm so tight all that was showing were the moons of his fingernails. In one quick motion he ripped off his shades and poked Mark in the chest.

"Are you Nate Mayes?"

Mark didn't say anything.

"I got a call that someone named Nate Mayes was in here trying to withdraw some money illegally."

Nothing.

"Oh, you want to play games, huh? Well, I don't play games. When I pulled up, your buddy here gave me the silent treatment too, but to my surprise" – he cracked his knuckles on his free hand – "he was much more cooperative the second time I asked. Told me his name was Jason Hopkins and he said he was waiting for his friend inside." He turned to Hop and jerked him forward. "So Mr. Hopkins, now that we're all here, tell me if this deaf-mute here is Nate Mayes?"

Hop looked at Mark, not sure what to do. He tried to stay loyal, but he didn't know now how long he could keep it up. Mark let him off the hook.

"No, sir. I am not Nate Mayes. My name is Mark Ragone."

The guy looked at him, incredulous, then looked over his shoulder. Mark turned around and saw Rachel standing there, arms crossed.

"This the one, Rachel?"

"Yeah." He could hear her snort behind him.

"Bring me his I.D."

Rachel walked over and handed him the drivers' license, side-eyeing the two of them the whole time.

"Well, well," the man said, taking a close look, then popping open the laminate sleeve and pulling out the card. "We got a fake." He reached into his pocket and flashed his badge, then pulled out a single pair of handcuffs that he split between Mark and Hop. As he walked them through the door, Mark watched the two of them exchange a look.

"Thank you for the call, Rachel," he said. "These two are coming with me."

"No problem, uh, Eddie," she said with a wink, then gave his shoulder a little rub. Another gesture that seemed a bit more familiar than it should have been. "Bye now."

The more Mark thought about it, the more the whole thing seemed a little too informal. No reading of rights, no back up cops, no radio chatter, and they were being led out to a pickup truck. Alarm bells were chiming, but it wasn't until he pushed the two of them in the second row of the cab that Mark realized something was truly wrong.

"You make sure justice is served on these boys, now, honey" Rachel said, smiling.

The man shut the door and spoke with his back to them, but Mark could still hear his muffled reply. "Don't you worry. And thanks for calling me to come out here."

She leaned up to him and whispered something Mark couldn't hear. Whatever this dude said in response did not make her happy, and she stormed back inside the bank without looking back. Then he climbed in, turned around and threatened to shoot either one of them on the spot if they made so much as a peep.

CHAPTER 75

T he telling of my experience in Hattiesburg didn't take nearly as long as Lance's, but I still burned some time getting into the details. Reliving it got me all whipped up again, and I still couldn't believe I pulled it off. It would have been much better received had Hop and Mark been there to hear it.

"What do we do next?"

"We give it another half hour," Nate said. "Then we go looking for them. Best-case scenario, we find them broken down on the side of the road. Worst-case scenario – well, I don't even want to think of a worst-case scenario."

"I'm ready when you are," I said. "I don't know how much longer we can sit on our hands."

"I know."

"Look," Lance said, getting up, "I'll be glad to go on a recon solo, or as a group if you want, but if y'all got it covered for now, I'm gonna head out for a bit. Kind of feel guilty leaving, but I invited a big crew of my home boys to come out to the party tonight, and I need to get ready."

"The party?"

"I am forever the optimist." Feeling the need for some decorum, Lance paused. "'Course if Mark and Hop don't get back, we ain't having a party, but I want to be prepared. Just in case."

"No problem, just keep today's events quiet for now."

"I ain't tellin' nobody. Ain't their business. You sure you don't need me to stay around here?"

"No, just call and check in when you get a chance, and I'll give you an update. If I don't answer, assume we are on our way to Wiggins. What all are you picking up?"

"Hayden's got a trailer loaded with pallets we're going to use for the fire. We also got to get some beer – I figure six coolers of ice cold Bud'll do it."

"No one's arguing there."

"My cousin's got a grill on a trailer. He's going to fire that up too." He was rolling now. "Gonna be a good one. Not as big as Fish Feeder's, but once I told them we were going to party down on my dime tonight, friends I didn't know I had started coming out the woodwork."

"Your dime?"

"Yeah, my dime." Lance smiled and peeled four one-hundred dollar bills out of one of the envelopes. "I'll call you in a bit."

I followed Lance out, then made a detour to the kitchen. I still hadn't eaten, and now that the nerves had worn off I was ready to chow down. Thanksgiving leftovers were always a treat, and even Nate's whacked-out folks seemed to have had quite the spread.

"You want anything?" I yelled from behind the refrigerator door.

"Nah, I'm good."

I carried an overstuffed plate down the hall, sampling the wares as I walked, and as I turned the corner into the office, Nate was standing up, one hand shuffling through the drawer, one hand deep in his pocket.

"Find anything good in there?" He nearly jumped out of his skin when I spoke.

"Uh, no," he said, exaggerating the digging. "Just adjusting my balls." He closed the drawer and leaned on the corner of the desk. "Been sitting way too long and my boys needed some attention."

"I mean the drawer. I really don't want to hear about your nuts."

"I was just checking it out to make sure I didn't miss anything. I don't think I ever really searched through all these drawers, you know."

"Well you're missing this sandwich. It is righteous. You sure you don't want half of it? Of course, you're going to need to wash your hands before you even get close to my plate."

"Nah, I've been nibbling all day. There still should be lots of food left for later," Nate said, "even with your gluttony." I raised a forkful of dressing in response and jammed it in my mouth. "Vicky had it all catered in, but my dad still complained about the turkey being too dry and the dressing being too runny, so both of them went their separate ways without eating. I knew I was going to be here by myself all weekend, so I put it up before it turned. Cold turkey breast on white bread with mayonnaise makes what could be the perfect sandwich."

"Add bacon and you're there."

I continued to eat while Nate slid back into his chair where he counted out the money and made entries in what looked like a notebook.

"What are you doing?"

"Have to account for everything – Lance's indiscretions notwithstanding, lots of eyes may be on these withdrawals."

"Oh, speaking of that, Nate. Back to what happened at Magnolia Federal. The manager told me when I went to take out the money –"

" – that a withdrawal had been made already that day?"

I put my plate down. "How'd you know that?'

"Did the other manager say anything along those lines?"

"No, but –"

Nate held up his hand. "I couldn't tell you before, Matt. If I did, none of you would have agreed to go out today."

"Tell me what? What are you talking about?"

"I did make a call. Several in fact."

Nate pulled a smaller, pocket-sized notebook out from under the one he had been writing on. He made one more quick note and was about to slide it across the desk when we heard the front door open.

"Lance? That you? You forget something?"

No response, but we must have gotten his attention, because footsteps started coming our way down the hall. I looked at Nate, and he shrugged his shoulders.

"Lance?"

When the pace quickened, and we still didn't get an answer, we knew it wasn't Lance. When the heel clicks blew up to a full sprint, we popped out of our seats and started to run, but we were too late.

Doc Mayes beat us to the door.

His hair was a mess; his clothes were dirty, and his eyes – half closed from fatigue and black with rage – locked in on Nate.

"You son of a bitch."

CHAPTER 76

At first, I expected a replay of the night Nate's dad busted in on us playing pool. The similarities sure were there. Nate breaking a house rule. Nate and a buddy hanging out. A surprise entry by a very angry man. All the boxes were checked, except one. This time Nate wasn't scared. Not in the least.

There had been a paradigm shift.

"Son of a bitch? Who do you think you are? Say something like that again and I will knock your ass out. I won't hold back like I did last time."

His dad's right hand twitched. "I've got a friend who works at Hancock Bank here in Gulfport." He took a step forward as he said it, but when Nate didn't move, his dad continued.

"A very close friend who looks out for me. I happened to give him a call today, and you know what he said?"

Nate didn't respond.

"He said 'I didn't expect to hear from you twice in one day, Dr. Mayes.'" He leaned into the desk, putting him an arm's length away from Nate at this point. "Imagine my surprise, considering he and I had not spoken in weeks."

"Maybe you should pay better attention to your business."

"You should have never interfered with my affairs, son. That can be dangerous."

"You should shut up while you're ahead. And by the way, you haven't earned the right to address me as *son*. You quit being my dad a long time ago. You know, right about the time mom died."

Dr. Mayes's shoulders stiffened and his head cocked slightly to the left. He may have not been physically punched right then, but he certainly felt the impact of what Nate just dropped on him.

"I've seen the picture, *dad*," Nate said, "you know the one." This time, it was Nate who took a step forward. "In fact, I've seen *all* the pictures from your little collection."

As soon as the words left Nate's mouth, his dad's eyes grew wide with surprise, then turned to slits with the understanding that Nate had truly figured it out. I thought I might have even seen a flash of muted admiration in between – his son wasn't a dumb ass after all – but it didn't last. A split second later, the two went at it like bull rams fighting over a mate on Mutual of Omaha's Wild Kingdom – and at that moment *I* was proud to see Nate hold his own. They tangled a bit, fists flew, and punches turned into grappling. After about a minute, both were breathing like they'd run up about ten flights of stairs, but Nate was in much better shape. If I were scoring the fight, I would have given it to Nate, hands down. He was bigger and stronger, and just needed one more push and it would have been done.

But the old man had other plans.

Nate went in for the pin, but his dad kicked the chair in his way and threw off Nate's leverage. Then he grabbed Nate and slammed him right on top of the desk. Luckily, Nate's momentum rolled him off on my side of the room. He tried to get his footing, but he was still off-balance and tripped on the couch, landing on the opposite side near the corner, causing what looked to be an antique sword fall and clang on the floor. When Nate finally popped back up, ready to go at it again, he took one step and stopped in his tracks when he found himself staring down the barrel of a 9mm Beretta his dad pulled from the desk.

The fight was over.

"What exactly have you done? Tell me everything now, and I might just let you walk out of here."

"Leave, Matt," Nate said, never taking his eyes off the gun.

I looked at Nate, then back at his dad – who hadn't budged.

"Leave." He said it again, and this time his voice was softer. "You need to meet up with Lance, okay?" He sounded like an elementary school teacher reminding the class to do their homework.

"Okay." I scooted toward the door, keeping my back against the chair rail the entire time. Before I stepped out, I turned back to Nate just to check one more time.

He looked me square in the eyes and gave me a nod. He didn't look the least bit scared.

"Go."

It was the last time I ever saw him.

CHAPTER 77

Kathryn's shopping excursion turned out better than she had hoped. At first she was a bit overwhelmed with the lingerie options available. Did people really wear some of these things? Uncomfortable was not the first word that came to mind, but it was one of them. It was different from shopping for cotton coverage panties and functional bras, that's for sure. Fortunately, the lady working the department was very helpful in finding something that fit Kat's needs. Sexy, but not slutty, and since everything was on sale, she was able to pick up an additional, if not more practical, outfit.

She made it to the gallery just before three, and was able to spend a few minutes getting organized before Emily showed up, perky and ready to work. Kat thought she might ask Emily about her boyfriend status but chose not to. They were getting along great, and she didn't want Emily to clam up or think Kat was weird. Plus, Emily would soon find out Kat was going to go after Nate, and she might look back and think Kat had been using her to mine information.

They chatted about Thanksgiving and their mutual successes at the mall before doing a quick walkabout to inventory what needed to be done. Most of the pictures were labeled, and the layout had been blocked long ago. Now they needed to do the build out, construct an additional riser for the quartet (the cellist needed more space), and pick the final two selections from Marty Deen's drawings. Kat also mentioned they should hang some Christmas decorations, but neither was interested, having spent the bulk of their day immersed in them. Since most of the construction had already been assigned to the men, that left them with one option.

The sketchpad.

"Here it is," Kat said. "I fully intended to have given this at least one pass by now, but things kept getting in the way."

"I understand that. We've all been busy. How many are in here?"

"Not sure; I think Marty's dad said about a dozen."

Emily started flipping through it but wasn't paying any attention. She was still tired from shopping and needed a few minutes to reset. "Should we wait until he arrives? I'd hate to have to redo this if Marty disagrees with our selections."

That worked for Kat. She was feeling it too. "Yeah, let's give it a few more minutes. You want to pick up some coffee? Triplett-Day always has a pot on."

"Sure."

Kat handed Emily two dollars. "That should cover us both. I like mine black, straight up."

"Yuck. I need milk. And lots of sugar."

"Different strokes."

"Yep."

"We can dive in when you get back. See you in a minute."

Kat stood at the door and watched Emily walk down the sidewalk until she turned the corner and drifted out of sight. She waited there for a minute staring at the parking lot, fully expecting the rest of the crew to show up, but they didn't. No Nate, no Marty, no Rick.

What could possibly be holding them up?

CHAPTER 78

The two boys sitting in the back seat had obeyed his orders well. Too well, actually. He expected the teenagers to protest, cry, curse, or at least ask a question or two, but he got nothing. He figured they took his threat of violence to heart, which meant he could use it again if need be. It was not until he instructed them to talk that they spoke up, and when they did, the floodgates opened – so much he could barely get the skinny one to shut up.

During the half hour trip back to Gulfport, he learned a number of things, and the more he heard about the real Nate Mayes, the more impressed he was with the kid. It was not easy to pull off what he did logistically, and the fact that he was able to recruit friends to help him spoke highly of his personal skills. Kat was right – he was a viable witness, on a number of levels.

He sure hoped he wouldn't have to kill him.

Time would tell, of course, and if the young Mayes was nearly as cooperative as these two, he might let them all live. They may have to survive a few nights bound and gagged in the woods during his exodus, but such is the price of freedom.

Rachel hit him up for some more coke on the way out, but he didn't have any to give her, which made her less than pleased. He had been trying to wean himself off of it and had been fairly clean since he took his last big hit after the Charlotte Gutherz incident. While the lack of cash on hand certainly helped him achieve his sobriety goals, he attributed most of his detox success to his commitment to reset his life.

He actually tried not to dwell too much on his new self, because he was not there yet. No more 'Fast Eddie', no more law enforcement, and a fat bank account were all heady thoughts, but they meant nothing until he had the money and was on a plane headed far, far away from the United States. Nate Mayes was going to get him there.

According to these two, all he had to do is go out to Gulfport Lake and Nate would come to him. It was going to be a party all right, but not the kind they had planned. Once he had them all together, he fully expected Nate to turn over the cash and the information for every single account. If Nate didn't cooperate, he would kill his friends, one by one, until he did.

In order to round up all the witnesses, however, he had one more stop to make. The timing was about right to make the pickup anyway, so he turned onto Pass Road and made his way towards Green Oaks.

"Hey, where are you taking us? This isn't the way to Gulfport Lake." It was the other kid – the loudmouth smart ass – who piped in.

"Did I say you could speak?"

"No."

"Then shut up."

He drove a few more blocks and double-checked the address Kat had given him. He smiled when he went through the four-way stop just past the tennis courts.

He was almost there.

CHAPTER 79

They decided to put up the two largest Christmas wreaths after all, and were soon back at the table. Kat made sure she sat facing the front door.

"We've given it some time. Should we just go ahead and sort through these now?" Emily asked. "I mean, it's up to you, but if we aren't going to do this, I may head out if that's okay."

"Yeah, let's take a look. We need to make it quick, though. If I don't see Marty's face in ten minutes, I'm going to have to get him myself. His parents would freak out if they knew he hadn't made it."

"I hope no one got in a wreck or had car trouble."

"Me too."

"So, his parents left Marty home alone?"

"Yeah."

"Wow, I bet he's worried sick he's not here yet."

"Probably. You never know with him, though. He'll surprise you sometimes."

Kat opened the book. The first sketch was a great blue heron, but it didn't quite look right. She couldn't tell if it was the shape of the beak or the colors he used for the wings, but it was off, so she flipped the page, and the second one – a barred owl – wasn't much better. Emily agreed.

"I hope we find a good one in here that works."

"Yeah, me too," Kathryn said and turned to the next one.

C'mon, Marty, Kathryn thought. Surprise me.

CHAPTER 80

M arty played *Spy Hunter* until his wrist hurt. It was a good afternoon – his best, actually – because for the first time he made it to the level where the car turns into a boat, and he hit the ramp at just the right spot. He entered his initials for the new high score in case anyone ever checked.

At three o'clock, Marty was ready. Fully dressed, bag packed, and two new batteries in the walkie-talkies. They used nine volts, and when he touched the terminals to the tip of his tongue, the metallic tingle told him they were good to go.

He was disappointed when his ride didn't arrive on time, but he wasn't mad. After all, the FBI agent could be doing an undercover sting operation trying to catch a drug dealer. Or maybe the FBI agent was running a secret stakeout waiting for some gangs to show up. Either way, it was important government business – way more important than taking Marty to an art gallery – so he could sit tight until justice was served. Even so, he hoped the car had a siren and a two-way radio he could use.

Marty was almost through rereading a Batman comic when he heard the sound of a vehicle slowing down in front of his house. He closed the book to listen, and sure enough, somebody was pulling in the driveway.

Marty hopped off his bed, buckled the strap on his bag, and grabbed his keys.

It was time.

CHAPTER 81

Rick Papania parked his truck right in front, climbed out and stretched. He was tired of the drive and was glad to be back in Gulfport, even if it was under these circumstances. It had been a long day covering lots of miles – and he still had work to do.

He looked at the door and hesitated. He wasn't quite sure what to expect, but he braced for the worst. Things had been easy – almost too easy – so far, and he hoped his streak would continue.

He stepped up to the concrete, took a deep breath and reached for the door.

CHAPTER 82

Out of the ten sketches Kat had reviewed, two were serviceable and one was good. The rest were not up to par. The mockingbird, however, was perfect. The attention Marty paid to the plumage was pretty amazing. It would sell, for sure, but she didn't know about the others. Maybe the gallery would use only one of the extras from the pad. That would be fine with her. There was plenty of inventory on the walls already, anyway. Still, another good one would be nice to have.

Emily flipped to the last page. "What is this?"

The drawing that lay open on the table wasn't a bird at all. It was a picture of a pickup truck and two men. One was holding a gun and the other was splayed out on the ground, like he'd been shot.

Kat looked at it closer and her throat clicked shut. She couldn't breathe. As a shaky finger traced the images, tears streamed down her cheeks.

"What is it, Ms. Cooper? Are you okay?" Emily asked. "Ms. Cooper?"

Kat grabbed her arm and tried to stand up. She looked Emily in the eyes, and a thousand thoughts raced through her head. She wanted to tell Emily to grab a phone, to call the cops, to go get her car and to leave.

But only one word came out of Kat's mouth.

"Marty."

CHAPTER 83

Marty slid the chain off the slide and turned the knob on the deadbolt. He pulled his pack over his shoulder and patted down his hair. He was ready to go.

He slung the door open and held out his hand to give a firm shake, just like his daddy had told him to do.

The bad man took a step inside, took his hand, and smiled.

"Hello, Marty. Good seeing you again."

Colored pencils, paper and a walkie-talkie spilled out onto the floor.

CHAPTER 84

The drawing couldn't be right. No way. Kat knew she had to pull herself together, but this cut her to the core. Suddenly, nothing made sense, yet everything made sense. She picked the pad up, but before she could take a second look, the chime beeped and a man walked in the door.

Kathryn took off so fast she knocked her chair over.

It scared Emily, and she started towards the alley exit in the back but stopped when she saw Kat running toward the man, still crying.

He looked as shocked as any of them. "What?" he said. "What is it? Are you okay?"

She thrust the pad into his hand. "Look." Kat could barely get the words out. "Look."

He studied the page. Within a matter of seconds, his face followed the same progression as Kathryn's – bewilderment, shock, then horror.

"That is Tom Chrestman," he said, pointing to the man on the ground in the drawing. "And this other person holding the gun is –"

Kathryn looked up through glassy eyes and tried to say the name of the man in the drawing, but the full scope of the betrayal crushed her, and at first, all she could do was nod. When she tried again, however, she was able to cough out a response.

"Ethan," she said in between sobs. Rick Papania drew her close and she buried her face in his chest. "It's Ethan."

CHAPTER 85

Much to Ethan Davis's surprise, Marty didn't put up a fight at all. No thrashing, screaming or running away. To the contrary, he became near-catatonic as soon as Ethan walked through the door. Ethan was happy he didn't have to resort to any violence, but it still wasn't easy. Walking Marty's dead weight out to the truck was like moving a queen-sized mattress alone. Ethan wrestled him to the truck and shoved him in. By this time, Ethan was pissed, thirsty, and not in the mood for conversation, so when the loud one popped off from the back seat and asked – for the second time – where Ethan was taking them, Ethan hit him with a quick jab so hard it cut his cheek and made the area around his eye puff up.

"I told you to shut up. From now on, you do not say another word, you understand?" Mark nodded his head.

Hop flinched when Ethan put his finger in his face. "Now you, on the other hand, you are the only one I want to hear from."

"Yessir."

"What time is your little rendezvous at Gulfport Lake supposed to start?"

"I don't know. We never said. I guess we were going to meet up between four and five. You know, when we got through at the banks. Party is supposed to start after dark – probably around six."

"You better not be lying to me, son." Ethan leaned in.

"I'm not." Hop wasn't lying. Not really. He knew he, Mark, Matt, Lance, and Nate were all supposed to meet at Gulfport Lake early, and he knew there was going to be a party later, but he wasn't sure about the particular times. Maybe it wouldn't matter.

"Good, because if you are, you're the one I'm shooting first."

Hop put his head down and prayed for a miracle.

Chapter 86

It took less than a minute for the shock to wear off and for Kathryn to snap back into FBI mode. It certainly helped that Rick was there, because as soon as she told him about Marty, he got on his radio and commandeered the phone. Yes, she was mad at him for not calling to tell her he would be late, and he knew he was in the doghouse for dropping that ball, but he apologized, and all was forgiven – for now. They had work to do, and watching Rick take charge motivated everyone around them. He used the sketch and Kat's description of Ethan's truck for the APB, and by the time he hung up, every cop, highway patrolman, and fireman on the Mississippi Gulf Coast, along with everyone else in the room, knew to be on the lookout for a six-foot two white male in his mid-thirties driving a 1984 light blue Dodge Ram Crew Cab.

Since Rick was busy chasing that lead, Kat turned to other issues – and recruited some on-the-spot help. "Emily, can you call Nate Mayes? I need to make sure he's safe and secure."

"Yes, ma'am."

"If you talk to him, tell him to meet me at GPD headquarters right next to city hall on 14th Street, okay? Right away."

"You got it." Emily went to the office and dialed Nate's home number. She let it ring until it rolled to the answering machine and hung up. She tried again and still got no luck, so she dialed Matt.

"Come on, Matt. Pick up." Nothing. Same when she tried to call Hop and Mark.

By now, the gallery was a flurry of activity and had morphed into a temporary ops center, with Chief Papania barking out orders right and left. Emily strolled around looking for Ms. Cooper, and when she didn't see her, she waited until he had an opening and jumped in.

"Chief?"

"Hey – Emily, right?"

"Yessir. Do you know where Ms. Cooper went? I can't seem to find her."

"She had to go to her office. Said she had to lock down some files. You need her?"

"Not really. She asked me to make some calls, but I haven't been able to reach anyone yet." She looked around, and there were already two other people waiting to speak to him. "You look like you have this under control. I'm probably going to go on home, okay?"

"You're welcome to stay, but I understand. It's pretty crazy around here and will probably get worse."

"If I do find out anything, should I call her or you? I don't know the number at her office."

He pulled out a card. "This number is to dispatch. If I'm at the station, they can ring me there. If not, let them know who you are, and that you are trying to reach me, and someone will get me on the radio, okay?"

"Yes, sir." He turned back to his work, and Emily headed to her car. She wanted to go see her mom and tell her everything that had happened, but before she did, she wanted to try to meet up with Matt. She had a lot to tell him.

She was sure his day had not been as interesting as hers.

CHAPTER 87

Since Nate still had my keys, I had no choice but to take Ferris, and I worked the horses under the hood like they've never been worked before. I flew down Highway 49, thankful no cops were running traps, and made it to Airport Road in fifteen minutes. Arguably, I ran one, maybe two, red lights, but they were close enough to yellow to not give me too much heartburn and not cause any wrecks. Of course, there were more than a few drivers who didn't appreciate my Indy skills, and one finger, two horns, and a very vocal obscenity later, I turned off onto the gravel road leading up to the lake and punched it.

I saw Hayden's obscenely large pickup truck and a trailer packed with pallets over by the beach area. He and Lance were pulling them off two by two.

"It's about time," Lance said. "We could use some help. I'm running a little behind, but it's my fault. Stopped at Elizabeth's to get a quick rub down before I met up with Hayden. What can I say?"

When I didn't laugh or come back with a comment, Lance realized something was going on. He pulled his gloves off as I told him what happened at Nate's. Hayden stopped to listen but didn't say a word.

"You call the police?"

"No. Not yet. I wanted to come by here first. With Hop and Mark still out, I didn't know if I should. Anything from them?"

"No."

"So, what do we do now?"

Lance took a drink of water out of his Igloo jug. "I don't think we have a choice anymore. We got to go to the police and tell 'em 'bout Nate. We know for sure he's in trouble, so he's first on the list."

"You're right. I should've thought of that."

"As for the other two, let's just play it by ear. For all we know, they could be right around the corner."

"Yeah," I said, "I guess we'll find out soon enough."

"I guess so," Lance said, looking up towards the road. "Let's roll."

CHAPTER 88

E mily thought she should start at Gulfport Lake in case Matt and his buddies were already setting up. If no one had made it yet, she would go to Bayou View Grocery and try another round of calls. It had the closest pay phone.

She clicked around on the radio to Power 108, and stopped when she heard the Go-Go's. A long line of cars coming her way temporarily blocked her from turning left onto the gravel road, so she took advantage of the delay to apply a fresh coat of lipstick in case Matt happened to be there alone. She pulled down her visor and twisted out "Chestnut Rose," a color picked out for her by the lady at the cosmetics counter. She was an autumn, after all.

By the time she flipped the mirror back up, there were just a few more cars left. She reached over to the passenger seat to put the tube back in her purse and stopped. Coming in her direction was a large blue pickup truck.

No way.

She tried to remember how Chief Papania described it. She knew it was blue and had a back seat because she had to ask someone what 'crew cab' meant. As it got closer, Emily ducked down behind the steering wheel, and as the truck made the turn, she peeked above her dash.

Marty Deen was sitting in the second row, looking out the window. He didn't see her.

Emily reached into her pocket, pulled out Chief Papania's card and floored it. She could get to Bayou View Grocery in three minutes if she caught the light.

CHAPTER 89

Lance's instincts must have been right, because as soon as we climbed into the truck, a dust trail rising above the pines told us someone was coming our way – and they were close. I squinted my eyes but didn't recognize the vehicle that breached the tree line.

"That one of your boys, Lance?"

He looked for a second then shook his head. "Never seen that one before." He leaned out his window. "Hayden?"

"Nope."

A blue crew cab pickup truck came down the drive and skidded to a stop right in front of us. Sitting in the back seat were Hop, Mark, and a man I didn't recognize. They all looked miserable, and Mark had blood all over his face.

"What is going on here?" Lance said under his breath. Before I could answer, the driver rolled down his window and pointed a gun at us. Up to that point, I had lived most of my life barely even seeing a gun in person. The fact that I had two pulled in front of me in the span of one hour was beyond comprehension.

"Out of the truck. All of you, and keep your hands where I can see them." He also ordered Mark, Hop, and the other guy – who I later discovered was Marty Deen – out, and lined all of us up, including Hayden, side-by-side in front of Hayden's truck.

"My name is Ethan Davis," He said, pulling out a badge. "I work for the Federal Bureau of Investigation. FBI for you retards – and yes, I meant to say that in the plural. From what I was told on the way over here, you boys have been engaged in some very serious activity today. Displayed some behaviors that could put you in jail for a long time."

He waited for a reaction but got none. I could tell Mark was mad just by the look on his face, but he held his tongue – for the time being.

Agent Davis continued. "Mr. Hopkins here tells me this whole enterprise was masterminded by a ringleader by the name of Nate Mayes. So, first things first. Which one of you is Nate?"

I raised my hand, and he walked in front of me. "Let me see some I.D. – real and fake."

"What do you mean –"

"Don't even start with me, son. I know all about it. Hand them over."

I gave him both, and before he even asked, Lance did the same.

"Well, well. Mr. Hopkins, despite their well-crafted paraphernalia, neither one of these miscreants appears to be Nate Mayes." He walked over and pointed at Hayden. "And unless Sloth here is my man – which I seriously doubt – the rest of you Goonies need to start talking, or –"

"Are we under arrest?" It was Mark.

"What'd you say, boy?"

"Are we under arrest?" Mark asked, enunciating each word. "Because if we are, you need to read us our rights."

Agent Davis jumped in Mark's face. "I thought I told you not to speak."

"I can speak if I want to. And if I am under arrest, I have the right to speak to my lawyer."

He looked at Mark then scanned the rest of us.

"I will tell you what you have the right to do and what not to do, and if you know what's good for you, you'll keep your damn mouth shut."

Mark scowled at him but didn't say anything.

"Mr. Hopkins, you did, in fact, tell me Nate Mayes would be here, didn't you?"

"Yessir," Hop said, staring at the ground.

"Surely one of you knows where he is, and if you tell me, I bet we can work out a deal. Who knows, I may even be able to keep you out of jail. If not, well –"

"You can't do shit," Mark said.

"Excuse me?"

"Nate told us all about it. He said there is a dirty cop on the inside." Mark leaned forward. "I think it's you."

Agent Davis clicked his jaw, and walked up to Mark, resting his hand on his holster and drumming his fingers across the grip. "Those are pretty strong words, boy. You better be careful."

"I know about the drop box."

"Shut *up*, Mark," I said. "Let it go."

"I know about the pictures."

Hop tried to jab Mark with his free hand, but Mark shook him off.

"And," Mark said, squinting as he spoke, "I know who you are. *Fast Eddie.*"

In what couldn't have been more than a second, Agent Davis drew his gun, engaged the slide and rested the barrel two inches from Mark's forehead.

CHAPTER 90

Emily made the call to the police station, and they patched her through to Chief Papania at the gallery. When she reported to him what she saw, he thanked her then told her not to go back out to Gulfport Lake as he would have officers on site within minutes, and it was just not safe for her to be out there.

Emily knew she should obey him and sit tight, especially if this Ethan guy was dangerous, but she just couldn't. The look on Marty Deen's face alone was enough to put her back in the driver's seat, and as she pulled off, she wasn't too terribly worried. A whole army of cops was on the way, and with their lights, radios and open roads, they would probably beat her there anyway.

* * *

When she turned off onto the gravel road, she didn't see where any dust had been kicked up, so she stopped and rolled down her window, listening for the cavalry. She didn't hear any engines revving or sirens wailing.

But she did hear someone yelling.

She didn't know who was doing it, and couldn't make out exactly what was being said, but it didn't sound good. Emily would never forgive herself if someone harmed Marty.

She jammed the clutch and worked the gears so hard, she was in third by the time she made it to the trees.

Chapter 91

Mark should not have pushed Agent Davis like he did. I really believed we could have gotten out of there in one piece had he kept his mouth shut. But when his last comment about Fast Eddie hit the bullseye, this guy – whoever he was – lost his freaking mind.

"Well, well, I think we have a winner," he said, his voice rising with every word. He pointed to Hop. "I told this one here, he was going to be the first to go, but I have changed my mind. It is your lucky day, son."

He looked back at Mark, and his eyes were feral and wild, much like those of my dachshund when I tried to take a stick out of her mouth. Then he started to yell.

"I didn't like you the first time I saw you." He licked his lips, and Mark stared him down, unmoving. "And I don't like you now." He looked around, happy to have an audience. "This one's going to be easy. Any last words, you little prick?"

Mark glanced over at us, then his eyes found the ground. He shuffled his feet and opened his mouth, but before he could speak, a white BMW came screaming down the drive, throwing rocks and oyster shells in its wake.

It drew Agent Davis's attention away from Mark just long enough for Lance to lean into the cab of Hayden's truck and hit the button.

Hayden told me at Fish Feeders he got that train horn off a decommissioned diesel locomotive at a rail yard where his uncle worked. I had forgotten just how loud it was, and when it blew, the vibration alone made my eye twitch.

It startled Agent Davis, too. So much that when he jerked, his reflexes drew his elbows in tight by his body, and he dropped the gun.

For a big boy, Hayden was quick, and before the pistol hit the ground, one of his arms had already disappeared into the truck bed.

CHAPTER 92

Historically known as the hardest of the hardwoods, hickory's practical applications have been manifold over the years. Native Americans bent hickory to make their bows. Early settlers to North America turned hickory into spokes for carriage wheels. Perhaps the most famous hickory aficionado was Babe Ruth, who favored Louisville Sluggers fashioned out of hand-selected virgin trees. Its most utilitarian and widespread application, however, had been in the fashioning of handles for tools and farm implements – none more prevalent than axe handles.

It was not until Hayden pulled Cousin out of the bed of the truck, however, that I was able to gain a full appreciation of hickory's physical properties.

When Hayden stepped up, it was as if the Babe himself had been lobbed an easy one right down the middle. Hayden swung Cousin like he was batting clean-up in the bottom of the ninth with the bases loaded and the game tied.

He hit Agent Davis from behind – broadside starting at his ear, with wood finding its mark through his temple and across his eye socket and cheekbone.

For a split second, Agent Davis's head dipped down into his neck in what was truly a grotesque display of physics, his face odd and misshapen due to the multiple acute craniofacial fractures. Several teeth flew out the other way, and when his head jerked back from the recoil, his body went limp, and he fell face first, timber style, just like a tree.

Hayden stepped up, sniffed, then wiped his nose off with the back of his sleeve.

"Got him."

CHAPTER 93

I am not sure just how many cruisers the Gulfport Police Department kept in its fleet, but I am pretty sure every single one of them peeled into the Gulfport Lake parking lot in the seconds after Agent Davis hit the ground. There were more than a few unmarked cars as well, and eventually an ambulance showed up to tend to the carnage. Agent Davis was alive, but it was going to be a long time before he started forming syllables again.

The first thing I did was hug Emily and tell her what happened at Nate's. The next thing I knew, I was in the back of a squad car with Gulfport Chief of Police Rick Papania and FBI Special Agent Kathryn Cooper screaming towards Nate's house. We were accompanied by two escorts and tailed by a SWAT van. You would have thought the president was in town.

On the way over, I told them an abbreviated story of all the laws we had broken and why. Agent Cooper said we would clearly have to face the music – and were not eligible for any of the reward money – but she likely had some wiggle room considering our actions with regard to the capture of Ethan Davis. She could barely say his name when she spoke, and when I called him 'Agent' Davis she told me to never to address him in that context again.

The gate was still open when we arrived, and I was instructed to stay put as the SWAT van unloaded. Like a clown car, man after man dressed in black and navy blue filed out and surrounded the house. Within minutes, the premises were secured, and I was given the all clear to go inside.

The house was eerily silent when I walked in the front door. The only sound was coming from the game room, where pieces of conversations creeped out into the hall. I wasn't sure I wanted to go down there, but Agent Cooper saw me and waved me over.

"Come in here, Matt. You'll want to see this."

No, I didn't. If Nate was dead, I most certainly did not want to see that. "No thanks, ma'am. I am fine staying out here."

"It's okay. I promise."

I eased my way in, and while Nate might not have been in the room, everything was most definitely not okay. Lying in the middle of the pool table was Doc Mayes, unconscious and bleeding. Next to him was the 9mm Beretta with a clip next to it. A cop was circling the table, taking pictures, and the strobe from the flash gave the room an ethereal feel. Before he could finish, an ambulance crew arrived and moved him and everyone away so they could start tending to his injuries. We stood around the table, all of us watching and wondering if he was going to make it.

Doc Mayes had been beaten to a pulp. His face had multiple bruises, bumps and cuts. The area around his eyes was puffy and purple. It was weird enough seeing him like that, but something about his wounds struck me as odd. They were uniform and looked like tracks or stripes. Some of the skin had split open, and blood oozed out onto the table, turning the felt from Kelly green to black. The EMT cut Doc Mayes's stained shirt off, and his back and stomach looked similar – parallel strips of bruises and marks, some several inches long, some still bleeding, crisscrossed his torso.

I looked up at Agent Cooper and shook my head. "What happened here?"

"Looks like he was whipped or beaten with something."

"With what?"

"Don't know, but someone was very angry with this man."

"You think? So, where's Nate?"

She crossed her arms and stood between me and the pool table. "We were hoping you would tell us."

I looked around. The cop next to her was watching me too. "You mean he's not here?"

"No."

"What about the gun?"

"Empty. Nothing in the chamber and not a single bullet in the magazine. Never fired."

I stared at it for a second, thinking. "But if Nate isn't here, then —"

"Mr. Frazier, can you follow me?" It was Chief Papania. He was wearing latex gloves and motioning towards Doc Mayes's office, which, frankly, is where I thought we would start.

When I got there, I found the office in even worse shape than when I left. Nothing remained on the desk or the credenza, one end of the couch was moved out away from the wall, and shards of glass, two drawers, and a shoe were scattered about. Blood specks peppered the floor and furniture like a Jackson Pollock painting. But that wasn't why Chief Papania called me in there.

Sticking out of the wall was a bloodied antique-looking sword. It had been jabbed through the canvas photo of Doc Mayes and Vicky, splitting him right between the eyes. Layered on the sword's blade, like a grisly shish kabob, were several Polaroids of people who had been beaten, maimed or killed. Bunched at the hilt was a stack of bank slips.

All three of us studied his work for a few minutes before Chief Papania spoke up.

"Do you have any idea what this means?"

I looked his way. "Why, yes, Chief. I think I do."

* * *

We sat down on the couch, and while his assistant wrote, I told them everything I knew. About the photos, the bank accounts, and about Nate's tortured history with his old man. As they inventoried and tagged each Polaroid, I noticed Nate's mom wasn't one of them. I kept that little nugget to myself.

A half hour later we walked outside. Multiple news crews were by the gate doing live feeds, and the lights from the rigs blew up the yard like a Friday night football game. The SWAT van, cop cars, two ambulances, and a few unmarked Crown Vics were parked all over. There must have been at least fifteen vehicles out there. I stood on the stoop with Agent Cooper and Chief Papania.

"Matt, do you have any idea where Nate could have gone?"

"No sir," I said, surveying the scene. I saw the two exchange looks out of the corner of my eye, and I knew I was in for some more questioning.

"Are you sure?" Agent Cooper asked.

"Of course, I'm sure. I don't know where he is. I wish I did, actually. Why do you keep asking?"

"Well, Dr. Mayes's car is still in the garage; his stepmom has not yet returned from Destin, and we found Nate Mayes's truck parked at Gulfport Lake, which is a pretty strong indicator as to his last known location. Since Gulfport Lake happens to be precisely where we found you and the rest of his friends, let me ask one more time. Do you have any idea where Nate Mayes went when he left here this very afternoon?"

As they talked, my eyes found a spot on the driveway, right in front of the little building Nate referred to as the potting shed. It is where I had parked earlier that day, before Nate gave me the keys to Ferris.

"Matt? Did you hear me? Do you know where Nate Mayes went when he left this afternoon?"

"No, ma'am. I do not."

I put my hands on my hips, checked the yard one more time, and smiled.

The Milk Wagon was nowhere to be seen.

CHAPTER 94

Three weeks later, police were called to investigate a 1980 white Suburban that had been abandoned at the Gulfport-Biloxi Regional Airport. It had been parked right in the middle section of the main lot, close to the terminal, and had remained virtually unnoticed until a cop moonlighting as a security guard pegged it as the one they had been looking for. The detectives combed through it, dusting it for fingerprints and looking for anything to tie it to the investigation and, specifically, to Nate and his possible whereabouts. They used a clean set of prints of Nate's from his house as a reference, and got multiple hits off the steering wheel, the back seat, the console, the door handles, the radio knobs, and numerous other places between the bumpers. Much to their frustration, his fingerprints were intermingled with what one detective estimated to be at least ten, possibly fifteen others – also scattered from one end of the vehicle to the other – and after a day's worth of documenting what they could, they moved on.

As for hard evidence, in addition to a few blood streaks smeared on the mat and on the bottom of the steering wheel, they found what the report described as a "worn pair of black and white slip on shoes – Vans brand, size eleven" and a "bloodied and torn light blue screen printed t-shirt" tucked under the drivers' seat. Rolled inside the shirt were eleven Winchester 115 grain 9mm bullets. Further inspection of the ammo garnered two matches: some faint latent prints from Dr. Ford Mayes, and some more recent ones from Nate. This got them all whipped into a frenzy, yet despite doubling up their efforts, it was the last piece of hard evidence they retrieved from the vehicle. After keeping it impounded a few extra days for good measure, they cut the Milk Wagon loose, and Chief Papania himself delivered it to my front door.

But that didn't mean they were done. Both state and federal authorities spent several days grilling me, Lance, Mark, and Hop, presumably looking for inconsistencies in our stories. They even spent half a day interviewing Marty Deen. All told, they were sorely disappointed. Each and every story matched; each and every story was factually consistent, none of us knew anything about where Nate might have ended up – and we certainly didn't know anything about the bullets they had found. The one theme that surfaced through all of the interviews that even remotely pointed to a motive was Nate's desire to end the criminal activity of his dad by avenging his mother's death – which eventually came to light, even though her Polaroid was never discovered.

It helped that our stories were corroborated by a second, concurrent investigation relating to the other Polaroids and rogue bank statements. Ballistics matched Ethan Davis's gun as the one used on Tom Chrestman, and the account information lined up to the dime with the missing transactions from Cape Island Compounding. Ultimately, new indictments for Ethan and Doc Mayes were served. Vicky left town the same day she gave her statement. Since she was still a potential person of interest, she wasn't allowed to leave the state, so she moved back in with her parents in Jackson, where she wasted no time filing for divorce.

There was not a whole lot we could tell them about Nate, although they certainly tried to squeeze it out of us. No one knew any more than Nate had chosen to let us know, and after several unsuccessful attempts to pin us down, they finally quit asking.

The six million was another story. Multiple rounds of interrogations took place on that front, culminating with a visit from the IRS.

"How much money did you withdraw from Magnolia Federal?"

"Fifteen thousand dollars. I told you already. We were all instructed to take fifteen thousand out of the banks we were assigned to, and that's what we did. At least Lance and I did. Mark and Hop didn't get that far." The guy was a supernerd.

"By my count, that puts the cash withdrawals at seventy-five thousand dollars. What happened to that money?"

"No idea. We gave it all to Nate."

"Do you know what happened to the remaining money in the accounts?"

"I didn't know there was any remaining money."

"Didn't know?"

"No. Nate didn't tell us."

"Didn't tell you?"

"No, sir."

That was the honest truth. Nate never told me exactly how much money was in the accounts, although he had alluded to it being rather large. The only inkling I had of any amount came from the exchange I had with the Magnolia Federal manager, but the nerdman already knew about that. Our withdrawals did trigger the IRS to take action – just as Nate had said they would – and agents were waiting at the bank offices when they opened the doors Monday morning. Much to their surprise, a heck of a lot more than seventy-five thousand had been moved.

What Hop, Lance, Mark, and I didn't know was that while we were making our merry way through South Mississippi doing our best Nate Mayes impersonations, someone else from a number originating from Nate's house called the banks and collectively wired $5.5 million dollars to a private, secure account in Nassau, Bahamas. The following Monday, the money was wired from Nassau to Vienna, Austria.

Two days later, the money taken from the banks disappeared, never to be seen again.

Most of it, that is.

CHAPTER 95

I had not put on a tuxedo since homecoming, and while the thought of getting monkeyed up again did not appeal to me, I have to admit that when the cufflinks went on without too much cursing, I kind of got excited. It was New Year's Eve; the night was cool, crisp and clear, and I had a date with Emily Miller, the most beautiful girl in the world.

She was pretty on any day, but something about the way she looked that night left me speechless. She had her hair drawn up and clasped in the back so it cascaded around the nuzzling part of her neck. Her dress was amazing – black, classy, and tailored right down to the last hint of lace that bordered the collar and sleeves. She was wearing her mother's pearls and her grandmother's fur stole. She looked like she should be walking the red carpet.

And walk it, she did.

The Holden Gallery went all out for Marty's exhibit, and it was *the* social event on the Coast that night. There was, in fact, a red carpet out front, and although getting out of the Milk Wagon was not nearly as exciting as slipping out of a limousine would have been, we did our best. Marty had a say-so regarding the guest list, so for better or worse, all of us involved in the great bank caper – including Hayden – were invited.

By eight-thirty, everyone had shown up with dates in tow. Mark and Wendy mingled like they had done this a hundred times, and Hop and Kristin – much to everyone's surprise – behaved somewhat like a normal couple, even holding hands as they perused the art. Lance and Elizabeth were together, as were Hayden and a different NASCAR girl. We all cleaned up remarkably well, and put on at least a pretense of good behavior, which was a nice departure from our usual routine.

Agent Cooper and Chief Papania were there, looking very much unlike two officers of the law. Like Emily, Agent Cooper also had her hair pulled up, but hers was affixed with what looked like some kind of sparkly thing laced through flowers in the back. She was working the crowd, making sure everyone's drinks were full, and that everything was where it needed to be. Chief Papania wore black cowboy boots with his tux, and while it was a look most couldn't have pulled off, he actually succeeded, even if he seemed somewhat ill at ease amongst the mucketys. The two looked happiest when they were together, and more than once I spotted them pawing at each other when they thought no one was watching.

We spent a good twenty minutes listening to Marty tell the story of when he was abducted and how he and the A-Team took down the bad guys. Hayden was Marty's reluctant hero, and more than once, Marty made Hayden recreate that final moment with the 'big stick' that saved all of our lives.

After we had heard the story twice, Mark pulled me aside on my way to the food table.

"Hey, where are y'all going to be at the stroke of midnight?"

"I don't know; hadn't thought about it."

"Why don't you meet us out at the Lake? Hop's on board and I already talked to Lance. He and Lizzie are in, too."

I looked across the room at Emily. "Okay. If she's up for it, I am."

"Good. You got any libations?"

"No. You?"

"Yep," Mark said, "I picked up some champagne mini bottles. Just enough for two."

"Save me one, okay?"

"Why don't you come and get it now? In case y'all don't make it." He looked back over at Emily and raised one eyebrow. "Believe me, brother, I won't fault you. Come on."

Mark had the bottles in a cooler in his trunk, and after the hand-off, I made my way down the street. I had purposefully parked a few blocks away from the gallery. The exhibit was a highfalutin event, and my vehicle stuck out like a sore thumb next to the Lincolns, Mercedes, and other old rich-people cars. Dropping off was one thing; parking that behemoth front and center was another.

Even though cops were out in force downtown, they were mainly directing traffic, so I didn't do too much to cover up the bottle as I walked. I knew that once we left the party, however, there would be roadblocks everywhere like there always were on New Year's Eve, so I needed to hide it. I hadn't used the Trapper since I retrieved those Polaroids for Nate. I felt around under the dash until I found the trigger. As expected, it popped open.

The ambient light from the street was just enough for me to see shadows, and I blinked at something tucked way down in the bottom. I reached over and pulled out a wrinkled manila envelope. Written on the front were four names: Matt, Mark, Hop, and Lance. I couldn't figure out what it was until I clicked on the dome light and saw Magnolia Federal's return address preprinted in the top left corner.

It was the same manila envelope I had dropped off at Nate's house not too many weeks prior on the day of the bank run. The envelope I pulled out of the Trapper, however, felt different in my hands from the one I gave Nate.

It was heavier.

Forty-five thousand dollars heavier, to be exact.

* * *

Later that night, we all met at Gulfport Lake, and the four of us and our dates sat barefoot by a makeshift fire. When I explained the circumstances surrounding my discovery and passed out the goods, the reactions were about what I expected.

Mark held his stack in his hands and counted it, then recounted it, then counted it again, saying, "Are you serious?" over and over. When the reality of it all set in, he got choked up and walked off to the pier to collect himself.

Hop took his stack, looked at me and said, "He knew what he was doing all along," then spent the next twenty minutes trying to explain everything to Kristin, who cocked her head as if she were hearing music for the first time.

Lance literally kicked his heels and ran around in circles in the sand, whooping and hollering until he fell down. Lizzie seemed emboldened by this new development and got really, really close to him. It was the beginning of a banner night for those two.

Emily was absolutely beaming, and she cuddled into me, pulling my coat tight around her shoulders.

"Well, there you go, Matt. You always said he was full of surprises, didn't you?"

"Yeah, but I had no idea this was coming."

"Well, he thought a lot of you. Of all of you, actually. He told me once he'd never had friends like this before in his life – ever. But he said it was you who turned things around for him."

"Oh, yeah?"

"Yeah. He said you put everything in perspective for him one day at school."

To Emily's credit, she didn't ask me what Nate meant by that, and I didn't volunteer it. I knew exactly what she was referencing, and at the time, it didn't seem like anything more than me saying something to keep Nate from losing his spirit. Then Em pulled my face down to hers, and I returned to the moment at hand, as it were.

All of us eventually reconvened around the fire and spent the next hour or so telling Nate stories. Before too long, we realized we totally missed the New Year's countdown, but decided we should do some toasts anyway. I grabbed the sleeve of cups I had lifted from the gallery, and with Mark's help, topped everyone off.

We toasted to the success of Marty Deen and his art show – no small feat thanks to Emily's efforts.

We toasted to our dates for knocking us out with their beauty and poise – and gave a special nod to Kristin for hanging with Hop all this time. She actually laughed.

We toasted to our friendship and vowed then and there to never break the bonds that tied us together – and to never again mention the money.

And finally, we toasted to Nate. The strangest, coolest, weirdest, and, of course, most generous dude we ever met.

"To Nate," I said, raising my cup, "Wherever you may be."

A chorus of voices echoed my tribute, and as I turned my drink up, I looked high in the night sky and thought that somehow, somewhere, Nate was toasting us, too.

Wherever he may be.

EPILOGUE

In spite of me and Hop taking the helm, our reunion was shaping up to be the best one yet. The ten-year was a little awkward, and the twenty was poorly attended, but by the time thirty rolled around, there was a lot of interest. Most of us had married; several of us had divorced; a majority had kids, and a few even had grandkids. No one seemed to care anymore about income, jobs, spouses, or the other outward indicators that seemed so prevalent in our first two gatherings. By that point in our lives, we were just genuinely looking forward to seeing each other – and were glad to be alive.

Hop and I broke up the primary responsibilities. He took care of the logistics – food, band, venue, and to a lesser extent, decorations. I was in charge of getting people registered and paid, which involved several months of running down emails and addresses.

All told, we had contacts for sixty-one people, which wasn't bad, considering only seventy of our original seventy-four were still alive. Of those, we had forty-three commitments – again, pretty good stats, considering jobs, geography, and that timing just didn't work for everyone. Emily was even coming, having missed the last one due to the fact that she had a newborn – her fourth – and couldn't make the trek over from Dallas. I hadn't seen her since our tenth and was looking forward to catching up. Who knows, we might even share a dance for old times sake.

One week out from the big day, I sent a final email to the group, reminding them of the time, the address, and to pay if they hadn't already done so. Just as I was about to hit send, my inbox pinged. I didn't recognize the sender, but the re: line caught my attention.

St. John High School Reunion – Attn: Matt Frazier

I opened it, and there was no text, just a large three-megabyte attachment. I hesitated to proceed in case it was spam or a virus, but the thought occurred to me that it could be a late responder needing to sign up. Plus, the message seemed a little too personalized to have been generated by a bot, so I double-clicked it.

When I did, a photograph I hadn't seen for over three decades came up.

There we were – me, Mark, Hop, Lance, and Nate at homecoming – standing in the St. John parking lot with our tuxes on, smiling as we waited for Emily to snap the picture. We were all skinny; we all had good hair, and seeing us together – along with Nate's very visible shiner – suddenly reminded me in vivid detail all that went down that fateful semester. As I studied it, I saw something I had never picked up on before. I always thought we had been arm-in-arm when the picture was taken, but upon closer inspection, I noticed Nate was not. He was there, standing on the end, but instead of locking up with the rest of us, one of his hands was flashing the thumbs-up symbol.

The other was pointing directly at the Milk Wagon.

I sat up in my chair and grabbed my phone.

Inscribed on the bottom, in that unmistakable loopy handwriting, was a message.

I told you I wanted one.
See you Friday.

Acknowledgments

First and foremost, I thank God for all of His blessings and for surrounding me with people who bring so much light to my world. It is truly a gift to have close family and friends, and I would not be the person I am without the support of those near and dear to me.

To those early readers of the manuscript who provided guidance, editing, and comments – I am forever grateful. Thank you Kay, Holden, Jack, Mary, Valerie, Nick, Erica, Jeff, Ron, Lance, Tara, Karen and Mom. The book is better because of you.

Thank you to "Fast Eddie" Appel for walking me through the ins and outs of money laundering, as well as the banking regulations in effect back in 1986. Any mistakes or inaccuracies on that front are mine and mine alone.

Thank you to the St. John High School Class of 1987. The impact you have had on my life continues to shape me in so many ways. What I wouldn't give to go back with all of you for just one more day. You, my fellow Eagles, are amazing.

To my best high school buddies Jeff and Ron – still two of my favorites today. I am so glad we grew up in the '80s, and I am incredibly thankful we got to do it together. I couldn't imagine it any other way.

Last, but not least, I must acknowledge the Milk Wagon, the old beat up Suburban that, in fact, transported us through those formative years – in more ways than one. I have never driven a finer vehicle, nor do I think I ever will.

Be good.

Made in the USA
Middletown, DE
18 December 2021